LET
HER LIE

Also available by Bryan Reardon

The Perfect Plan
The Real Michael Swann
Finding Jake

LET HER LIE

A NOVEL

BRYAN REARDON

CROOKED
LANE

NEW YORK

Published in the United States by Crooked Lane Books, an imprint of The Quick Brown Fox & Company LLC.   .

Crooked Lane Books and its logo are trademarks of The Quick Brown Fox & Company LLC.

Library of Congress Catalog-in-Publication data available upon request.

ISBN (hardcover): 978-1-64385-569-1
ISBN (ebook): 978-1-64385-570-7

Cover design by Melanie Sun

Printed in the United States.

www.crookedlanebooks.com

Crooked Lane Books
34 West 27th St., 10th Floor
New York, NY 10001

First Edition: February 2020

10 9 8 7 6 5 4 3 2 1

To Michelle, as always.

ACT ONE/SCENE 1

EXT. THE BEACH—NIGHT

A full moon shines down on the rolling surf of the Atlantic Ocean. We see the pale rise of a sand dune, a patch of yellow daylilies and—a nightmarish figure appears out of the darkness. A CHYRON flashes across the jet-black sky: AUGUST 12, 2016.

In the darkness, the sound of the surf was hypnotic. It drew Jasper Ross-Johnson like a beckoning finger or a dog's leash, tugging him as his feet dug into the soft, pale sand of the dune. As he crested the rise, the horizon spread, the contrast between the inky Atlantic and the hint of a rising sun as sharp as his thoughts.

Find a perfect daylily before dawn. Shape it into a crown and place it in the freezer. Ask the question.

Jasper had not visited this exact stretch of the beach for just over twenty years. And never to harvest a flower. Something had drawn him back this morning. A fleeting memory of the weathered wood planking leading toward the beach. Wispy, straight-trunked pines lining the walk almost up to the base of the dune. As he remembered, the plantings, perfectly random, sprang up just past the trees, as they had so many years before.

Jasper could have knelt under the cover of night, pulled out his perfectly edged sheers, and cut the brightest daylily of the bunch. That done, he should have returned to his powder-blue electric moped and slipped silently away. The ocean, however, had other plans for him tonight. It drew him up the dune with whispers from the past. To the top. And that's when he saw her.

She walked at the water's edge, just where the surf had darkened the sand. Still a quarter of a mile away, she appeared as nothing more than a darker shadow. Jasper stood frozen, staring. For the first time, he wondered if it was the call of the tide that had lured him to this place. Or could it be something different? A ghost singing from the past. Something so foreign that it caused sweat to bead his perfectly smooth forehead.

He certainly felt the danger. For the first time since his first time, this was unplanned. He was unprepared. He'd left things unfinished. And he had never heard the call before with things still unfinished. He looked back down the winding path, back toward his moped. He glanced at his feet, noting the leather thong sandals, their perfect fit. He had not cleansed. He had no gloves with him, not even stowed in the compartment of the moped. It was all wrong. All very wrong.

Jasper's eyes returned to her. The briefest flash of yellow, neon, seemed to catch his eye. The hint of a halo circling the woman's head. His chest tightened, a flutter running through his body. Despite his basest instincts, or because of them, he took that first step over the dune, down toward the beach, toward the woman walking obliviously closer.

PART ONE

THE HALO KILLER

CHAPTER

1

June 5, 2017

WHEN I WAS a kid, I used to pray for snow. All winter I would watch the weather. Every chance, no matter how small, filled me with hope. That a storm would hit. And we would get to stay home.

Then, one evening, it would come. I'd look out the window and see those first flakes dancing down from the night sky, playing under the streetlamp at the edge of our yard. I'd watch, my eyes almost watering with excitement, as it stuck to the pavement. Turning the world outside white like the clouds of heaven.

The phone would ring. I'd hold my breath with anticipation. Then I'd hear it. School had been canceled. The euphoria would burst out like an eruption. I'd bounce on my bed. Slap a hand on my ceiling and cheer. What seemed like the most important dream of my childhood had come true.

But there was this one storm. A blizzard. It swept through my town, dumping two feet of powder. School closed along with everything else. Our front door wouldn't even open. For two days, we hunkered down inside the house. My parents seemed to love it. For me, my dream shifted to a nightmare. The walls seemed to close in on me, pushed by gnawing fingers of utter boredom. Life reduced to a pinpoint focus— my house, my bedroom, my bed, and eventually my own mind. With no distractions, my full being turned inward. I picked apart my family, my friends, my life. All my faults. All my failures. Although I didn't know it at the time, that amount of attention so narrowly focused on anything only leads to the darker corners of our lives.

Ironically, in less than a day, my prayers had changed. I found myself begging for the snow to thaw. For school to open. So I could get out of my house. Out of my head. And return to the normal, somewhat numbing rhythms of life.

The summer I turned thirty-two , I started to think a lot about that memory. My life, in many ways, had turned into that storm. My dreams had been flipped into nightmares. For my entire life I'd dreamed of fame. And, as you might know, that wish had come true. My documentary *The Basement* hit big in 2015. Overnight, everyone in Hollywood knew my name. Invitations poured in to all the parties in the hills. Every-one knew me. Watched me. If I had remembered, I might have known that all that attention could only lead to something bad.

For me, it was a scandal. Like all the good ones, it involved lies, sex, and money. And it ruined my career.

Maybe I ran. Or maybe I just needed a break. But that June, I decided to move from Los Angeles to New York. I thought it was the right place for me to get my head straight after what I was calling the Bender incident. As I settled into my new apartment in Hell's Kitchen, so much became clear. Most importantly, I could see the line between fame and infamy again. And I knew I needed to get back to my roots. I was born to be a filmmaker. I had made an award-winning, critically acclaimed smash hit. I was Theo Snyder! I just needed to find the next story I was meant to tell.

It was at that time that the Halo Killer, Jasper Ross-Johnson, entered my life. At my agent Steph's encouragement, I was chasing leads again. I was working two potential subjects at the time—a mother who had driven her kids off a cliff into the Pacific Ocean, and a Mississippi politician who'd spent five years in prison for statutory rape before his release due to a procedural misstep. Then I received his letter. It came forwarded from Steph's office with the return address Howard R. Young Correctional Institute in Wilmington, Delaware. The note was concise and simple. Jasper stated that he had added me to his call list and would like to talk. It took me a week to navigate the circus of setting up a pre-paid account. But I eventually contacted him and he told me about that night on the beach, the one where he was harvesting a flower and he saw a woman at the waterline. Even after that, though, I wasn't sure he was the one.

At first blush, it may seem as if the Halo Killer would be an easy choice for my next documentary. He was notorious, mysterious, and frighteningly good at his sinister hobby, having left almost no physical evidence behind for two decades. Unfortunately, he was also old news. He had been captured just under a year before, on August 14, 2016. His story had already run on every true-crime program from network to YouTube Red. I was late to the game. But I, and other filmmakers like me, didn't just throw up the quickest story we could. Art took time. Jasper's story was in that dead zone. Past the viral stage, it needed time to gestate until it could be told the right way.

After hanging up with him, I can't say I was initially sold. But the Halo Killer's voice, soft and slippery, pumped back into my thoughts like the burn of a slow injection. A hitch in his tone at one point during our conversation, the hint of an unexpected emotion, caused me to close my browser and listen again to the audio of our conversation. When I did, the idea sunk into my brain like a barbed hook. Jasper had me on a line. Maybe I would fight, thrash around a bit. But, eventually, I'd tell his story. That's how it works, really. We don't have a choice. The great subjects always find us.

I had a problem, though. I tried not to admit it, especially to myself, but following the incident, I was a pariah. I needed a camera operator, which was no big deal. I still had the cachet to convince some NYU student to handle that. Probably on spec. The real problem would be finding an investigator. To tackle something as big as the Halo Killer, we'd need to find new angles. New evidence. Or, more accurately, new doubts. I needed help in that department if I wanted this to be my redemption. I knew that the usual suspects were off-limits. That the best investigators, the big fish, had cleaner, less complicated waters to swim.

So I called my friend Kent. He was in New York, too, and part of the reason I'd moved there. His father owned one of the largest production companies in Hollywood, one that was particularly interested in documentaries. In fact, they'd produced *The Basement*, which was how I'd met Kent. He didn't work for his dad. He didn't really work, I guess you'd say. Instead, he was the most connected person I knew who would take a meeting. When I called, he insisted on going to Nobu Downtown. His choice made me hesitate. My scandal was still fresh. Though

I could walk down the streets of New York without being recognized, lunch at Nobu was a different story.

I nearly said what I was thinking. The words almost slipped free.

Are you sure you want to be seen with me?

But some of the old Theo was still inside, even then. That Theo had swag. He used his charisma to move people. That's what I told myself. So I kept the worries and insecurities bottled up as best I could and accepted his invitation.

When I walked in, I found Kent right away. He sat in one of the six seats at the bar in the middle of the restaurant. As always, the place was packed. Walking over to him, I passed three celebrities. My cheeks burned, but I made eye contact. With friendly nods, I moved past them as casually as I could and headed for Kent.

"Hey," I said, breathing for the first time since stepping inside.

He swung around in his seat. Kent was short, no more than five six. He had an international look to every inch of him, from his Italian shoes to his Cartier glasses. When he popped out of the seat, he wrapped me up in a hug. Then he pulled back. His surprisingly long fingers encircling my wrist, he looked me up and down. His mother was Jamaican, and every so often the accent would slip out.

"You look good, Theo. Almost like your old, badass self."

"Thanks."

"Do a spin for me?" Kent winked. "Just kidding. Sit down, you animal."

We took two of the six seats at the bar. I looked at the other four.

"Maybe we should sit at a table," I said, looking around. "There are a lot of ears here."

Kent laughed. "This is about as private as it gets, my dear."

"What about—"

"I reserved all six, silly."

"Are you serious?" At my peak celebrity, I couldn't have done that. "I guess you are."

"So," Kent said. "What's up?"

"I might have a new project, but I wanted to talk to you about it."

Kent glanced at me, side-eyed.

"No," I continued. "I'm not looking for a deal or anything. I want to do this one unencumbered."

"You mean unfunded," Kent said, smirking.

"Both."

"Why the meeting then?"

I tried to pour on the charm. In the past, it had just happened. I would compliment his glasses. Share a subtle take on his dad's latest project or verbally jab at one of Kent's enemies. That day, though I managed to go through the motions, they didn't seem to hold the same sway.

"And?" he asked when I was finished.

"Come on," I said, looking hurt.

"Theo," he said. "I like you. You're funny. Reckless as hell, but that's how you hit it big in the first place. No one could have done what you did with *The Basement*. When you left a hot mic on that creep. That confession while he was taking a piss?—that shit was crazy. But I know you need something. And I'm just saying that I want to help. That's all I ever want to do. Who's your target?"

I looked over my shoulder. No one was paying me any attention, to be honest, but a number of eyes lifted in Kent's direction. So, I leaned in closer, whispering as best I could over the noise of the restaurant.

"The Halo Killer," I said.

Kent's reaction was exactly as I'd expect. He knew everything, all the time. Whenever I passed any information to him, I could see his mind clicking, making connections. It was what made him Kent.

"The Halo Killer," he repeated, a little louder than I wanted him to. "That's crazy. Kind of on the old side, though. Or do you have one of your signature new angles?"

I knew it all came down to that moment. I would sink or swim on my one true gift. The substance behind all my success. I needed to perform. Give Kent the perfect pitch. And I knew he was waiting for it. Judging my pause.

I closed my eyes in a deliberate blink.

Come on, I urged myself silently. *You can do this.*

Suddenly, it came back. I came back, if maybe for just a moment. I spoke, my voice low but ominous.

"The Halo Killer was a ghost. The cops had absolutely nothing on him. He played with them. Teased them. And they were powerless to stop his rampage. He was better than them. All-powerful. The Superman of serial killers.

But who cares? We've seen that doc already. It's all over Netflix. Bundy, Dahmer . . . all of them. They're white noise at this point."

I took a drink, like those past stories didn't matter. Then I focused my eyes on Kent's. I held him hostage. Slipped into his psyche and plucked at his true desire.

"I have no interest in what makes Jasper Ross-Johnson tick. What made him a killer. No, the real story isn't about Superman. He's too perfect. Too boring. The real story is about . . ." I let it hang for a second before finishing. "His kryptonite."

Kent didn't say anything. The silence spread out between us, and my insecurities crept back to the surface. It was a dumb idea. Stupid. I was finished.

"Love it!" he finally blurted out.

"Are you serious?"

He squinted. "Of course I am. Shouldn't I be?"

"Yeah, definitely."

"That's my old goddamn *Theo*!" He slapped my shoulder. "So, what is it?"

"What?" I asked, giving myself a second to think.

"His kryptonite."

I teased him. "I'm not telling anyone yet. But I have a lead. A good one."

"Nice," Kent said. "You're going to need an investigator. Top-notch. I was just talking to someone. Do you know Zora?"

"Monroe?" I asked, with a little more excitement than I had meant to show.

Although I had never met or worked with her, Zora Monroe was far and away the best investigator in the business. And the most connected. Not just among producers, who loved her, but with seemingly everyone else too, from the feds to the local police to the neighborhood grocer. Most people seemed to owe her a favor.

"The same," he said. "In fact, we talked about that nutjob."

"She asked you about the Halo Killer?"

"Yeah," he said. "She said she caught the *Dateline* piece on it. And she was surprised no one was on the case. It was no big deal. We were just having drinks and it happened to come up."

"Did you get the sense she was interested in working on a project?"

Kent shrugged. "Have you ever met her?"

I shook my head, and he laughed.

"She's a tough read. I didn't get the sense she was fishing. She really doesn't need to."

"I know, I know. I didn't mean—"

"I'm just thinking about it," Kent said. "No, I don't think it had anything to do with work, really. It was more like she just knew someone would be on it soon. And it happens to be you, my friend. I think that's a great fit."

"Really? And you haven't heard anyone else nosing around the story?"

"No," he said.

I took a deep breath. "Do you think she'd . . . work with me?"

Kent leaned back. He looked me in the eye, a troubled expression on his face.

"Theo, baby, none of that. You made *The Basement*. The fucking *Basement*. She should be wondering if you would work with her."

I laughed. "I love you, Kent."

His smile was only slightly salacious. "You better."

I touched his arm. "Can you introduce us?"

Kent chortled. "You know I can do better than that."

* * *

Three hours later, as I sat alone in my apartment listening to my recording of Jasper's story for the hundredth or so time, I got the text. It was from Kent:

She's expecting your call. Be yourself and she's yours.

There were a bunch of emojis too, but I had no idea what they meant. My hand shaking just a little bit, I called Zora Monroe.

"Hey," I said when she answered.

"Who is this?" she asked.

"This is Theo Snyder. Kent gave me your number. Said you might be interested in the Halo Killer case."

There was a pause. I think I might have held my breath.

"Thought you were out of the game," she said.

"I . . . No, I've just been focused on finding the right target."

"Huh," she said. "And you decided on the Halo Killer?"

"Yeah," I said, feeling a touch off-balance. "I actually spoke to him already. He told me this story that . . . just stuck . . . I guess."

"You spoke to him already?"

"Yeah," I said. "You want to hear the recording?"

"I do," she said, and I pictured her leaning forward in anticipation.

I played the audio, the part when Jasper spoke about the woman on the beach. It was subtle, but there. I was sure of it.

"Did you hear that?"

"What?" she said.

"When he said he had left things *unfinished*. Before that, I just assumed the woman on the beach was his first victim. They always talk about their first one, you know? Especially how he talked about that woman. About seeing her. Being drawn to her. But when he said 'unfinished,' I think he was talking about someone else. A victim he hadn't . . . finished with."

"That's a big assumption."

I smiled. "Assumptions are my business."

"True." She paused.

I closed my eyes. Scenes began to take shape in my head.

"I see the beach. Moonlight playing on the rolling surface of the tide. Silence, then the sound of someone moving in the darkness. And Jasper's voice. His words penetrating the night."

"Okay, I get it. What are you thinking?"

"So, let's assume he sees this woman on the beach while he already has his last victim, the one that got away. Her name was . . ." I shuffled through the stack of papers beside me until I found it. "Barbara Yost. She's the only one who lived. The only person the Halo Killer touched but didn't kill. If I'm right, his story took place the day he was arrested.

"Zora, he had been unstoppable. The police didn't have a shred of evidence that tied one murder to another, let alone that led to Jasper Ross-Johnson. He was a master. What happened, then? He runs into this woman on the beach, and he gets caught two days later. What changed? Who is she? Could she be the reason they finally caught him? And best yet, Yost is alive. We can talk to her. Maybe she can give us a clue."

Zora paused. I listened to her even breathing, envying her calmness.

"Huh. Maybe," she said.

"Are you interested?"

She didn't answer right away. I had enough time to decide that either way, I was moving forward with this one. My next film was going to be about the Halo Killer. Whether I worked the case alone or with the best investigator out there.

"I'm in," she finally said.

I jumped up from the edge of my bed, pumping my fist. Just as quickly, I put my hand down, flattening the front of my shirt.

"Excellent. I'm going to get as much research done as I can. You're based here in New York, right? Do you think you can meet me in Brooklyn later this week? I'm heading to the prison tomorrow."

"To see him?"

"Yes. For the first time."

Zora paused. "You seem pretty far along."

I sensed something, like I might be losing her. "I can cancel."

"Why would you do that?" she asked.

I took a slow breath. "How about we meet the day after tomorrow? Tuesday. Maybe at the Hungry Ghost?"

I don't know why I suggested Brooklyn. Only that it seemed more fitting, cooler. For some reason, that seemed important in the moment.

"Sounds good."

I ended the call, feeling amazing. I had my subject. I had the top investigator out there. And somehow I knew it would be my best film to date. The game changer. My personal phoenix! I'm not sure my feet touched the ground as I grabbed my wallet and rushed out of the apartment. I had a lot of work to do before Tuesday.

2

I HAD SEEN JASPER Ross-Johnson's picture in the newspaper, obviously. But that didn't prepare me for the man that shuffled into the visiting room at Howard R. Young Correctional Institute. He moved with a heaviness that belied his birdlike stature. I'd seen that a million times before, in almost every prison I'd ever visited. Criminals, especially of the notorious variety, were never as physically imposing as I'd expected. On top of that, prison—the confinement, the stress, and most of all the horribly unhealthy food—sapped years of life in the span of days. But the true killers always made up for that when I looked into their eyes.

I turned to look at my camera operator. She stood over my right shoulder, filming. We'd just met that morning and I'd forgotten her name.

"You're getting this, right?" I asked.

She nodded. When I looked at him again, the same disjointed feeling struck me. Maybe it was the fiery red of his skin. Or maybe the thin layer of lightly colored stubble that seemed to cover his entire body, from his head to the backs of his hands. It could have been the way his drab prison-issue clothing draped on his frame. The way it was perfectly pressed, as if it were hung from the tracks at the local dry cleaners, waiting to be picked up.

As he neared the window, his eyes met mine. Tiny and dark, they delved deep. I forced myself to breathe and keep eye contact until he looked away. His eyes slipped to the camera, and I was able to take a breath. Then he sat down heavily across from me. His legs tightly crossed, Jasper rocked forward before speaking.

"Nothing has caused the human race so much trouble as intelligence."

I shifted in my seat. "Excuse me?"

He frowned, watching me. Something about what he'd said struck me, though it came with no context whatsoever.

"That's from a movie," I said.

Jasper's dark eyes shined. He clapped his little hands together. I smiled, caught off guard by his childlike excitement.

"Do you know who?"

I thought about it but shook my head.

"Hitchcock," he said.

And it came back to me. *Rear Window!*"

Jasper clapped again. "Exactly."

The guard turned his head toward Jasper. The little man noticed the attention and his demeanor changed immediately. He slumped down in his chair, almost as if he was returning to the character he had been playing when I first saw him enter.

"Nice to meet you, Theodore," he said, his tone changing back as well. "I've seen your work."

"You have?"

"Of course," he said with a soft laugh. "I watched a good amount of television . . . prior to this. My incarceration." His eyes flickered. "Three hundred eleven days . . . six hours . . . and thirteen minutes." A sharp focus returned. "I wish I could have enjoyed your second film, the portrayal of Joseph Bender's life."

"That film wasn't released," I said tersely.

"I know. You failed to stay appropriately nonbiased. Something about his sister. And a lawsuit. I read *Variety*."

I flinched, and he smiled. "She . . . misled me."

He barked out a laugh. "She was an exotic dancer, correct? I'm sure she did far more than mislead you." He paused, shaking his head. "I don't know why every article mentioned that. We do love the tawdry, don't we?"

My voice grated a little, but I fought to soften it. Play it cool. "I try to let the story tell itself."

Jasper leaned forward. "Is that what you call it?"

"Excuse me?"

"A story," he said. "I guess that's the truth of it. Life is just a story. Though we write our own script, you never really can predict the ending. Regardless, I guess you're here to talk about my early years. That's how you handled your first film. And I believe that's how you would have handled your second. You certainly have a gift for the cinematic scene."

My teeth clicked together as I forced my mouth shut. He must have watched the clip I put on Twitter. The one from the Bender film that got me in so much trouble. Breathing in through my nose, I told myself to slow down. He was testing me. They always did that, in their own way. That's why he was bringing up Bender and the incident. But I could handle it. I just had to breathe.

That's when I realized my mistake. I'd broken the cardinal rule of making a documentary. I'd arrived that afternoon with an agenda. That story of the woman on the beach was like a needle in my brain. I needed to know who she was. And if she had caused him to slip up after so long. What was it about her? Could she be his kryptonite?

That's not how it works, though. I should have learned that from Geri Bender. I'm not calling the shots. I'm not some novelist sitting in a coffee shop, staring out the window at the passing world, and playing God on his laptop keyboard. No, I am the light-shiner. This was not my story. It was his.

So, I leaned back and tented my hands. "Is that where you'd like to start?"

Jasper looked thoughtful, then nodded. "Yes, that seems appropriate."

*　　*　　*

ACT ONE/SCENE 3

EXT. THE BEACH—DAY

We see the same beach in daylight. Happy families—dads with mutton-chops and moms in high-waisted bikinis—lounge on the sand and splash in the green-gray surf. The camera pans past the dunes to the opulent mansions overlooking the coast, focusing on the childhood home of the Halo Killer.

A CHYRON appears on the perfect blue sky: MAY 29,1971.

The Halo Killer's life began in a beautiful beachfront home. With floor-to-ceiling windows cracked open to let in the crisp, briny breeze and fill the house with the sound of the rumbling surf, his parents held court. Deeply plugged into the socialite culture, they threw parties every month, and invitations were highly coveted. Moving among the beachy yet modern furniture and the original art hanging on freshly painted walls, one would expect to cross paths with CEOs, politicians, even a certain local boy turned Hollywood movie star.

During one of these parties in the early seventies, Franklin Johnson and Clara Ross stood on the landing of their great room, a perfect ocean view over their shoulders, and she clinked a fork lightly against the rim of a champagne flute. Everyone's attention turned to Clara as she stood next to her impeccably dressed husband, holding his hand and smiling.

"We're having a child," she announced.

Franklin gave one of his speeches, quoting *Breakfast at Tiffany's* and making up a rousing yet quirky limerick on the spot. There was laughter and a spattering of applause, as well as a few raised eyebrows. It was the seventies. Even among this mostly enlightened crowd, their marriage was considered *of convenience*. The addition of a child didn't seem to fit. Maybe one or two attendees that night noticed how tightly Clara gripped Franklin's hand. Or how she looked away as he recited his poem. In the end, the party continued, and everyone shared the couple's joy deep into the night.

*   *   *

At six, Jasper Ross-Johnson would build his first memory, one that would stick with him his entire life. By then, his mother's dabbling in real estate had turned into a thriving business, one Clara Ross dedicated more and more time to each year. It was a Sunday, though Jasper didn't realize it at the time. His mother had left early that morning to host an open house at one of her properties. His father moved through the house, singing to himself.

From that day forward, the smell of a certain men's fragrance would bring him back to that memory. It would call up the feeling of walls closing in around him. It would return him to an utter, unforgiving darkness. Every time the scent slipped into his nostrils, it would be as if he could feel the gentle press of padding against his ears and the steady rhythm of classical music dancing in his skull. That morning, however, he simply smelled the cologne as he stood in the hallway watching his father primp.

Franklin noticed his young son through the mirror over his sink. He turned, his smile shining brighter than the exposed bulbs above the vanity.

"Want a squirt, my little man?"

Jasper nodded. With a laugh, Franklin knelt down and misted the fragrance into the air between them.

"Step through. Quickly!"

Jasper did as he was told, his bare toes slapping on the perfectly finished hardwood floor. He danced, lost in his father's joyful reaction.

"That's my boy," Franklin said, tousling Jasper's thick, strawberry hair.

Taking the boy's hand, he led him into the kitchen. As young Jasper watched, Franklin opened the refrigerator and removed a china plate. Pulling back a layer of Saran Wrap, he uncovered a cheese sandwich and some baby carrots.

"Huh," he said, staring at the perfect little lunch.

Franklin snatched the sandwich off the plate and took a significant bite. Chewing, he muttered something to himself and placed the plate on the granite counter. Jasper watched him chew, waiting.

"No crumbles," Franklin said.

His father walked away, returning to his bathroom. Jasper watched him until he disappeared around the corner. Then he pulled the high counter stool out and carefully climbed onto it. He touched his sandwich with a pale finger, looked back the way his father had gone, and then picked up a carrot as carefully as he could. Leaning forward so that his mouth hung over the plate, he took a delicate bite.

When Franklin returned, Jasper hadn't touched his sandwich. His father never looked at the plate as he whisked it off the counter and back into the refrigerator.

"Come on, buddy," he said.

Jasper climbed down off the stool and followed his father into one of the guest bedrooms. The window was open, and he heard the ocean rumbling as it rolled over itself and hissed back onto the cool sand. He took a step toward that pure sound, only to be stopped by his father's hand on his shoulder. When he turned, Franklin crouched, his face close as he spoke softly to his son.

"It's naptime," he said.

Jasper remained utterly silent as his father opened the closet door. Grabbing a yellow Sony Walkman off the shelf, he turned to his son. Jasper never hesitated. Maybe this was their routine. Maybe he'd done the exact same thing a hundred times before. Either way, he stepped into that closet. His father hit play and slipped the earphones over Jasper's head. Smooth jazz masked the sound of the door locking. The darkness wrapped him up. Jasper didn't move. He didn't sit. He certainly never napped. He stood until the tape reached its end.

When the music stopped, Jasper's eyes widened. Confused, he remained still for a time. Then, tentatively, he took a step toward the door. His tiny hand reached up for the knob. He grabbed it, trying to turn it. But it wouldn't open. His chest tightened. The muscles of his forearm twitched. Jasper tried to open the door again and again and again.

He didn't stop until he heard the voice. It boomed out, a man laughing and speaking loudly. Jasper's eyes widened. His hand fell from the handle and he took a step back, knowing at once that it was not his father's voice.

CHAPTER

3

J ASPER'S EYES MET mine through the glass. "I've never told that story before."

"I know," I said. "There is almost nothing about your past out there."

"I'm a private person." He smiled. "Nothing happened to me, of course. Martino was a very nice man."

"Martino?" I asked.

Jasper's lips thinned. He broke eye contact with me. "He was a friend of my—"

"Time," the guard announced.

Jasper stopped midsentence. A raptor's focus returned to his eyes. He muttered to himself, words I could just make out.

"Patience, planning, purpose."

It sounded like the mantra of a madman. But I wasn't ready for the interview to end. I leaned forward. As much as I needed him to tell his story in his own way, I needed to know.

"Jasper," I said, as he rose from his chair. "How did they finally catch you? What happened that night on the beach?"

He had already turned away from me, but he spun back, very slowly. The focus left his expression, as if he was searching the past for an answer to my question.

"It was a *miracle*," he said, and that childlike look flashed in his eyes once again.

* * *

The next day, Tuesday, I was up by four o'clock. Truthfully, I'm not sure I slept at all that night. I took the subway to the Hungry Ghost, pushing the door open almost two hours before I was scheduled to meet Zora. Bypassing the brighter corners of the shop, with its French white and black floor tiles and patisserie seating, I chose a dark corner, one surrounded by rich wood paneling and a New York City sense of privacy. Taking the seat facing the entrance, I spent my time trying to find some trace of the man Jasper had mentioned, Martino.

I found nothing. Normally, that would set off a red flag. To be honest, though, I was distracted. Nervous. And I knew it. My past still haunted me often then. And the idea of meeting Zora brought me back to why I'd left Hollywood in the first place. How quickly the mighty can fall.

*   *   *

In the moment, I didn't even realize that my fame had reached its peak. It was the night of *The Basement*'s premiere. Through the window of the Town Car, I stared ahead, up Hollywood Boulevard. At the crowd held back by lush velvet ropes. The eyes turning, staring hungrily. I could hear their voices rising up. And above it all, I saw my name in lights—THEO SNYDER. I couldn't believe it. It felt like a dream.

"Theo," my date, Veronique, whispered in awe. "They're calling out your name!"

I couldn't even say anything. I just stared out the window, a stupid smile on my face. And a raging torrent of emotions burning inside my chest. I had dreamt of this moment since I was six. Made my first movie on a refurbished Super 8 when I was eleven. Lost over fifty film competitions by the time I was fifteen. I'd been rejected over a hundred times by age seventeen. Moving out to Hollywood six years before that night, I'd begged, groveled, and kissed the ass of what felt like everyone in that town. I'd left my close-knit family behind. I had three nephews and a niece back in Virginia who I'd never even met. All for that moment. My dreams miraculously come true.

"This is so hot," she said, more to herself.

The driver eased us to the curb outside the massive sandstone columns lining the entrance to Grauman's Egyptian Theatre. An usher dressed in a vintage uniform opened our door. I let Veronique get out first. Flashbulbs popped. A reporter beckoned to her. After a pause, I followed her. And everything went nuts.

"Theo!"

"Over here."

"How does it feel?"

The voices all mingled into a rush of heart-stopping intensity. I felt a hand touch my shoulder and turned to find my publicist, Frankie, smiling like he couldn't believe it any more than I could.

"Come on," he said. "You need to talk to E."

I grabbed his sleeve. "This is crazy!"

"What?" he said, unable to hear me over the crowd.

I leaned closer. "This is crazy."

"I know," he said. "*Variety* ran your distribution deal with Netflix this morning. And Hanks mentioned you on the *Tonight* show last night."

My eyes widened. "Tom Hanks?"

Frankie nodded. "We sent him a screener last week."

"Of *The Basement*?" I asked.

He laughed. "Of course, Theo. And you need to look like you've been here before. Get used to this. You're A-list, buddy."

I swear my feet floated off the concrete. I did a short interview with E! Entertainment. After that, three big-league producers sought me out. They all filled my head with gushing compliments.

"*The Basement* is a classic, Snyder."

"How did you get that ending, man. Blew my mind."

"Call me."

"Let's do lunch."

All of that, and I barely heard a word. I couldn't comprehend it. The entire moment was surreal.

Before I entered the theater, I got a text from my mother. My sister, Michelle, had shared the clip from the *Tonight* show with her. She was so excited. So proud. Her words full of love. I read the text. It touched me. It really did. But, in all the excitement, I forgot to respond.

Eventually, my posse appeared. Mikey and Dale, both filmmakers. Eric the actor. Mel and Steph, my manager and agent. Everyone surrounded me. Pumping me full of light and love and drinks. For one night, I was the talk of the town. The hottest ticket in Hollywood.

*   *   *

Two years later, on a rare rainy day in June, I walked down that same street. Past that same theater. I was alone. My phone was silent. I hadn't seen Mikey or Dale in months. Eric had just been the source of yet another scathing online interview about my scandal. Mel had moved on. My mind spun out of control, trying to figure out how it all went so wrong. Wondering if I could even fix it if I tried. And I heard someone call out my name.

My head whipped around. For a torturous moment, I was back at the premiere of *The Basement*. The lights were popping. The compliments flowing. I was trending on Netflix. And, as in life, a single blink of the eye, one very bad decision that I just can't talk about, and it was gone again. A heartbreaking tease from the past.

A group of three people stood by the entrance to the theater, two guys and a woman. All about my age. I got the sense, right away, that they were with the media. Something about the glint in their eyes. Like a pack of lionesses spotting a newborn wildebeest.

"Theo Snyder," one of the guys said. "It's you, isn't it?"

I lowered my head and kept walking. I heard the slap of his Toms catching up to me from behind.

"Come on, buddy," he said. "Let me ask you a few questions. You got the time."

"Fuck you," I muttered.

He heard me. His tone got even more predatory.

"Come on, Theo. Have you talked to Pepper? Are you still seeing that Bender lady? How's the lawsuit? Come on."

My teeth grinding together, I shook my head. My pace quickened. And it was in that moment that I knew I had to get the hell out of that town.

*　*　*

Sitting in the café, I lost track of time. I was still daydreaming when she walked in. Zora Monroe could not be missed. She had to be about six feet tall, because when I shook off the malaise and stood to give her a quick hug, I had to look up. Her height was one thing, but her eyes were something else. Hooded in a way that made me assume she'd grown up in some charming southern town, they could change on a dime. One second, you might wonder if she was even paying attention. The next, she was picking at your soul with a pair of sharpened tweezers.

Otherwise, she fit the place. Her bleached dreads rose in a haphazard knot atop her head, adding even more to her imposing height. She wore the effortless style of an unpretentious hipster, the kind of clothing that rose above brand names and magazine ads, a disheveled perfection. Swinging her pack onto the table top, she sat, stretching her long legs across to my side of the table. I shifted, making room, deciding that Brooklyn had definitely been the right choice.

"I thought you were someone else," she said.

"What?"

"When Kent mentioned you, I thought you were that other guy. The one that did the one about the drunk aunt."

"Grey? Really?"

"Yeah," she said.

It was strange. Unlike with Jasper, I sensed no intention behind her slight. I have to say, though, that I felt it nonetheless.

"Anyway," I said. "Let's get started."

Since our first call, we had been digging. I'd amassed three boxes of files back in my tiny apartment. For her part, Zora had located Jasper's surviving victim, Barbara Yost.

"A friend of mine helped me track her down through her cell."

I squinted. "A friend?"

"Yeah, he works for one of the big carriers."

"Is that legal?"

She rolled her eyes and I let it drop.

"Have you reached out to her?" I asked.

"Left two messages."

"Hopefully she'll call back. I've dug up background on all the victims. But I'm hitting a wall on Jasper. He told me a little about his childhood, but there is nothing out there."

Zora nodded. "I know; that's part of what interests me. I want to dive deep. I'll find something, or find out why there isn't anything to find."

"He told me he is a private person." My eyebrows lowered. "But he mentioned a man named Martino. I couldn't find—"

"I got that," she said. "You stick to making your movie."

I couldn't tell if she was kidding. Either way, my gut told me it was right. That the two of us working together would lead to something truly special. For the second time since the scandal broke, I found my old self. My mouth opened and I got lost in the story.

"I can't stop," I said. "The scenes just keep falling together in my head. Act one can open with a shot of Jasper walking up to our interview. The gray walls. The orange jumpsuit hanging on his tiny frame. The score rumbles. Something dark but strong. Something Hitchcockian. He'll start his story, and as his voice chills the audience, the shot changes. We cut to that cabin where they rescued the Yost woman. Those trees, like the devil's fingers pointing up at an ominous sky. Then back to him. Smiling. Picking at the stubble of his eyebrow. Then right to a still of one of his victims."

Zora watched me as I spoke. Nodding along. Tilting her head.

"Nice," she said. "I get it now."

"The film?" I asked.

"No, you," she said.

I might have blushed, but Kent's words rang in my head. *She should be wondering if you'd work with her.*

"Okay, then, let's get to work," I said. "The more we find out about this guy, the more I'm sure about this. I keep going through the victims' names. Where they were from. Trying to find a pattern. But . . . it's strange. All of them are from the same place. All were found along a twenty-mile stretch of the coast in Delaware. I've never seen anything like it. How could he have gotten away with doing the same thing again and again and again?"

"They weren't all the same," Zora said.

"I don't know. There was the first one. It was different. In fact, it wasn't until his sixteenth confirmed murder that they attributed her death to him. What was her name? I can't . . ."

I pulled out my phone and skimmed through my emails, looking at an article I'd breezed past earlier.

"Theo," Zora said.

I looked up. "Yeah."

"I need to get going," she said. "Where do you want me to start?"

"Barbara Yost," I said. "We need to find her. And maybe that Martino guy he mentioned. Set up some interviews."

"Excellent," she said.

Zora started to stand up, but I kept going.

"That last thing he said. When I asked him how they caught him. He said it was a *miracle.*"

She paused. "He's a megalomaniac, like all the rest."

"Didn't you hear it? The way he said *miracle?*"

"No, I didn't."

I ignored her. Instead, I just heard the word repeating in my head, in the Halo Killer's unsettling voice.

"There's something there. I'm sure of it."

"Maybe," Zora said, openly assessing me. "But I need to go. I'll call you when I get something."

"Of course," I said. Then I squinted, noticing a look on her face. The way her eyes left mine as she spoke about her next steps. "This is personal to you."

Zora's eyes widened. I saw it, but she recovered almost immediately.

"This case?" she said. "I don't know—"

"No, I mean your job. You became an investigator for a reason. Something happened to you. Did you lose someone?"

She scoffed. "Not exactly."

"Was your father a cop? No, that's not it. Too obvious." I nodded, my interest hooked. "It's something, though. Tell me."

Zora smiled for the first time. Her head shook.

"Wow, they told me you could sniff a story out. But I really need to go."

"Next time," I said.

"Maybe."

"No, promise me," I insisted. "Next time."

She laughed. "Okay, okay. You are an interesting one, Theo Snyder." And she got up and walked away.

* * *

Walking back to my place after the meeting with Zora, I questioned everything. I think it was the first time, really. I found myself thinking back, again, about who I was prior to *The Basement*, before my fame. I'd heard so many people in Hollywood say that they always knew. That they were born with the knack. That by their third birthdays, their mothers had noticed. Had enrolled them in acting class or some movie club at the local library. Neighbors commented on their coming greatness, as if success had been preordained.

Was it true?

When I asked myself that question, I wasn't talking about their stories. I could never know their truths. What troubled me, though, was that I couldn't easily provide my own answer. Sure, I watched a lot of TV. And, at least before the whole Bender thing, my mom liked to tell everyone who would listen that she knew I'd make it. That I had been driven. Gifted.

Nearing my apartment, thinking once again about how I ran away from Los Angeles, I couldn't just accept that. I worked hard, definitely.

But I'd gotten lucky, too. Early in my time out west, I met Kent. I think he might have had a crush on me. Whatever it was, he took a liking. He looked out for me. Introduced me to some amazingly connected people. He paved the way for *The Basement* to reach development.

I knew I'd made a good movie. That the ending was something special. But so many great projects never make it. And most of the ones that do don't go viral like my film did. For whatever reason, people started talking about it. Word spread. It was almost a hive-like phenomenon. Like the greater public deemed my story to be the "it" thing. So much of it was luck. I knew that, though fame certainly fills your head with delusions of grandeur.

By the time I reached the elevator, the question in my mind had changed. I wondered what it was that I really wanted. Was it just the fame? Had it always been that simple? Or could it be something more, some need to validate my existence? Some misguided effort to fill a hole in my psyche? Something more insidious?

"God," I muttered, rubbing my eyes.

When I got like that, there was only one way to break the cycle. I needed to get back to work.

Once I got inside, I went straight to the makeshift work space that was my kitchen counter. As I sat down, I grabbed a stack of reports. Turning on a small desk lamp, I hunched over them, picking through each sheet like I expected an answer to jump off the page. Frustrated, I kicked one of the three cardboard boxes on the floor, each filled with more paper.

"I need to get organized," I said out loud.

I got up and walked over to my bed. Pulling it away from the wall, I slid the giant corkboard I used as a headboard out into the room. In LA, before I lost the house in the hills, it had hung on the wall in my study. In Hell's Kitchen, I had no choice but to lean it against my one window, turning the apartment into a prison. Sort of like Jasper's.

As the day turned to night, I got to work. In a case like this, I needed to study the victims. Understand each crime. As I found the files I'd arranged, I felt like I was piecing together a jigsaw puzzle. The names started to meld together as I thumbtacked photos to the board— Jennifer Moffa, Lori Grant. But the faces stared back at me, an unspoken accusation behind each unmoving eye.

What do you want? they asked.

Who are you? I asked in turn. *Why did he choose you?*

Time slipped by. Eventually, I made it to the Jane Does. In Jasper Ross-Johnson's case, there were eight. Eight human beings who slipped away in crushing silence. Eight humans who no one looked for. Who no one missed.

*   *   *

The phone woke me up. When my eyes opened, I found myself prone on the floor. A police report stuck to my elbow as I reached for the cell. I answered without looking, for some reason expecting it to be Zora.

"Hey," I said.

"A collect call from Jasper Ross-Johnson, an inmate at the Howard R. Young Correctional Institution. Call forwarding is unauthorized and may result in disciplinary action to the inmate. To accept charges, press five now."

Shocked, I fumbled with the screen, trying to bring up the number pad and hit five before I lost the call. For a second I thought I was too late. Then the automated voice spoke again.

"Thank you for using the Secura prepaid system. Your call can begin now."

My hands shook like mad and I held my breath. The line remained silent.

"Jasper?"

I heard breathing then. Waiting, I stood up, trying not to step on any of the files littering the ground. My eyes caught on the faces covering my corkboard. A sudden wave of sadness swept through me, and I had to sit down heavily on the edge of the bed.

"Ja—"

"Did you believe me?" he asked, his voice flat and soft.

"About your childhood? Of course I did. Why would you—?"

"Some people don't. I imagine when you visit subjects like me, they claim their innocence." He laughed. "I imagine they tell you that the system abused them. That the deck was stacked."

"Sometimes," I said. "Definitely. Do you mind if I record this conversation?"

"Sure," he said, distracted. "I did it. I killed all of them. And I pled guilty to every charge. I put up no defense. In the end, the state will end my life, like I ended theirs. It will come full circle. Nothing could ever change that."

"Why did you—?"

"I'm sorry. I just needed to ask you that one question."

"Whether I believed you?"

"Yes."

"Why?"

"Because I need to know who you are. I agree to be in your documentary. I will give you every answer I have. When it's all done, I'm going to ask one thing of you. Do we have a deal?"

"I . . . yes, definitely," I said, before I had time to really consider what I was getting into.

"Excellent. Then I will let you get on with your day."

"Wait," I blurted out. "When we spoke yesterday. What was the *miracle*?"

He laughed. "You're asking the wrong question."

"What do you—?"

He cleared his throat. "It's not *what* was the miracle, Theodore. It's *who* is the miracle."

The line clicked. The automated voice returned, telling me how much my credit card would be charged. And I knew that somehow, I'd just taken an incredible leap forward.

4

WHEN THE CALL ended, I realized it was morning. I had no idea how the hours of the night had slipped away from me. I stared at the giant board, at all the pictures of young women, some taken from high school yearbooks, some from the cold metal surface of a medical examiner's table. I dug knuckles into my eye sockets, then pulled out my notebook.

> STEP ONE: Find Barbara Yost—the only survivor
>   Gut feeling: She can shed light on the woman from beach, from Jasper's first story
>   Gut feeling: That woman caused Jasper to slip up
>   NEED TO KNOW WHY!!!
>   Who is the miracle???

"Who?" I whispered to myself.

Then it hit me. Not all at once. But I felt a tickle in my memory. I flipped the page and spoke out loud as I wrote.

"Who would a serial killer think of as a miracle? Family? Someone from his past? What made them special?"

A banging on my door startled me. I spun around, so lost in my work that I imagined Jasper Ross-Johnson bursting into my apartment, a yellow flower in his pale, deathly fingers.

"Hold on," I said, standing up.

Before I could move toward the door, though, it opened. Zora appeared, stepping in without the slightest hesitation.

"It was open," she said, looking around. "Who were you talking to?"

"Nobody," I said, looking away. But then my excitement stormed back. "Come here! Sit. I was just organizing, and I think I'm onto something."

Zora closed the door behind her. She turned to look at me, that unreadable expression on her face.

"Jasper told me that the miracle wasn't a thing but a person. It must have something to do with the woman on the beach."

"Why do you say that?" Zora asked flatly.

"But what made her a miracle? What was special about her?"

I stumbled to my laptop and replayed the recording. Zora stood motionless, listening patiently. When it was over, I slammed the laptop closed.

"His MO was to grab them and then find the flower, and he was out collecting one when he saw the woman on the beach—that means he already had someone that night. Probably Barbara! The woman at the beach must have thrown him off. Just like I thought. That's how he got caught. How Barbara survived. That woman, the one on the beach, she's a hero, Zora. But who is she?"

Zora put a hand up. In that gesture, she reminded me of my parents for some reason.

"Look, I know I just met you and it's the first time we've worked together. I mean, I heard the stories about you. That you're intense . . . But I have to be honest. You are totally scattered."

"Whoa," I said, caught off guard.

"I understand," she went on. "I really do. And I've seen it before. From great filmmakers. I think you're on the edge. It's a dangerous game. Hard to come back from. But it's impossible to make an unbiased documentary when you're down there."

I took a deep breath, needing to think. Turning my back to her, I paced across my tiny apartment. Her comment probably had something to do with my scandal. She didn't trust me. But she was right. I was deep. So, I wasn't sure it mattered. I could do it myself, alone. Maybe I didn't need an investigator at all. Maybe that would be best. I knew, somehow, that the Halo Killer was my one chance. It was all or nothing. And after Bender, I didn't know if I could trust anyone else.

I turned back, about to speak, but my eyes wandered to the pictures pinned to the corkboard against the wall. I found myself staring at the closest photo, the grizzliest of them all. It showed the Halo Killer's alleged first victim. Her body, badly decomposed, lay prone on a field of large, jagged rocks. Unlike the other victims, she had not been found with a flower around her forehead. But there was something in the picture. I moved closer to get a better look and noticed it was a set of headphones, askew but still covering one ear. Like Jasper's story from when he was a child.

"I don't know. Maybe it's best if we go our separate ways."

I wasn't really looking at Zora when I said that. And I didn't see her expression. By the time I noticed, she had turned her back to me as I had done a moment earlier. Her shoulders were tense, her hands balled into tight fists. When she spoke, when she told me her story, she never once looked back at me.

"I promised you I would answer your question from last time. Why I do what I do." Her voice grew distant as she continued. "When I was little, I was a real daddy's girl. He taught me to play basketball before I could walk, I think. Started coaching me when I was six. We spent so much time together that, even when I was little, I remember feeling bad. Like it would hurt my mom's feelings. But we . . . I never really understood her. She just wanted us to be happy. Especially my dad.

"By the time I was ten, I started to notice things, though. Little stuff at first. There was this one girl's mom. It started with conversations that would go on too long. Me and the girl would get bored shooting baskets or whatever. And we both would nag them to stop talking so we could leave the gym.

"Then it got more obvious. I saw her touch his hand. She was always laughing at everything he said. And they would whisper sometimes. One day, I smelled her perfume in his car."

She moved at that point, past me and to the window. Surprised by her frankness, I stared, openmouthed, devouring her story like it would be my next project.

"Maybe I had the bug already. I liked those stupid Hardy Boys books from the library. And I used to watch reruns of *Magnum P.I.* every chance I got, even though it was cheesy as shit. Whatever gave me the brilliant idea to follow him, I don't know. But that's what I did. One night, I slipped out of my room and got the keys to my mom's car. It was parked out on the street, and I got into the driver's seat and just waited.

"It was after eleven when he came out. When he drove off, I pulled out behind him. He never—"

"Wait a second! You said you were ten," I interrupted.

"Or eleven," she said, still not looking back. "I was always tall. And my dad let me drive all the time. It was no big deal. Anyway, he went straight to her house. I parked and I snuck out. And I saw them. Through the window."

"Oh, shit," I said. "That's crazy."

Her head shook, sadly. "No, that's not the crazy part. I did it again. The second time, I brought my IPod with me. And I took a picture of them. They were just kissing, but I did it. I was just so mad at him. I felt like everything I ever thought was a giant fucking lie."

"You showed your mom?" I asked.

"I did," she said, softly. "Maybe I should have thought about it. Noticed how she was. She was southern. All the charms. I think that's why we never really saw eye to eye. But when I showed her, she . . . slapped me. And she took my IPod."

"Are you serious?"

"She never really spoke to me again. I mean, pleasantries every chance she got. But nothing real. Nothing that meant anything. To be honest, I don't even know if I cared about that. But my dad? That broke me. He was never the same with me again. He stopped coaching. Stopped playing basketball with me altogether. Never went to another one of my games."

Zora turned, and her eyes met mine. "I lost them both, then. All because of the shit people hide."

"I'm sorry," I said.

"That's not why I told you that, Theo. I meant it when I agreed to work with you. I just need to know that you won't hide anything from me."

"I won't," I said, so totally caught up in her story. "I promise."

"Okay," she said, nodding to herself. Then she nodded at me. "I found someone."

"What?" I asked, my eyes widening. "Who?"

"Martino."

"Are you kidding?" I rushed over to her. "I couldn't find a scrap on him. I was starting to think Jasper made the whole thing up."

"He's in Delaware. I talked to him already. He's willing to meet you halfway on the day of your next visit with Jasper Friday morning. For lunch that afternoon in Dover, Delaware. Can I confirm?"

The blood rushed to my head so quickly that my scalp itched. I wanted to hug her, but one look into her hard eyes wiped that idea completely away.

"That is so awesome. So, when you talked to him, did you learn anything?"

"He was Jasper's father's lover. For over twenty years."

"Gold," I said.

"Maybe." Zora let out a sigh. "Just remember, Jasper Ross-Johnson is a very dangerous man."

*   *   *

I took the Amtrak to Delaware early Thursday afternoon. Dropping into one of the last open seats in the quiet car, I slipped my bag to the floor and pulled out the files I'd brought along. Something had been gnawing at my brain. Something about that word—*miracle*.

And I couldn't get the picture out of my mind, the vic with the headphones . . . were they connected? I dove into her file and found what I was looking for almost immediately. It was a small local news article that had come out a couple of weeks before Jasper's arrest. If I'd been more careful when I first saw it, the file wouldn't have been labeled a Jane Doe. I shook my head at my own carelessness as I read the headline: HALO KILLER'S FIRST VICTIM IDENTIFIED. Under that, in a lesser type, was the subtitle JANE DOE MOTHER OF THE 1996 MIRACLE BABY. As I read the article, my mind drew the scene. And my film found its *miracle*.

*   *   *

ACT ONE/SCENE 6

EXT. EMPTY PARKING LOT—DAY

Cracked pavement bakes under the early-autumn sun. Faded white lines lay out a half-dozen empty parking spots. In the corner of the lot, we see a run-down outhouse. A baby's broken cry shatters the silence. A CHYRON appears on the screen: SEPTEMBER 12, 1996.

The newborn had been abandoned to die in an outhouse sink. It was a hot September night. The restroom sat in a little hut off the parking lot of a remote state-owned beach. Outside, a translucent ghost crab sidled up the dune, sending granulates raining softly down the side. At full speed, it disappeared into a perfectly rounded hole, a darker circle

surrounded by countless scratch-like markings left by its frantic legs
during a long night's work. A second later it popped back out, returning
to the hunt. When the scream echoed out of the open door of the small
building, the crab disappeared again in a flash of white.

Inside, as her scream faded into the lonely night, a woman moaned.
She had a name but would be known as Jane Doe for far too long.
Utterly alone, she labored in the darkness. The bones of her elbows
looked sharp enough to slice clean through the graffiti-covered walls of
the single stall. The smell of fresh blood mingled with the brine and
musk, so pungent that even she cringed. The pain struck again. Her
narrow fingers clawed at her exposed belly, as if she might rip her life
away, like she might start over somehow. A clean slate. All the past mistakes unmade.

The baby was born five minutes later, slapping to the tile floor. A
final scream tore from the woman's mouth. Her eyes closed, and her
back slid down the stall wall as her bent knees gave out. For an instant,
a heavy silence fell over the scene. Then the baby wailed. And the placenta slipped to the floor.

The sounds were enough to resurrect the woman, if only for a
moment. Quickly she snatched the baby off the floor, cradling her
against her chest. Blood and mucus stained the white fabric of her bikini
top. The woman took a step but stopped, feeling the tension tugging at
the baby's umbilical cord. Her eyes returned to the floor, to the organ
that had once been hers. A dazed emptiness clouded her eyes as she bent
and scooped the placenta up in one hand.

Her feet barely left the tiles as she shuffled to the one sink. Sweat
covered every inch of her skin as she stood before a clouded, cracked
mirror, staring at her half-naked self. At the baby against her chest. And
the raw, red mass morphing around her fingers.

Did she intend what happened next? Had the woman known what
she would do in that bathroom by the sea? Maybe her instinct moved
her to the sink, where she could clean the birth off her newborn child.
She could leave that place. Together, they could start a new life.

Tragically, miraculously, that is not what happened that night.
Gently, lovingly, the young woman placed the baby and placenta into
the basin. Her bloodied hands moved with an agonizing slowness as
they pulled away. She took a step backward. Then another. Grabbing a
meager pile of belongings, including a pair of cutoff jean shorts and a
battered neon-yellow Walkman, the shattered young woman turned

and hurried through the open door, out into the night, tears of heartbreak tracing down her cheeks.

So many questions haunted that tiny shack below the dune, carried out into the harsh world on the back of an infant's calls. In a way, those questions were both a beginning and a beginning to the end.

*   *   *

Four days passed. Doctors would later say that the conditions were as perfect as possible. An unseasonably warm week in September. The cool porcelain of the sink. The fact that babies are born with fluid and glucose stored in their liver. As unlikely as the baby's survival was, what surprised everyone was the vitality of her scream.

The tourist season had just ended. The small beach, never crowded, did not see a visitor until Friday evening. A white Toyota pickup pulled into the small lot. A man exited the truck and moved around to the back. As he reached for the first handful of fishing gear, he heard it. A baby crying.

At first, the man thought nothing of it. He pulled rods out of the bed and placed his stocked Igloo on the ground. When he heard her again, he paused. Casually, he turned his head, taking in the entire lot, noticing that his truck was the only vehicle there. His head shook as he gathered what he needed and took his first step toward the path across the dune. The third time, he stopped dead in his tracks, realizing that the sound came from the small outhouse on the other side of the crackled asphalt.

The fisherman dropped his gear and his cooler. He sprinted, his mind straightening into a narrow line of action. The door remained open. As he reached it, a smell struck, one he knew to be rotting flesh. He flinched but pushed through it. His hand grabbed the jamb and he took his first step into the bathroom.

What he saw in that outhouse sink changed his life. For years, he would awaken at the witching hour to a flashback image of her, mouth gaping like a dark hole cut through the gaunt lines of her face. The bare, twig-thin arms and legs. And, most memorable, the two, tiny hands clenched into menacing little fists. As if this baby was not screaming for rescue but in defiance. As if she was saying she could take anything this life might dish. Now and forever.

The fisherman never touched her. Instead, he fumbled his flip phone out and dialed 911. He stood a foot away from the abandoned, malnourished, dehydrated newborn. His hands hovered closer, as if at any minute he might finally sweep her into his arms. His eyes found the dried umbilical cord still attached. Then the shriveled placenta. This father of three, a man who could gut a bluefish in less than a minute, swallowed down a mixture of revulsion and panic.

Three minutes later, the police found the man in that exact same position, his hands eternally reaching for her. The first officer, a man three months from retirement, pushed past the angler and rushed to the sink. His years of service vanished. He spared not even a single thought to crime scene procedures. To contamination of evidence. Instead, the officer scooped her up out of the cool basin and hugged her to his warmth. Her head turned with surprising strength. Her mouth opened. And this abandoned child, left exposed and without nourishment or fluids for four days, attempted to nurse from his crisply ironed uniform.

For the first time in his long career, the officer cried. The fisherman took a step back toward the door just as the ambulance arrived.

"It's okay," the officer said. "It's okay."

She felt like air in his arms. Like she might float right out of his grasp, right up to heaven. When he moved toward the exit, her tiny bones called to him. His mind counted those he could see until he had to stop. Jogging carefully, he crossed the lot, meeting the first paramedic halfway to the ambulance.

"It's bad," he said, softly, as if he did not want her to hear his words. "Had to be here for days."

The paramedic reached for the baby, but the officer would not let go. A second technician pulled the gurney from the back, the wheels clanging down to the pavement.

"We need to help her," the paramedic said.

In a daze, the officer lowered the baby girl onto a sterile white blanket. As the medics burst into action, the officer watched her through a film of tears.

"A miracle," he kept whispering. "She's a little miracle."

5

I EASED OUT OF my imagination, out of the script I'd written in my head, and back into the real world. Lowering the article, I called Zora. She answered on the second ring.

"He's toying with us," I said.

"Shhhh," someone hissed behind me.

"Oh, sorry," I said, standing up. To Zora I whispered, "Give me a second."

As the train rattled through New Jersey, I made my way out of the quiet car.

"I found it!" I blurted out once the door closed behind me.

"What?" Zora asked.

"The miracle. It's a person. The daughter of Jasper's first victim. I don't have details. I guess she was left in a bathroom. And survived for like three days or something. That's where the name came from. Her mom was murdered, but they didn't ID the body until right before Jasper's arrest . . ."

"Huh," Zora said. "Okay, I'll get on this. See if I can find anything else out."

"I need to meet her," I said. "You need to find her."

"I'll do my best, Theo. Like I always do." She paused. "Oh, shit. I forgot. I talked to Martino."

"Did he have second thoughts?" I asked.

"No, he wanted to see if you could meet him earlier. Tonight. And he can't make it up to Dover. He wants you to drive down to Rehoboth Beach."

"That's two hours from Wilmington. I don't get in until four."

"An hour and a half, actually. Okay," she said. "I'll tell him you can't make it. We can reschedule. He said he could meet up in a couple of weeks."

"No," I snapped. "No, I'm good. I need to rent a car. I can probably get there by seven."

"I'll let him know."

"Text me an address where he wants to meet up. Okay?"

"Definitely." She paused again. "Are you sure this isn't too much? There's no rush."

"No, I need to see him. It's all good."

"Okay," she said, sounding unsure. "Just drive carefully."

"Of course," I said, looking out the window again. "Definitely."

* * *

My eyes burned as I neared Lewes, Delaware. It was six thirty and Waze told me I was fifteen minutes from the address Zora had texted me.

I hadn't yet organized what I wanted to ask Martino. When I pulled into the restaurant parking lot, I eased into a spot away from the other cars but didn't get out. Instead, I built a timeline in my head, like I was storyboarding the Halo Killer's movie.

Twenty years prior, Jasper Ross-Johnson had taken his first victim. It would be sixteen years until that murder was attributed to the Halo Killer. And another four before his victim would be identified as Abbie Henshaw, the woman who abandoned the Miracle Baby.

Ten months ago, after abducting Barbara Yost, the ghostlike Halo Killer had slipped up after seeing a mysterious woman walking on the beach. He was captured and incarcerated, and Yost was rescued from a dingy cabin in the marshland bordering Delaware and Maryland.

And his words filled my head:

Miracle.

Not what, but who.

Could that baby, a local legend with a shocking tie to the Halo Killer, have something to do with his capture? The perfect emotional counterpoint to Jasper's madness. Storytelling gold! I fought the urge to plot the rest of the story, fictionalize it. That wasn't my job. I played in facts. Truth.

Why bring Miracle up at all? Could Jasper feel remorse? As he faced death, could he be regretting what he'd done? Could Miracle represent the pinnacle of that guilt? Maybe he needed to see her. Talk to her. Apologize for killing her mother.

As I sat in the car, my brain started to frame the shot. Jasper sitting behind the Plexiglas shield, his expression vacant and cold. Then, a door opens. Miracle appears, a grown woman. Jasper sees her. And in that instant, humanity slips into the eyes of the worst murderer in recent history. A generation of viewers raised on Disney movies melt in front of their smart televisions.

"That's *Beauty and the Beast* shit," I whispered.

As if in answer, my phone went off. It was a text from Zora.

Are you there? Martino just texted me.

I glanced at the time. Twenty minutes had passed. Instead of texting her back, I rushed out of the car and across the parking lot. I threw the door open and scanned the tables as I approached the host.

"Hi, I'm looking for—"

"Martino," the man said, a huge smile of his face. "He told me you'd be here. I . . . I just want to say, I loved *The Basement*. It was amazing."

"Thanks," I said, looking away.

As I moved in behind him, I saw Martino for the first time. He sat in a shadowed booth in the far corner of the mostly empty dining room. Bright-blue eyes looked out from a tan face. His expression was flat, but more from Botox than from lack of emotion. When he stood to greet me, he moved with a youthful grace that made me feel older, though I knew he had to be close to twice my age.

"Theo, it's so great to meet you," he said.

"Hey . . . Hi . . ." I wanted to use his name as he'd used mine, but I still wasn't sure if it was his first or his last. "Thanks for meeting with me."

"My pleasure. Sit, sit." He smiled at the host. "Thanks, Stephen."

Stephen blushed and stammered something before walking away. I took a seat, but I couldn't take my eyes off Martino. The perfectly trimmed silver hair. The long fingers, like a musician's. The androgynous quality of his mannerisms. He caught me staring.

"He's got you under a spell, I see."

"What? Who?"

"Jasper. Don't worry, I don't blame you. He is a very complicated man."

"Yeah," I said, taking a slow breath. "I'm . . . yeah. Hey, is your name . . . ? Should I . . . ?"

"Martino," he said, his smile showing shining capped teeth. "Just Martino."

As I nodded, a server passed the table. She almost bowed to the man as she passed. I stared at her, then turned back to him.

"I'm not famous," he said, laughing. "Not like you. Or like Jasper."

"Oh, I . . ."

"I own three restaurants. And I understand that I'm considered a nice boss. They all want to work for me, that's all."

"I'm sorry," I said, rubbing at my face. "It was a long drive."

Martino squinted. "I'm sorry."

"No, it's great. I really wanted to meet you. And . . . yeah . . . he has gotten under my skin. Just a little, I guess."

"He's always been like that," Martino said.

That's when I noticed the sadness in his eyes. It made me think of a parent who has lost a child.

"Where would you like me to start?" he asked.

"Wherever you want," I said.

"There's so much to say, I guess. I don't want to take your entire evening."

I laughed. "I'll listen to everything you want to say. Everything you can remember." I paused. "What was he like?"

Martino's eyes grew distant before he answered. "I don't think anyone really knew."

* * *

ACT ONE/SCENE 10

EXT. BEACH RESORT MAIN STREET—DAY

MARTINO struts down the sidewalk, past kite shops and colorful eateries. His feathered, shoulder-length hair bounces as he nods and chats with nearly everyone. The bronze Adonis carries a bottle of champagne under his arm, and the most carefree smile imaginable, as he hurries to a party, one hosted by the parents of a killer.

Martino rushed down Rehoboth Avenue, the heart of Delaware's most popular beach resort. The town was big enough that not everyone knew each other, but everyone certainly knew him. He was a fixture at local parties, along with the Ross-Johnsons. That was where he headed, across Silverlake to the edge of Carpenter's Beach. To Franklin's sprawling beachfront home with its crystalline windows and salt-touched breezes. He would be early, but that was okay. Clara wouldn't mind the help getting everything ready.

When he reached the house, he opened the front door without announcing his presence. He heard voices from the hallway but turned instead to the bar in the great room. Humming to himself, he fixed a dry martini and plopped two pearl onions in before swirling it around.

"Hello," he called out.

No one answered. So, he moved toward the bedrooms, walking slowly, a warm smile lifting his sun-bronzed cheeks. His lips parted, about to call out again, when Clara's voice rose up, shrill and near manic.

"Get over here!"

Martino froze. His smile faded. He loved Clara. She was his favorite type, unpredictably fabulous. But as he stood there, overhearing, he thought for the thousandth time that she should never have been a mother. It didn't suit her. Nor did it suit the boy.

"Hold still."

Martino disliked the tone. On the balls of his feet, he inched past Jasper's room. The door was open. Despite himself, he peeked within. It was just a flash, but he saw Clara kneeling, one hand gripping the frail child's shoulder so tightly that her knuckles whitened. With her other hand, she racked a fingernail across the sharp edge of his collarbone, cutting into the skin. Blood beaded and Jasper flinched.

Martino turned his head, slipping past. His pace quickened as he headed to Franklin's room in the back. But he was not fast enough to avoid hearing Clara's venom.

"Really? Really! What? Are you a little baby? Are you? You're just like your father," she hissed. "Just like him."

6

"IT HAPPENED THAT night," Martino told me, his bright eyes distant.

"What happened?"

He looked out a darkened window. "You have to understand. Clara knew everything. They had an understanding, even before the marriage. She had no interest in a husband. She just needed a partner. And Franklin being Franklin, he liked the show of it all. The look of confusion. He was a trickster." Martino laughed, lovingly. "As was often the case, I stayed the night in his room. Once again, everyone knew. Except . . . the boy. He must have heard something. I don't know."

Martino paused. I waited, admittedly impatient.

"I don't understand."

"He must have heard something. That's all I can think. It was late. Franklin had this charming slit of a window above his bedroom door. I remember seeing the boy's face in it. Like a ghost, really. I had a second to wonder how he got up that high. Then the crash.

"We rushed out into the hallway immediately, but Clara was already there. The boy was crumpled on the hardwood. He wasn't moving . . . He must have climbed all the way up there, then slipped. Fell to the floor. She grabbed him . . . picked him up. And he was so limp. I . . . I thought he was dead."

He stopped again. A single tear left a track on his right cheek.

"She kept shaking him. Screaming at him . . ." Martino's voice rose. "'*Be a man! Be a man!*'"

I flinched. Everyone in the place stared at us. At the same time, I was enthralled.

"But he was out cold," Martino said. "Poor little boy."

"Are you saying he had a head injury?"

Martino squinted at me. "I believe so, yes. But she kept screaming at him. She shook him and shook him. Slapped his face. His eyes never opened."

He covered his mouth with a hand. I had questions, but I stopped myself.

"I'm sorry," Martino continued. "But it was horrible. I truly thought the boy lost his life. She took him away while he was still unconscious. That's when I saw the stepladder. He must have climbed up to peek through the window. At us."

The lines of his shining face sagged. It was as if a light had flickered out inside the man. But I couldn't stop myself. As he faltered, my excitement grew.

"He had a brain injury. Are you sure about that?"

He nodded. Maybe my humanity should have outweighed the need I felt. But I reached out and touched the top of his hand that rested on the tabletop between us.

"You blame yourself, don't you?"

Martino closed his eyes and nodded. "He was never the same after that. Something inside him broke. Like a lightbulb shattered in his soul."

A lightbulb in his soul? That might have been the corniest thing I had ever heard. I imagined it coming out of some overly dramatic soap opera script. But I hid my reaction, instead focusing on the interview.

"Listen, I've been doing this for a long time. I've met so many people like Jasper. And I've learned one thing for certain. It is no one's fault. Sometimes"—my voice lowered to a whisper—"I'm not even sure it's their fault. But a head injury? I've never seen that mentioned in any of the articles about Jasper. That can be a factor. There was a study not too long ago, a highly respected one, that found a correlation between brain trauma and acquired sociopathy."

Martino shook his head. "The boy was always a little strange. But . . ."

"*Strange* and *murderer* are surprisingly far apart on the spectrum of human behavior. It takes something for a person to cross that line, to stop seeing people as equals and start seeing them as something different. Experiments, toys, dolls, voices—there are so many different variants. So many different patterns to these cases. It's true that their choice in victims tends to show something about their past. Abuse, isolation, fear—those things can influence the *who*s and the *how*s. But they don't create a killer. Something else does. Something more . . . biological."

I watched Martino for a moment before continuing. I could tell he didn't really buy what I was saying. I could see how deeply responsible he felt for what Jasper had done. For the people he had hurt.

"Trust me. You didn't have anything to do with it. I promise. Not to be too personal, but his victims were women, Martino. If that night had any true influence on Jasper, he'd have killed men. I'm . . ."

"Or boys," Martino interrupted.

"What?" I asked.

"Boys," Martino repeated.

"None of Jasper's victims were male."

His head shook slowly. "I don't know about that."

I leaned forward. "What do you know?"

"There was a boy once. His name was . . . Danny. And a book. An awful, awful book."

*   *   *

ACT ONE/SCENE 13

EXT. FRONT PORCH OF RESTAURANT—DAY

Martino holds court at a café table just off the sidewalk, surrounded by smiling faces. His eye wanders and he catches sight of YOUNG JASPER. His blood chills.

After that night, Martino felt a heightened sense of responsibility for the boy. He kept his eyes open. His restaurant sat like a hub at the center of the community. Once fall hit and the season ended, however, it became an enclave. Locals wandered onto the porch or into the bar, depending on the weather. He would sit among them, holding court, each and every day, one eye on the conversation, the other on the street, watching everyone that passed.

It had been years since Jasper's injury, and the stories filtering back to him grew more and more troubling. Odd behaviors turned strange. Strange turned dark. Dark seemed to be heading toward dangerous.

That day, as he sat at a six-top, surrounded by friends and two of his bartenders, he was almost lost in the moment, enjoying the warm September air against his taut skin. The conversation flowed easier than the cocktails. He was in his element.

Then one of the bartenders facing north craned his neck. "Isn't that Frankie's kid?"

His stomach jittered as he spun around. He saw Jasper immediately. Something had changed about the way he moved. His thin arms bent at smooth but odd angles as he walked, almost mantis-like. The boy with him, small for his age, dwarfed Franklin's son. That one had wide, slopping shoulders and a massive tuft of jet-black hair atop his narrow head.

"Who's that with him?" Martino asked.

His friend who owned the three arcades on the boardwalk answered. "That's Danny."

"Danny?"

"I have no idea who his parents are. Never seen them. Someone mentioned that his mom might live in Seaford. But no one even knows how he gets into town every day. But he's always there. Spends most of the day at my place. Begs quarters from the changemakers. They like the kid, though. He's sweet, but dull. I think there's something wrong upstairs."

"Huh," Martino said.

He stared as the two boys passed the porch. Though Jasper didn't look at the bigger boy, his head tilted closer. And Jasper's thin lips moving constantly, almost hypnotically. For his part, Danny stared straight ahead, never blinking, nodding over and over again.

"That might be trouble," Martino muttered.

"What?" his friend said.

At the same moment, a waiter joined the table, carrying a large silver tray loaded with fresh drinks. Martino helped spread them among the crowd. Their conversation lifted over the clank of glass on the metal tabletop, and he turned his attention back to his friends.

* * *

Less than a half hour later, Jasper returned. When Martino saw the boy turn off the boardwalk, alone, he sprang up from his seat.

"Where are you going, boss?" a bartender asked.

Martino put a hand up. "I'll be right back."

He raced off the porch toward the boy. Jasper never looked up. He carried a book that seemed half his size, open between his two small hands. His nose nearly touched the pages as he headed straight for Martino, oblivious that anyone was in his path.

"Hello there, son."

Jasper startled. He slammed the book closed but recovered almost instantly.

"Hello, uncle," he said in a monotone.

"What do you have there?" Martino asked.

Jasper appeared to consider bolting. Instead, he blinked once, then handed the black-covered book to Martino, who turned it over, looking at the cover picture. It showed the corner of a dingy room with what looked like blood splattered over every surface. Martino read the title aloud, the words slowing as he realized what he held.

"Blood Stain Evidence."

"It's mine," Jasper said. He blinked again. "I found it."

"This isn't for you, kiddo," Martino said, forcing a smile.

"Can I have it back, please?" the boy asked.

"I'm sorry. No."

Jasper stood looking up at him, stricken, his disappointment palpable.

"Run along home. And tell your father I said hello."

The boy remained frozen. With a shake of the head, Martino turned and headed back to his porch. He climbed the three plank steps but stopped at the top, wrapping a hand around one of the whitewashed posts as he turned. Jasper still hadn't moved. The two stared at each other for a moment longer until the boy finally walked away, heading back toward Carpenter's Beach.

"You coming back?" someone called from the table behind him.

Martino shook his head. "In a minute."

Shielding the cover of the book from his friends, Martino headed back down the stairs. Walking quickly, he hit the boardwalk and then turned onto Rehoboth Avenue. Two blocks west, he pushed the door of the bookstore open and marched up to the counter.

"Hello, Jan," he said.

"Hi, Martino," the owner of the shop said from behind the register. She looked at him over the reading glasses she wore halfway down the bridge of her nose. "What do you have there?"

"I just ran into Franklin's boy. Did he buy this from you?"

Martino passed the book across the counter. Jan lifted it, giving it a calm once-over.

"No, he didn't," she said. "He was wandering around the store on Wednesday, but I haven't seen him since."

"Then how'd he get it?" he asked.

Jan clucked her tongue off the roof of her mouth. "That other boy just bought it. Danny, I think his name is."

7

S ITTING ACROSS FROM me in that dim, peaceful restaurant, I could feel Martino's sadness thickening the air between us.

"That boy went missing," he said, his eyes closed. "Not long after that day."

"You said his mother had it hard. Maybe something happened. Maybe she had to leave town. Maybe child services found out."

When his eyes reopened, I saw guilt and loss entwined within his expression.

"I never said anything."

"Why?" I whispered.

"Because I loved him," Martino said.

"Jasper?"

A dark laugh burst out between his impossibly white teeth. "God, no. His father."

We sat in silence for a while. When I finally glanced at the time, it was later than I expected.

"I'm sorry," Martino said. "I didn't mean to go on as long as I did."

"Please don't apologize. Thank you so much. I . . ." It was my turn to laugh. "I don't even know what I'm thinking. I have to be at the prison early tomorrow morning. But can we stay in touch. I'd love to hear more."

"Of course," Martino said. "Anything you need."

We stood. I gave him a friendly hug. He walked me to the door. And as it closed behind me, I somehow knew I'd never speak to the man named Martino again.

* * *

At just past one AM, when I was thirty minutes away from Wilmington, my phone rang. I knew it was him, even before I saw the now-familiar prison number on the screen.

"Hello, Theodore," Jasper said. "Are you in town?"

"I am," I said, my eyelids feeling heavy. "I'll see you in, like, seven hours . . . Wait a minute! How are you making this call right now? It's the middle of the night."

"I'm well liked here," Jasper answered with a hint of amusement. "They know I'm a bit of a night owl."

"That's scary," I said.

"How so?" he asked, sounding genuinely curious.

"Um, I hope they don't like you so much that they let you walk out of there."

Jasper laughed. "Are you giving me an idea, Theo?"

"No, I . . . God, I'm exhausted."

"Running yourself ragged?"

My visit was scheduled for nine in the morning. With the change to the Martino meeting, I wasn't even sure I had time to make it to the hotel room I'd reserved. And decided to drive straight there and take a nap in my car. So the answer would be a resounding yes, but I left it unsaid.

"I have something for you," he said next. "Are you recording this call?"

"Not yet," I said. "I'm driving—"

"You have thirty seconds," he said. "I'll wait."

Despite the confusion that flared up and sent a tinny taste to the back of my tongue, I swerved to the shoulder, slamming on the brakes. Someone laid on the horn, but I ignored it. Instead, I set the app I used for telephone interviews as quickly as I could.

When I got back on the line, he was already telling a story. I rubbed at my eyes, half listening now that the recorder had been turned on.

"I was a dermatologist. Did you know that? No?" He paused. "A very successful one. My patients thought I had alopecia. That explained my lack of hair. Can you imagine? They thought my profession was a deep and noble passion. How quaint.

"Did I mention that I volunteered at an animal shelter as well? For years. I . . . Are you there, Theodore?"

I blinked. "Yeah, definitely."

"Good," he said, his tone suddenly sharp and purposeful. "I have a present for you. There is something hidden on my property. Something I want you to have. You'll thank me, Theodore."

"Seriously?" I leaned forward so fast that my knees slammed into the steering wheel. "Where is—"

"One-seven-four-seven-three."

"What does that even—"

"Three Sapling Drive, Frederica, Delaware."

"Jasper, what—"

The line went dead.

*   *   *

The second part of Jasper's puzzle was solved easily. I put it into my GPS app. The destination calculated as an hour back the direction I'd just driven. Regardless of how tired I felt, I didn't really hesitate. I just turned the car around and drove.

Eventually I found myself on a deserted back road and eased onto Sapling Drive. It wound behind a thicket of oaks and white pine until a modern but dilapidated split-level came into view. As the lights from my rental panned across the front, I saw cedar siding and large, cloudy windows looking out into the woods. When I got out, I stumbled in one of the many deep ruts carved in the yard, as if heavy vehicles had rolled in and out a number of times.

Stepping outside the beam from the head lamps, I felt exposed. Reaching back through the open window, I killed the lights. Slowly, my palms sweating, I inched closer to the house, following a brick walk to the entrance. A set of massive oak doors appeared in better shape than everything else. When I tried to open them, the handles simply rattled.

"Shit," I whispered.

With a quick glance back toward the road, I slipped off the walk and moved along the perimeter to the side yard. I tried every window, every door, but the place was locked up tight.

Finally, I moved to the edge of the woods and found a good-sized fallen branch. It took me three swings, but I finally sent it through one of the long windows. The sound of glass shattering tore through the night. I froze, half expecting an alarm to sound or a police siren to come screaming down Sapling Drive.

Nothing happened. Everything remained deathly quiet. Using the branch, I cleared away the shards. As I climbed through the window, though, my shirt snagged. I felt something cut through my side, just above the hip. Not deep, but when I flopped to the floor inside the house and slid my hand under the fabric, I felt warm, sticky blood between my fingers. I pushed myself up, leaving a rust-colored palm print on the cool floor tiles. Evidence of my breaking and entering, I knew, but it was too late to worry about that. The Halo Killer's home was pure gold.

I had to get it on film. Wiping my hand on my pants, I slipped the phone out and used it as a flashlight. As I switched on the beam, it made a lazy arc across the room. I hit record on the camera at the same time, sure the footage would be priceless.

Over the years, I'd worked projects with every type of person. I'd visited the homes of hoarders, dog fighters, the morbidly obese, agoraphobes, heroin addicts. Everyone you could imagine. Yet I'd never seen anything like what I saw that night.

I stood by one window. From there, two doorways could be seen. Both were sealed with cloudy plastic sheets that hung still in the stifling air. That was the most normal aspect of the space. The entire place was a motley patchwork, sections of every flooring imaginable spread out around me—shag carpet, tile, Berber, cork, poured concrete, and the strip of bathroom tile under my shoes. Atop it, in haphazard positions, furniture with as many different surfaces filled almost every open space—a leather chair, a suede recliner, a lush velvet footstool. The walls hadn't been spared either. Swatches of wallpaper with different textures ran up against sections painted in matte, eggshell, and gloss.

"What the hell," I muttered.

And I pictured Jasper, as I'd seen him at our first meeting. I truly believed I could smell him in the air. I sensed him in every inch of that bizarre place. I couldn't get myself to move. It was as if his ghost hovered just over my shoulder. And if I turned, if I looked into his beady, flat eyes, he would slip into my soul. I would become him. He would devour me.

But time brought me back. It was past three thirty and I had no intention of missing my visit at the prison. So I found the courage to move. I walked as softly as I could, crossing from carpet to tile to cork. I noticed a television on a small stand by another window and remembered Jasper telling me he liked to watch Netflix. A chill ran through my body when I pictured him sitting there on one of those off pieces of furniture, watching *The Basement*.

After that, I moved more quickly. Peeling back the still flap of plastic, I followed a short stub of hallway into a bare kitchen. From there, I made it around to the front doors. Standing in the foyer, I saw another room, one that would have been meant as a study. Following the light from my phone, I stepped in and froze again.

If the other room had been Jasper's funhouse, this one was his lab. Shelves lined the entire space, most holding vials and test tubes, beakers and every size of microscope. As I took a step, glass shattered under my foot. I swung the beam downward and saw the ruined mess of more equipment, likely broken during the police search of the home following his arrest.

"Wow," I couldn't help saying out loud.

As I moved the light again, I saw a metal crate. A sticker across the top read OHIO FORENSICS TRAINING CENTER. Above that, more shelves hung on the wall. Books filled those, every single one having to do with the science of evidence collection. I scanned the titles, shaking my head slowly. My heart missed a beat as my eyes took in one title above the crate. As I read it, I heard Martino's voice in my head—*Blood Stain Evidence*. I couldn't believe it. My hand shook as I reached for the book. It felt cold to the touch as I slipped it off the shelf. I saw the cover photo, the white corner and the splatter of blood, just as Martino had described.

"I can't . . ."

The words caught in my throat. As I lowered the book, my light shined up into the space it had occupied on the shelf. It reflected off a keypad. As the glare moved off the silver surface, I saw numbers from zero through nine.

I fumbled with my phone, listening to Jasper's call again, remembering the random list of numbers he'd told me. It took me three loops of the audio to convince myself to touch the buttons. Listening a fourth time, I entered the code and heard a locking mechanism release. A small metal door, like an access panel for a water valve behind the wall, swung open, catching on one of the shelved books.

Frantic, I tossed them to the floor, including the one from my hand, *Blood Stain Evidence*. The compartment opened and I reached in without a thought. Inside, I found a USB drive with a cheery green plastic cover. I pulled it out, pinching it between two fingers, and just the thought of what I might find on it turned my stomach.

In a flash, I was out of that house, racing to the rental car. Sitting in the front seat, I opened my travel laptop and inserted the USB. Thankfully, there was only one video. Holding my breath, I accessed it and hit play. For a beat, there was only a blank screen and a date stamp— *Sept 11, 1996.*

ACT ONE/SCENE 15

INT. HALO KILLER'S HOUSE—NIGHT

Shot from a security camera hung in the corner of the room, we see a nightmarish funhouse. A million textures cover every surface, shining in just as many shades of gray. Plastic over a doorway rustles and a monster appears—the Halo Killer wearing a hazmat suit.

Jasper's strange room appeared in shades of a night-vision lens—black and washed-out gray. Though the grim image diluted the cacophony of textures, colors, and contours, it heightened the utter wrongness of the floors, the walls, and the furniture. Bizarre moved to creepy, then escalated to downright fear when the ghostly image of the Halo Killer skittered through one of the draped plastic doorways.

In choppy stutter steps, Jasper moved toward one of the couches. He carried something in his right hand, maybe a plate of food, which he placed on a tiny table. Straightening, he turned, his head tilting up. The lens focused as the light shined off his perfectly smooth, hauntingly pale features. He wore a strange, skintight suit, likely latex, that covered him from his chin to the soles of his feet. Though he did not have gloves, a thin sheen covered both hands, as if he had dipped them in liquid bandage. With a heart-stopping smile, he looked directly into the camera and nodded. Then he sat down on the couch. Using a remote, he turned on the television, which glowed disconcertingly in the night-vision shot.

Jasper picked at his food for a few minutes. Though there was no audio, his head shook as if he was laughing. He clapped at one point. Then, carefully, he placed his meal back on the table and rose. With his eyes still locked on the television screen, he moved around the room. Like a young child, he crawled across the floor, passing over each of the random surfaces. He rolled back, climbed on every piece of furniture, rubbed his slick hands across every wall. All the while, he watched his show, laughing at times, his brow furrowed at others.

As if a switch had been thrown, he stopped after exactly twenty minutes. His back stiffened. His neck tensed. Like an automaton, he collected his dish and marched from the room. The television's blinding glow continued in one corner of the shot, the intensity waxing and waning. Otherwise, the room remained empty, eerily still for a time.

Then the plastic rustled again. Something that appeared inhuman entered the room. A tall, peaked head. A strange alien illumination. Billowing arms ending in large black fingers. The figure stepped closer to the camera, its head tilting up and nodding again. It was no monster. No demon from the underworld—not entirely, at least. Instead, it was Jasper, dressed in a full hazmat suit.

For over an hour, Jasper collected evidence. He dropped small numbered tents. Using tweezers, he plucked fibers from the carpet. He dusted for fingerprints. Jasper moved each piece of furniture. He bagged the remote. Eventually, his back straightened. He stepped out of the room, returning with a metal gurney. With painstaking care, he lined the specimens on the surface and wheeled them from the room.

For a moment, the shot remained empty again, the TV off, the plastic shifting slightly from his passing. Then, abruptly, the shot cut off, and a new one flashed to life. The room changed from Jasper's funhouse to his lab. He entered, pushing the gurney carefully up to a sterile table. One at a time, over the course of an hour, he processed each one. When finished, he lifted the hood and visor off his head. Turning, the Halo Killer looked up at the lens a third time. His mouth formed a single word.

Perfect.

CHAPTER

8

I BLINKED, UNSURE OF what I had just watched. But it took only a
second for a hearty laugh to slip out between my dry lips, nearly
shaking the inside of the compact rental.

"Holy shit," I yelled, slapping the wheel.

It was pure gold. I imagined this footage fitting into the storyboard
that suddenly filled my mind. I imagined a snippet, Jasper lifting the
hood off his head and staring up at the camera, his eyes the devil's
black. That shot would be the perfect ending to a teaser reel.

"Fucking gold!"

Still nearly out of my head with excitement, I caught sight of the
time: five thirty AM. I blinked again, my eyes suddenly burning with
exhaustion.

"No way," I muttered to myself.

Ripping the USB out, I tossed the laptop onto the passenger seat.
With a final look at my new treasure, I stuffed it into my front pocket.
Then I drove like a madman. I had to be at the prison by nine.

* * *

I'd come directly from Jasper's house. Sitting in the waiting area at the
prison, I slapped my knee, still nursing a simmering euphoria. The footage I'd shot just kept repeating in my head.

"Fucking gold," I muttered.

"Excuse me?" someone asked.

Startled, I looked up to see a prison official, someone I'd never met before. He was tall, with a straight back and a shock of white hair atop his head. When he spoke, his voice had the timbre of a radio announcer.

"Hello, Mr. Snyder. We've been expecting you."

"Um, hi," I said. "Is it time to go back?"

"Of course," the man said.

I groaned as I rose to my feet. The man watched me with a thin half smile lifting a corner of his mouth.

"You look tired."

I scoffed. "You could say that."

"Well, Jasper is waiting to see you."

I frowned, thinking about what the Halo Killer had told me on the phone hours earlier.

"Jasper, huh? You're on a first-name basis, then?"

The man laughed. "I'm sorry. I've just recently started working here and I've forgotten the necessary formalities. Inmate Ross-Johnson is ready to see you now."

*   *   *

When I finally got to the actual visiting area, Jasper wasn't there waiting for me. Before I could even question the old man, he was gone too. Only a guard stood on my side of the viewing room glass, staring straight ahead.

"Does it matter which booth I take?" I asked.

"No, sir," the guard said flatly.

I took a seat. Within a minute my camera operator, Jessica, entered, carrying her equipment.

"Sorry, my train ran a little late."

"It's okay," I said. "You can set up right behind me." I turned back to the guard. "That's okay, right?"

"Yes, sir," he replied.

I watched him for a second, once again remembering my call with Jasper earlier that morning.

"Hey, what time is lights-out, anyway?"

The guard looked at me then. "Here?"

"Yeah."

"Twenty-one hundred, sir."

"So, inmates can't make a call at—"

The sound of chair legs scraping on the floor interrupted me mid-question. I turned and found Jasper sitting across from me, his legs tightly crossed and a cloying smile lifting his razor-thin lips.

"Scare you?" he asked in that voice of his.

"Sorry," I said, and a yawn slipped out.

Jasper leaned forward. "Theodore, are you feeling well?"

I blinked. "Excuse me?"

"Did you find my safe?" he asked. "Did you watch the footage?"

"Of course I did," I said. "That's why I—"

"Did you notice the date?"

"Yes," I snapped, but I couldn't recall it at the moment.

"Did you?" he asked, his head tilting.

"Sure," I said.

"Excellent," he said, punctuating the word with one of his excited claps. "Then you noticed that it was the day before my first."

I could only stare at him as a layer of context built around the security video I'd watched. Jasper had been practicing. Testing his process. Making sure he left no evidence behind. That nod. The smile he gave. He was ready. To start killing.

"Wait a second," I said, my mind flipping back to what he had just said. "That can't be right. What about Danny? He was your first, right?"

Jasper blinked. "Who have you been talking to, Theodore?"

I leaned back, taking a deep breath. I even tented my hands. "A friend of your father's."

"Martino?" Jasper scoffed. "He's a fool."

"Do you think so?" I asked. "I found him to be very heartfelt. And earnest."

"Like Bender's sister?"

I recoiled despite my best effort. It was Bender's sister who'd led me down the rabbit hole. I blamed her for the scandal, 100 percent. Our affair was common knowledge, but nothing else. As far as the reports went, It had been an anonymous source that I had failed to vet. One that led me to conclude that Bender had been falsely accused. Which led to the defamation suit by the sheriff's department in Tulsa. The Twitter exchange between me and the producer. None of that mattered, though. What hit me was that he shouldn't have known that.

I took a breath, steadying my nerves. "Jasper, we don't have time to go into that. All I'm saying is that you were much younger when you . . . for your first victim. Thirteen or fourteen. Correct?"

"Danny was no victim," Jasper spat back at me.

"What would you call him?"

"A horrible mistake."

"How so?" I asked.

"How so? Are you serious?"

I just nodded and waited, trying to regain my composure. Jasper's eyes nearly cut right through mine. But I held my ground. I let him make the next move.

Jasper shook his head slowly. Then he looked past me. Maybe at the camera; I couldn't be sure.

"It wasn't supposed to happen. But I had read some books and looked up a number of articles. I just assumed that it would be boys. Because of my father, maybe. I just overthought it. When it happened—when I . . . chose . . . Danny—I knew it wasn't right. It was all wrong. I felt no relief. No, the voice just got angry. It yelled at me. Like she did.

"So, Danny isn't real. He's not part of this, Theodore. You need to understand that, or you won't understand anything else. She was the first one. I knew it the minute I saw her on the beach." His head shook slowly. "And none of my preparations mattered. Not that time."

When he mentioned seeing her on the beach, my heart thumped against my chest. I grabbed the edge of the table between us.

"Are you talking about the woman on the beach, from that first story you told me?"

"No," Jasper said, frustrated. "Please, listen to me. I'm talking about the first one."

My thoughts spun. "She was on the beach too. Jane Doe—or, I mean, Abbie Henshaw? The Miracle Baby's mother?"

"Yes! Precisely. I believe that was her name. Can I continue? It happened right after I learned my father had passed."

* * *

ACT ONE/SCENE 17

INT. DOCTOR'S OFFICE—DAY

We see an entirely new side of the Halo Killer. As Dr. Jasper Ross-Johnson, he sits behind an immaculately clean desk. Over his perfectly pressed shirt and tie, he wears the white coat of a doctor, a healer. The light from his lamp sparkles off his frighteningly smooth skin. The phone rings. It is a call from his mother.

As he sat behind his desk, waiting for his first patient of the day, Jasper had no idea it would begin later that night. He had been busy, perfecting his trade. Recording his practice. But he did not feel ready. In his studies, he still left faint traces of evidence behind, particularly on fabric surfaces. Such things would get him caught. Thrown behind bars. And Jasper knew he could never abide captivity.

In the moment, he wasn't even thinking about it. Not directly, at least. The hunger was always there, but at work he could keep it below the surface and focus his attention on the necessary skills: Lift the corners of your mouth into a smile. Don't forget your brows. Make eye contact for three seconds, no more. Laugh and glance out the window. Comment on the weather.

Jarringly, his phone rang. He snatched it up.

"Yes."

"Dr. Ross-Johnson," the nurse/receptionist said, her tone nervous. "Um, there's a woman on the phone. She says she's your mother?"

His eyes widened when he heard that. The movement was minute, barely perceptible. Yet his reaction made him angry, for it was unpracticed.

"Put her through, please. Thank you," he said, with purposeful inflection.

The line clicked. He let out a silent breath before she spoke.

"Hello, Jasper."

"Mother," he said, looking out the window at a cardinal sitting on the branch of a pine tree.

"I'm fine," she snapped. "Thanks so much for asking."

"How are you?" he asked, his eyes unblinking.

She laughed. It was a bitter sound, one he had not heard in a wonderfully long time.

"Your father is dead."

She dropped the news like the strike of a weapon. Jasper did not flinch. Nor did he respond.

"Did you hear me?"

"I did," he said.

"The funeral is on Sunday. At the church on Rehoboth Avenue . . . of course."

"Are you attending?" he asked.

"Of course not."

"I can buy you a plane ticket."

She laughed again. "No, thank you."

"Okay."

The line remained silent for a few seconds. Jasper could hear his mother's breathing. In it, he also heard her unspoken words. *BE A MAN, Jasper!*

"Will you be going?" she asked, as if she could not care less.

"No," he said.

"No? Are you serious? Whatever he was, he's your father. Doesn't that mean anything to you?" She left space for him to answer. When he didn't, she continued, "I assume I can expect the same from you. I don't really care, Jasper. You need to understand that."

"I do, Mother."

"*I do, Mother,*" she mocked. "Do you? Do you have any idea what it's been like? Your father's . . . behaviors . . . were bad enough. But you . . . Whatever! It doesn't matter. I felt compelled to tell you. Now I have. Enjoy your life, *Dr. Ross-Johnson.* You pathetic little . . ."

Her voice trailed off, muffled by the sound of her hanging up the phone. Jasper laid his receiver gently in the cradle and continued to stare at the blood-red cardinal until it flew off. When it did, his hand seemed to move without permission. Two fingers pinched together where his eyebrows used to be.

*   *   *

Late that night, Jasper moved along the empty beach. The surf ran up the sand to his left, hissing to a stop a few feet from his path before retreating once again. Though he stared straight ahead, south along the coast, he felt utterly alone. As if all the people throughout the world had simply ceased to exist. There was Jasper. And there was this place. Nothing else.

Eventually, he saw the first twinkle of light coming from the windows of a dozen homes that sat atop the dune, overlooking the ocean as if they owned it. At one time, this had been his home. Jasper kept moving as names listed in his head. D'Angelo, Frantz, Cheever, the past owners of each fabulous home. Maybe they were gone, the houses sold to the nouveau riche. Maybe not. In a way, it didn't matter to Jasper. He wasn't walking in the present anymore. Since his mother's phone call, he had slipped through time. Somehow trapped in a past he had no desire to revisit.

He stopped in front of his childhood home. Standing just where the dune slowly rose, he stared up at the behemoth and felt nothing but an icy finger tracing the line of his spine. Then a flash of movement in the shadowed night caught his eyes.

Jasper's body tensed as he made out the figure of a person, wispy and frail, as it rose from the ground. His hands balled into tight fists as he watched her move. There was something off. Something wounded about her gait. His predatory instinct locked on.

A gull shrieked overhead. He did not flinch. He leaned forward. His lips parted. His mouth watered. And Jasper took that first, silent step. The base of his brain, that part that had remained unchanged throughout the evolution of his species, took control. It evened his breathing. It tensed and loosened his muscles. It drew in every stimulus through his focused senses, every sight, every sound, every smell. Even the feel of the sand under his shoes. It calculated distance. Risk. And most of all, reward.

Closer . . . closer. . . .

A part of him remained. A sliver of humanity in the frontal lobe. The truth is, however, even that part of him did not ponder morals or ethics. Love, kindness, empathy—none of that factored into the silent, almost one-sided struggle inside Jasper that night. Instead, his intelligence tried to slow the near unstoppable momentum of his instincts.

"I'm not prepared," he whispered. "I don't have the latex. I didn't shower and lotion. I only shaved once today."

But his pace did not slow. Instead, he heeded the stronger call. Jasper inched closer and closer to her.

"Patience, practice, purpose."

Closer . . . closer!

That drive drowned out all the rest. Time skipped jarringly forward, and it was over. He was panting, looking down at what he had done. At the limbs bent at marionette angles as if playing among the jagged rocks. At the neon-yellow headset hovering like a halo above perfectly lifeless eyes. He was no longer Jasper Ross-Johnson. Instead, he was something else. Something entirely different. And it would be that reality, more than anything else, that he craved more and more, for a very long time. For, on that dark night, the Halo Killer was born.

CHAPTER

9

I WAS LOST IN his words when my eye caught sight of the guard on his side of the glass. He moved toward Jasper and my hand came up, like I might stop him. Force him to give us more time.

"There was an outhouse?" I blurted out, interrupting him.

Jasper stopped midsentence. His head tilted as he stared at me. The guard seemed to inch closer in slow motion.

"What did you say?"

"There was an outhouse. And the baby. Did you know about that?"

Jasper's eyes narrowed. He stood, one palm against the glass. Inching closer, the corner of his mouth lifted in a primal sneer.

"You stay away from her," he hissed.

I lurched back, my own hand coming up defensively. "What? Who?"

"I'm warning you, Theodore." Right before my eyes, Jasper Ross-Johnson transformed into the Halo Killer. "You think it's safe, don't you? That I'm locked away in this abomination. Not everything is at it appears."

His mouth gaped into a pantomime smile. When his teeth clicked together again, he hissed a final, mortal warning at me.

"Stay away from that girl, or you'll regret it."

PART TWO

MIRACLE JONES

CHAPTER

1

MIRACLE JONES—IT WAS so hard to understand her, how she fit into the story. Jasper's warning lit the fuse. A need flared inside me. I had to find her. Know her. But there was something more to it too. Some deeper connection.

I should have reached out to Zora, asked her for help. Instead, as I left the prison, I searched the internet for an address and phone number. When I found it, I didn't call first. Despite not sleeping a minute the night before, I drove almost two hours and pulled into a neighborhood, counting the houses until I reached number twelve. It was a nice little cottage with a view of the bay between the two homes across the street.

As I stepped out of the rental, I looked around. She'd grown up in that neighborhood. Lived in that house. Jasper's warning turned to dust. I didn't even think about how amazing the footage I'd taken the night before would look on the screen. Instead, I felt alive with an uncanny excitement, though I couldn't explain why.

I stepped up to the door and knocked. No one answered, so I tried again, leaning close to see if I could hear anyone inside. It was quiet, so I turned to leave. That's when I saw the woman standing in the middle of the street, staring at me. She looked like someone's great-aunt.

"Can I help you?" she asked, clearly suspicious.

"Oh, hi," I said, moving closer. "My name is Theo Snyder."

Not even a hint of recognition crossed her face. I thought that might be for the better.

"I'm looking for someone," I continued. "Miracle . . . um . . . Jones."

The woman squinted. "Are you from the *Daily Whale?*"

"What? No," I said, having no idea that she meant the local paper. "I'm a documentarian. I made the movie *The Basement.*"

Her eyes brightened. "The one on Netflix?"

"Yes."

"That was so scary. I've watched it three times. In fact, we acted out one of the scenes in my drama class."

I forced a smile. "That's great."

"Are you making a movie about Miracle?"

I paused for only a second. "I am. Do you know her well?"

The woman approached quickly. "I've known her since she was a baby. My name is Virginia Harris, but you can call me Ginny. Do you want to come over? I can get you some orangeade. The stories I could tell you."

I smiled. "That sounds delicious."

I followed Ginny Harris inside her house. She spoke to me for an hour, telling me secondhand stories of Miracle's childhood.

"Meg told me the story of how little Miracle learned about her abandonment," Ginny began. "In the sixth grade, if I remember right. She had just bought those fancy new shoes she loved so much . . ."

As she spoke, my mind shot the footage. Another scene slapped into place on the sprawling storyboard in my head.

* * *

ACT TWO/SCENE 1

INT. GROCERY STORE—DAY

A YOUNG MIRACLE JONES stands beside her stalwart mother in the produce section. The nine-year-old girl is small for her age, and the woman speaking with her mom looks her up and down, as if the little girl's very existence defies reality.

When she was young, Miracle loved her name. Her mom, Meg Jones, would take her to the grocery store on Coastal Highway during the off-season, after all the tourists had left. They'd run into neighbors, business owners, the guy behind the deli counter with the amazingly bushy gray eyebrows—everyone in town, really. They would all make a big fuss, talk about how big she'd gotten. How good she looked. What a smart little girl she was. And they all pronounced her name as if it belonged to a queen or a movie star.

By the age of nine, when the comments did not slow, Miracle felt the first gnawings of suspicion. On the surface, she remained that happy-go-lucky kid who smiled and spoke to every adult who passed. Her maturing mind, however, plucked certain words from the comments—*big*, *good*, *smart*. Something about them clung. Why shouldn't she get bigger? Every kid did. Why would they comment on how a kid looked, right in front of her? When they said *smart*, they always sounded a little surprised.

Then there were the semiannual doctor's appointments—the way her height and weight were charted with agonizing care, the questions about her appetite and her general thoughts concerning food. For a time, Miracle considered this normal. The more she played with other children, however, the more she wondered. She sensed the differences. At times she would glance over her shoulder, as if the shadows of her past were ready to pounce.

At the same time, she would not let herself believe that her parents held the answers. Miracle never noticed her mother's furtive glances, her near-hidden grimaces. The way she swept her small daughter away from certain conversations before they moved too close. Before they homed in on the truth. Because Miracle's infamy hung over all of them like a threat. One that her mother and father knew they had to address but couldn't figure out how, or when.

*   *   *

With middle school fast approaching, she and her mom took a mother-daughter trip all the way north of the canal to the Christiana Mall. Miracle walked through the vast building with her eyes wide and her hand clutching her mother's.

"Are those trees real?" she asked.

Her mother, Meg, laughed. "They are."

"This is amazing!" Miracle said with every ounce of her beautiful innocence. Her sheltered naïveté.

"It is," Meg said, smiling.

Their day could not have been more perfect. Miracle moved among the racks of clothes, in awe but restrained. Often her mother had to talk her into purchases, especially if she noticed the price tag beforehand. When they entered one of the shoe stores, though, her manners could barely slow her reaction to seeing the platform flip-flops that had been all the rage among some of her classmates over the summer.

"Oh, Mom," she said. "I . . ."

"You like those," her mother said.

"I do."

The shoes were expensive. Meg hesitated.

"It's okay," Miracle said. "I don't need them."

Her head down, she moved away from the shoes. She didn't pout, nor did she act the martyr. Even when she was a small child, Miracle had never seemed to ask anything of anyone. Instead, she tended to spread her smile and joy freely, without a thought toward compensation.

Meg's hand rose, as if to stop her from walking away. Miracle turned back, the lines of her face set. Later, her mother would tell the story over and over again. How, in that moment, she thought of her daughter's birth. Her amazing story. Strangely, it was in that instant, over a pair of shoes Miracle would outgrow in a matter of months, that Meg saw the resolve and understood how her daughter had survived.

"I'll pay for them," Miracle said.

"You don't have any money."

"Mrs. Harris asked me if I could weed her flower bed. She said her back hurt."

Meg laughed. "Did she?"

"Yeah," Miracle said. "I already said I'd do it. She said she'd pay me."

"You don't—" Meg tried to protest.

"I will," Miracle said, her face as serious as stone.

*　*　*

Her first day of middle school, Miracle came down the stairs, her new clothes perfect, her shoes a treasure. She laughed and spoke quickly, filled with a nervous energy that would last until later that day. The day the mouth of a preteen preempted all her parents' planning.

It started with a question, but Miracle didn't ask it. No, the question came from someone else. Her name was Madison. She was probably more popular than Miracle. Miracle thought she was prettier. But none of that really mattered. In truth, she was just the first one—the student with the weakest filter, really. Or the most insecurities.

That day, Miracle stood by her locker, talking to two friends. One was Gemma. They stayed friends all the way through high school and beyond. Miracle never remembered who the other one was. It made no sense to her; she could recall so many exact details from that moment. The lockers were a vibrant blue color, both dark and bright at the same time, like the paint was still wet. The hall smelled like hand sanitizer and chocolate cake—her locker was the closest one to the cafeteria. She wore black tights and a white top and those horrible platform flip-flops that, for some reason, everyone loved. She was so excited, and sort of nervous about school. Everything felt new and scary and full of a potential that she didn't really understand. Then Madison walked up.

Miracle could remember what Madison wore, too. Down to the exact shade of her hemp surfer's choker. She could still hear the sound of her footsteps. *Clack, clack, clack*, like a horse on an old cobblestone street. The way she smelled, like that Paris Hilton perfume. And the way she smiled at Miracle. Like she had just pulled up a crab trap full of a dozen keepers.

"Hey, Gemma," Madison said, but she stared at Miracle.

All three said hi to her.

"I like your necklace," Miracle even added.

Madison smiled and told them where she'd gotten it. The other girl seemed to drift out of the moment. Maybe she left. Maybe Miracle just didn't notice her again.

"I saw it there," Gemma said.

"I like your shoes," Madison said to Miracle.

"Thanks."

Madison's eyes narrowed. She looked at Miracle in "that way." Kids love attention until the first time someone at school looks at them that way.

"You're adopted, right?" she blurted.

Somehow, in her sudden panic, Miracle noticed Gemma's eyes widen and took a step backward. More of a shuffle.

"Yeah," Miracle said, the words sticking in her suddenly bone-dry mouth.

"And your mom left you in a bathroom sink."

As if for the very first time, the Miracle Baby blinked. As she stared at Madison, frozen, the lines of the girl's face seemed to melt away. But her eyes pierced Miracle. Violated her. She felt sick and exposed and, worst of all, unsafe for the first time in her life . . . that she could remember, at least.

"What?" she whispered.

That's when Gemma pushed Madison. Right on the chest, below her throat. Miracle never forgot. In that moment, when she felt the first tremor of the quake that would pulverize her childhood, her friend stood up. Gemma actually hit another girl, which in anyone else's story might be the absolute best moment of the sixth grade. For Miracle, it was something else. A tether that seemed to keep her present, despite the sudden darkness flooding her insides. It also would become a source of guilt. She'd never thanked Gemma for that. Because, like Gemma, Miracle acted as though it had never happened. Like it was just some horrible dream.

*   *   *

The instant her friend's hands hit Madison, Miracle's day might as well have ended. She could remember almost nothing as she haunted the halls of her school, drifting from one classroom to the next. Maybe friends asked if she was okay. Maybe rumors started to drift, slower before cell phones but no less indomitable.

One memory, however, clung from that day forward. It was a feeling like every inch of her being had become suddenly, excruciatingly alive. The thin fabric of her white top hung like chains. The thongs of her shoes, the ones she had loved so much before, threatened to sever her toes. Her eyes burned, boring into every perceived intention around her, leaving the rest of the world dull and out of focus.

Somehow, the day ended. Miracle wandered home from school, making it to her neighborhood. Without even a hitch to her step or a turn of her head, she walked past her house, continuing to the thin beach that ran along the coast of the bay that backed up to the houses across the street. Slipping out of her sandals, she let the coarse sand scratch the bottoms of her feet as she moved south.

Small docks ran out into the bay behind a few of her neighbors' tiny yards. Soft little waves rolled up onto land, hissing against the beach. An old dinghy, white and blue paint flaking off the sunbaked sides, knocked against one of the half dozen crab traps attached to the pier. Until that moment, the sound had been as much a part of Miracle's life as bedtime and the summer tourists. That day, it raged inside her skull. Tears came to her eyes as she hurried away, following the contour of Rehoboth Bay until the houses slipped out of sight.

At one point, the gravel gave way to stones. The stones became dark, slick rocks. Miracle picked her way among them until she was utterly alone. Then she climbed atop one that jutted out. The surface was wet and the air so briny that the salt seemed to cling to her face, burning her hot cheeks.

There she sat, solitary, staring out at the water. She paid no mind to the beautiful sunset. She didn't hear the distant calls as gulls fought over the overturned remains of a horseshoe crab. Nor did Miracle watch the fishing boats chugging in through the inlet. Instead, she pulled her knees up and let the dampness soak through her pants, cooling her skin as Madison's words repeated over and over again among her storming thoughts.

And your mom left you in a bathroom sink.

Miracle reached down and found a smooth stone nestled among the crags. With a shout, she sent it rocketing over the waters, as far as she could. It hit the surface, skipping once before cutting through the sparkles and sinking to the dark, silty bottom.

"That's not right!" she cried out. Then, more quietly, "That can't be right."

* * *

"Hi, Miracle!"

Mrs. Harris waved from her back porch as she cut through the woman's yard. Miracle tried to smile and wave. Mrs. Harris put her hands on the perfectly white railing and leaned forward.

"Are you okay? Your knee's bleeding."

She glanced down, noticing the tear in her leggings. There was blood, too. She had caught her leg on a rock while climbing down and never noticed.

"I'm good," she said, her voice empty.

"Do you need me to call your mom?"

"No thanks, Mrs. Harris."

The second she left her neighbor's yard, Miracle knew the older woman would do just that. News passed quickly through their tight-knit neighborhood, especially if it involved the handful of children living there. The retirees watched any activity out their windows like it was television. So, by the time Miracle reached her driveway, Meg Jones stood in the threshold, her hip propping the storm door open.

Liar.

The word flared in Miracle's head like an eruption. It burned so hotly from her eyes that she looked away, trying to hide it from the only mother she had ever known.

"What happened?" Mrs. Jones asked.

"I'm fine," her daughter snapped back.

"You're hurt. And your clothes."

Miracle looked at herself again. Muck stained her top. Her leggings were torn. Her feet were bare. She glanced over her shoulder–casually, really–when she remembered that she'd left her favorite shoes back by the rocks.

Then Miracle stormed past her mother, into the house. "I said I'm fine."

*   *   *

The next morning dawned with a deadly tease. Miracle opened her eyes to the rising sun, and for one glorious but fleeting second, the words had never been said. Her usual smile greeted the day. For a flash, her life was as it should have been. As if her past belonged to someone else.

A tick of the clock and it came back like an electric shock. Her stomach flipped, and the pain turned the skin of her face cold and wet. She sat up, swallowing down the nausea, and felt the first tickle of a new thought. One that ticked the back of her internal dialogue. Taunting her. Asking her, softly, if this was all just a bit too much. If it was worth fighting.

But Miracle was still young then. She still owned that famous resilience. Rising through the weight of it all, she pulled her thick, dark hair back into a loose ponytail. Standing in front of her mirror, she stared at the ends, which curled almost into bananas. Normally, that drove her crazy and she would straighten her hair before heading downstairs. That morning she simply closed her eyes and moved away. She spent a fraction of her normal time picking clothes for the day, settling on a T-shirt and sweats from the surf shop in Bethany Beach. Slipping on a pair of low-top white Converse, she made her way out into the hallway, pausing only at the top of the stairs, and only for a moment, before making her way to the kitchen.

The instant Miracle walked into the room, her mother seemed to react. As if she somehow knew.

"I can make you toast," her mother said, standing with her back to the sink.

"No thanks."

Miracle moved to the table, still not making eye contact.

"You're not wearing your new sandals," her mother said.

Miracle just stared at the floor, somehow fighting back the tears that threatened to sweep her into the bay. A crack formed in that moment, a fissure that would build slowly for years. "I lost them," she blurted out.

For a second, Miracle did not lift her head. Tears filled her eyes, but she refused to blink. Refused to let them out, to let them trail down her cheeks. Then she looked at her mother. Meg stood, as she had most of Miracle's life, with a solid purpose, like a farmer ready to seed, or more accurately, a young yet grizzled crabber preparing to check her traps. For the first time, though, Miracle noticed the sun damage. The gray hairs pushing a pale dye job up from the roots. She saw the glasses precariously clinging to the reddened end of Meg's Roman nose.

That was the first of the changes. As she turned her eyes away again, Miracle thought about her brother. He was fifteen years older, living upstate and working as a civil engineer. Whereas Miracle was birdlike in bone structure and energy, her brother was a country boy with a slow drawl and a slower temper, the first to smile from his comfortable seat in front of the television. He had that same nose. So different from hers.

Her next thought hit like sharpened glass.

I'm not a part of them.

It was too much, at least for that moment. Without a word, she rushed out of the kitchen.

"Are you leaving?" her mother asked. "It's early. What about breakfast?"

Before she finished, Miracle was already out the door, heading to school as if it might be better there.

* * *

Overnight, her school had transformed. The halls were darker, lonelier. The shadows deeper, more dangerous. The eyes that watched her walk the halls seemed to taunt her with the kind of crushing silence that only a middle schooler can truly understand. Every glance cut through her skin, setting her nerves on end and making Miracle want to jump out a window.

The day inched on, and it only grew worse. She felt fat, ugly, weird. Her mind convinced her that every whisper shared some piece of her past. A heartbreaking truth that left her raw and exposed. Worst of all, she had no idea what those truths might be. Not really. For though Miracle knew she was adopted, she had never asked for anything more.

As she stood alone in the hallway with her head almost tucked into her open locker, she wondered—for the first time in her life—why. Her parents had been open. She'd never felt they wouldn't answer anything she asked. But she never had. Never wanted to. Instead, she had felt a stable contentedness. And that had been torn from her, as it had to be. For it wasn't real. And lies can last for only so long. Though Miracle didn't make the connection that day, she would in later years. In fact, she would spend a lot of moments, the lonely moments that speckled her daily life, contemplating the difference between resilience and denial.

The tardy bell for third period rang. She heard it. She knew she had to get to math class. But as the seconds passed, a fury built inside her. It raged harder than the Atlantic during the worst nor'easter of her life. Without realizing it, she held her breath. Her fingers gripped the edge of her locker door, then slammed it so hard that the entire row rattled. Spinning, Miracle sprinted down the hallway, away from her math class. Her hand struck the exit door by the tech closet. Pain shot up her forearms, but Miracle didn't care. She didn't even feel it over her anger.

Once outside, she ran. Panting, her face burning, she didn't slow until she reached her front porch. Steps from her door, she planted her foot. One hand grabbed the support post. Struggling to catch her breath, she doubled over. Her resolve faltered. Exhaustion, and possibly fear, tempered her fury. The confrontation she so suddenly needed seemed even more dangerous. So much so that Miracle took a step back down the stairs.

That's when the door swung open. Meg Jones stood with her back straight. Her chest out. Her eyes sharp, as if she somehow knew what the day would bring.

"Are you ready to talk?" her mother asked.

As anger often does during the crushing moments of life, Miracle's rage vanished as quickly as it had erupted. The strength left her, slackening the muscles of her back and draining the blood from her face. Meg saw the change. She had been waiting for it, maybe since the day of Miracle's adoption. She did not hesitate, nor did she question. She simply swooped to her daughter and held her as she cried.

* * *

Often, through the years, Miracle would think back to that day and wonder. Should the moment have been different, more like one of those movies her mother watched on the Lifetime channel? Meg could have taken her by the hand and walked her out to the park by the water. With the sun shining down on them, her story could have been told in a hushed whisper and a voice trembling with emotion. Or maybe Miracle could have rushed home from school to find her entire family waiting, sitting in a circle. Meg's empathetic eyes taking in her daughter's fears, her pain, just before the love in the room surrounded her in a warm embrace.

Those moments in life, the pivot points where the future is written less by choice than by circumstance, never happen like that. They are neither planned nor perfect. Instead, much as Meg did, people stumble through them, making it up as they go. As each word slips out into reality, the doubts immediately follow, flooding our best efforts, making them brittle and thin. Afterward, every second can be picked raw, but it changes nothing. The path is set. The future hits like a tsunami, washing everything away without warning.

For Miracle, there was no family meeting. In fact, there was no conversation. Instead, Meg pulled back from her daughter and nodded. Without a word, she turned and hurried into the house. Confused, fighting to catch her breath, Miracle followed. In the living room, her mother reappeared, holding a folded piece of paper in her hand. It was an old, yellowed clipping. When Meg handed it to her, it felt brittle in Miracle's fingers.

Their eyes locked through films of unshed tears. Meg's mouth opened. Words might have tried to push their way out. She took a step back, and the change Miracle saw in her mother was more frightening than whatever words might be on the paper. Until that moment, and to everyone who knew her, Meg Jones was unflappable. Dressed in her customary shades of brown and her trusty angler's vest, she stood solid and firmly rooted in reality. She took in others' pain but never showed her own. Till now.

Suddenly, she spun and hurried from the room. Shocked, Miracle watched. As the seconds ticked past, the news clipping between her fingers grew heavier. Her eyes lowered and she saw the tail end of a headline. MIRACLE BABY. Standing alone in her living room, or what she had always considered *her* living room, she peeled back the corners of her past. As she read, as the weight of it settled over her, she knew she would never truly be Miracle Jones again.

2

Ginny Harris stood at her front door, looking down at me. Whereas I felt exhausted, disjointed, as if caught between spans of time, she appeared the opposite. The stories filled her with energy. Her eyes almost shined with it as she stood under the porch lamp.

"Thank you," I said. "When Mrs. Jones gets back, can you give her my card?"

"Of course. Are you okay to drive?" she asked. "You keep yawning."

"Definitely. I'm great. I really appreciate your time. Can I ask you one more thing?"

"Anything you'd like," she said with a smile.

"Do you know when Miracle learned about her mother—her real mother?"

"Oh," Ginny said, her cheeks flushed. "I really . . . I guess I couldn't tell you. I mean, I don't know. The last two years or so, she's been . . . different. Quiet. Very private."

I nodded. "It's been so great meeting you."

"I hope it was helpful," she said, or maybe asked.

"It was . . ."

Ginny Harris stepped out onto the decking. "If you need anything else, please let me know. I'm not sure about being filmed and all . . . but I could probably manage. If that's what you need."

"Of course," I said. "I have the recording of the interview. But we'll need an intro shot. Maybe out by the water. I'll be in touch."

She watched me for a moment. Then her helpful smile returned. "Drive carefully."

"I will."

I backed toward the car. She hovered, so I opened the driver's side door. Nodding, Ginny Harris slipped back inside her house. Once she was gone, I closed the car door without getting behind the wheel. Instead, I moved through her yard and out to the water. It was dark by then, and I found Rehoboth Bay more by sound than by sight. When I saw the sliver of moonlight dancing across the dark, calm surface, I stopped, taking a deep breath. The air felt so clean inside my chest, so unlike the city. At the same time, the space around me, the silence, closed in tighter and tighter. I pushed through it and turned left.

I walked carefully along the coast until I saw an outcropping of rocks. It had to be the same one Miracle had climbed across that day. I've never been the outdoor type, but something had come over me, drawing me closer and closer. I stepped up to the first stone, and my shoe slipped. I dropped to a knee and felt the fabric of my chinos tear.

That should have been enough. It was so dark that night. I had no idea what I was doing. For some reason, though, I rose back up and picked my way along the outcropping, getting farther and farther away from the sandy shore behind the neighborhood. As I did, it was as if I slipped out of myself and into the shade of a young girl. The mean girl's words filled my head. I felt the betrayal, not just by her classmate but by her family, her entire existence. Her life was a lie.

At some point I sat down on the stones. Moisture wicked through my pants. I shivered, but even that didn't break the spell. I watched the gentle lapping of the water, and something jumped a few yards out, sending a ripple of pale light across the surface. At the sound, an icy finger ran up my back. I turned quickly, expecting to find someone behind me, close, watching. My eyes strained to fight the darkness. Nothing moved. Nothing made a sound. But I couldn't shake the feeling that someone was out there.

"Hello," I called out softly.

I swear I heard the shuffle of a foot. I tried to get up, too quickly, and slipped again. My shoe sank into a small tidal pool.

"Shit," I hissed, stumbling to find more solid footing. "Who's out there?"

There was no answer. I remained frozen. I could walk any street of New York at three in the morning and not feel even a fraction of the threat I did in that moment. With nothing near me but space, I felt exposed, naked. Yet I could feel her out there—Miracle Jones. Despite the Halo Killer's threat, or because of it, I knew I'd find her. And uncover the mysterious tie between the famous Miracle Baby and the infamous Halo Killer.

3

THE TRAIN RUMBLED north, leaving Newark, New Jersey, the last stop before Penn Station. I stared out the window at the empty darkness, processing everything that had happened. Jasper's warning and Ginny's voice seemed to dance inside my skull, pulsing down the veins of my neck, tightening the muscles in my arms and legs. One calf suddenly cramped. With a grunt, I thrust that leg out into the aisle, pulling my toes back as best I could.

The pain subsided and I repositioned my body. As I sat there, staring out at the night, I placed my palm on the window. It felt cold and real under my touch. In a way, it grounded me. I focused all of my attention on taking in a breath. Feeling my diaphragm expand and contract.

Before I realized it, I was under the city, pulling into Penn Station. I must have slept, but it certainly didn't feel like it. It was as if time had jerked forward with the suddenness of a startle. I blinked, over and over again, trying to refocus my sense of place.

With a rattle, the train stopped. I remained seated, watching everyone depart into the tunnel. A conductor leaned over and spoke to me.

"You need to detrain, my friend."

"Sorry," I muttered.

When I rose, I felt light-headed. I had to reach out and use the seat tops like ski polls to keep my balance. I followed the masses out and up the escalator.

"Theo!"

The sound of my name, the surprise of it, woke me up a bit. My head whipped around and I saw, of all people, Zora standing above me, waiting.

"Hey," I said with a heavy wave of my hand.

At the top, I stepped out of the crowd and joined her. She looked so—I don't know—awake. At least to me.

"How'd you know I would be here?" I asked.

Her eyebrow rose. "You texted me the train number. Remember?"

"No," I said. "I mean, sure I do. It's good to see you."

"What did you want to talk about?" she asked, appearing only a little impatient.

I had no idea. I definitely didn't recall reaching out to her.

"Let's start walking," I said. "I need to get back to my apartment so I can sleep."

"Okay," she said. "It's on my way."

Together we rose out of Penn Station and headed north on Ninth Avenue. I told her about my meetings with Martino and Jasper. She got excited when I showed her the video I'd retrieved from Jasper's house.

"You broke in?" she asked, after watching it.

"Not really. He sent me there. Called me on my way back from Martino's. Had me running up and down that little state." I laughed. "Oh, shit, I almost forgot. I talked to this other woman. Ginny Harris."

"Who's she?" Zora asked.

We turned left on Thirty-Seventh. I could almost feel how comfy it would be to climb into bed and sleep for days.

"She's Miracle Jones' neighbor," I said. "She gave me some great background on her."

"And why would we need that? I thought we were doing a film on the Halo Killer."

"We are," I said. "But she's a part of it. I'm sure."

"Maybe," Zora said, but I caught the change in her tone.

"What's wrong?" I asked.

"You promised not to hide things from me."

"You mean my trying to find Miracle? I . . . should have called you. Sorry, I was running on adrenaline."

Zora continued to walk slowly away from me.

"Come on. I need to get home too," she said.

Something was off. I really didn't know what it was that I had picked up. Hesitancy, maybe. Distance. Distraction. I wasn't sure, but my storyteller instinct had fired. And I needed to know.

"I'm not moving until you accept my apology."

"Jesus, Theo, it's cool."

"Nope. Something is definitely up."

"I was just thinking."

"Tell me," I said.

"Fine." She threw her hands up. "But only if we keep walking."

"Excellent," I said, hurrying to catch back up with her.

She shook her head. "I was just thinking how crazy these investigations get. I was a private detective first. I trained with this old guy in Queens. It was wild stuff. But always the same, you know. Mostly like my dad, really. I found myself in some seedy places. Surrounded by bad people. I was still in high school, although my boss had no idea. I would skip so much he thought I'd already finished. I was too young, but I just needed to get away from my house. My parents. Especially my father.

"The longer I did it, the closer I got to bad stuff. Eventually, I gave pills a try. I shouldn't have, but I thought I was unstoppable. Like every other kid my age. Pills turned to shots, if you know what I mean. And I ended up spending more time chasing hits than I did running down dirty old men cheating on their wives."

My mouth hung open for a second. "Are you talking about heroin?"

She nodded, but gave me a look like I shouldn't have said it out loud.

"Yeah. I lost that job. And my parents kicked me out. I hit the streets, hard. Got bad, fast. Then . . . she found me."

"Who?"

"No one you know. But she was like you. A filmmaker. She was doing a story on the opioid epidemic. She ended up talking to these guys I hung around with sometimes. When she saw me, with my hair, and my height—"

"And your beauty," I said without thinking.

"God, Theo. I didn't mean that. I just mean I looked like the perfect character for her story. She started interviewing me. But . . . I guess . . . it went off script. We got personal, you know. She started caring about me. And I started caring about her. The closer we got, the more I wanted to help her too. I started bringing people around. Finding new angles for her. She just kept telling me how good I was at it.

"She got me my first job in the business. And . . . she got me clean. Everything . . . just kind of happened after that." She laughed. "Not that you asked or anything. Wow, what is it about you? I never tell anyone this kind of shit."

I stared into her eyes. "You loved her, didn't you?"

Zora stiffened. "What?"

"That woman. You fell in love wi—"

"Enough," Zora snapped. "I have to go."

At the corner, she turned south, away from me. I called after her.

"Zora, I'm sorry. I didn't . . ."

But she wouldn't slow down. She just left me there. With a shake of my head, I turned toward my apartment. I really needed to sleep. Maybe grab something to eat first. I'd fix things with her in the—

My phone rang. I yanked it out of my pocket, expecting it to be Zora, but it wasn't. It was my agent, Stephanie. I checked the time before answering it. When I noticed how late it was, I grunted.

"Hey, it's Steph," she said.

"Hey." I tried to sound upbeat. "How are you?"

"Good. Are you in the city?"

"Just got back."

I hadn't spoken to her since the day I left Los Angeles. And she knew I was behind in repaying Pepper. That wasn't what had me nervous, though. The truth was that I hadn't told her about the new project. I should have, and I wasn't sure why I hadn't. Somehow I could already tell she knew, though.

"Huh," she said. "Well, I thought we should touch base. I wanted to see what you were up to."

"Me?" I asked.

I felt like a fool. Or a cheater. Maybe both.

"Yeah. Look, I ran into Kent Barre tonight."

I closed my eyes. "You did? Are you in the city?"

"Yup."

I swallowed. "I was going to call you."

"No worries, Theo. Let's catch up. Can you get a drink at the Ace?"

"Right now? Oh, geez, Steph. I haven't slept in like three days. Maybe I should—"

"I totally understand," she interrupted. "Get some sleep. But hit the pause button on your project until we can—"

"What?" I shouted.

"Just until we talk," she said.

"I'm heading to the Ace right now," I snapped. "Don't leave!"

*   *   *

By the time I reached the front entrance of the Ace Hotel, it was after midnight. I had never been there before, and the place reminded me of an art deco university library. Given the late hour, I had to slip past a surprising number of people bunched around a large table that ran across the entire space. A full coffee shop took up the far corner. I scanned the crowd, but Stephanie wasn't anywhere in sight. As I moved toward the barista, intending to order an Earl Grey and maybe a muffin if they looked good, my phone went off. It was a text from her.

At the bar.

Stuffing the phone back into my front pocket, I moved across the room behind the long metal table and up the stairs to the restaurant. I found her immediately. Then I noted the Scotch on the rocks in front of her. Stephanie turned and smiled at me.

"Hey there."

I took a seat, my eyes moving off of hers quicker than I'd meant.

"What do you want to drink?" she asked.

"I'm . . ."

I paused. Aside from a couple of granola bars I'd bought at the train station in Wilmington, I hadn't really eaten in more than a day. I could barely keep my eyes open. But I knew I needed to have something. The thought of stomaching a bourbon, or even a beer at that point, felt like too much. But I did it anyway. She ordered the drink and turned back to me.

"Is this about the money I still owe Pepper? I'm getting it together."

"Not that," she said. "I hear you're working on something new."

"Yeah. I meant to drop you a note; I just . . ."

"The Halo Killer?"

I nodded, knowing Kent had told her. My drink arrived, and I took a large swallow of bourbon, more than I intended.

"You should have talked to me," she said. "There were other people looking at that story. Important people."

My eyes widened. "Kent told me that no one . . ."

"I'm not sure you understood him." She took a breath. "There was a producer big on it. About to fund a young director. But they got cold feet when they heard you landed Zora."

"Good," I said, with the last of my bravado.

"Not good. Cassandra was the filmmaker," Stephanie answered.

"Oh, shit," I whispered.

I'm not going to use her last name, although everyone knows it. Cassandra's father is an icon in Hollywood. In one choppy motion, I finished my drink, then put my head down on the bar. "Are you kidding?"

"No," I heard her say. "And she knows you jumped her. And now Kent's hearing stuff. And he's not the only one. It seems Zora has too."

"What do you mean? I just saw her tonight."

"When I saw Kent today, he told me she's nervous about the chatter. She might be out."

"That's just not—"

"It's worse than that."

My head shot up. "How? How can it be worse?"

"Kent heard another rumor. It's not good. Really not good."

Every ounce of energy leaked out of my body. "What?"

"Seems Cassandra is out for funding on a new project."

"Okay . . . ?"

Stephanie actually looked sad. "Kent said she wants to do a film about Joseph Bender . . . and you."

4

"I GOT TO GO," I moaned.

Standing, I lurched toward the stairs. Steph followed.

"You okay?" she asked.

I nodded, but my head spun. I moved ahead of her into the lobby. I felt dozens of faces turn, eyes boring into me. I put a hand up, waving Stephanie off. As I did, my stomach cramped, causing my eyes to water. Through a glassy blur, I searched for the restrooms. When I saw the sign for the elevators, I hurried in that direction.

"Theo?" she called out behind me.

"I'll call you," I managed to answer.

From there, I lost track of her. Despite the continued feeling of being watched, everyone around me disappeared, as if they'd slipped behind a rising curtain. All I could see was that sign.

"Excuse me," someone said.

Maybe I'd bumped them. I have no idea. Luckily, the bathrooms were back there. I broke into a sprint, hitting the door hard as I stormed into the men's room. The stall was open. Sliding to my knees, I was sick, horribly. Sweat stung my eyes and rolled down my sides, under my clothes. I moaned, then heard the bathroom door swing open and close again.

When it was done, I couldn't get up off the cold tile. With effort, I swung a heavy hand up and managed to flush the toilet. Then I rolled to the side, my shoulder resting against the shining metal divider.

"She won't do it," I muttered.

I wanted to cry. Or scream. But I had the energy for neither. Instead, my eyes still watering, all I could think about was Bender. And his sister.

*   *   *

After the instant success of *The Basement*, I was supposed to be living the dream. It had been released to shocking fanfare. Everyone was talking about it, in the business and across the country. In the blink of an eye, I went from obscurity to fame. My dream had come true.

On top of that, I had what I thought at the time was an amazing start for my next project. I was waist-deep in the story of Joseph Bender, a man accused of a murder I believed he hadn't committed.

One second I was on top of the world. The next, I sat across from my film's producer, calmly watching her view dailies from the past week. I felt excited, untouchable. Until she stopped the reel.

"You can't use any of this," she said.

Pepper was a friend of Kent and his father. She'd been producing films for only about five years before that day. But she'd outbid everyone else for the chance to support my film.

"Excuse me?" I asked, shocked.

Pepper leaned forward, the Italian leather of her desk chair making the softest, smoothest hiss. Though a blush rose on her cheeks, her eyes pierced mine.

"Maybe I'm missing something." She tented her hands. "Maybe, over the last six months, you've amassed hours of film, mountains of proof. But . . . I hear that's not really the case."

If that meeting had taken place prior to *The Basement*, I would have been appropriately nervous at that point. More importantly, I wouldn't have kept my financier in the dark for so long. I certainly would have given her thoughts and opinions the proper consideration. Instead, my hackles lifted.

"You hear, huh? And who might you be hearing from?"

Pepper took a deep breath. She was younger than me. But her tone hid any hint of that fact.

"Theo," she said softly. "It's a small town. I thought you'd know that by now. Look, you have some cachet. This isn't a disaster. In fact, I understand you have the foundation of another winner. But this stuff with his sister. What she's saying about the police. It's great. But I don't think there is even a touch of truth to it. Did you vet her at all?"

"Are you serious?" I snapped. "Geri is amazing. Better, she's right. The cops basically tortured Bender. They held him for almost two days in a shitty little interview room. Pumped him full of sugar and nicotine to keep him awake. Pressed him, mercilessly, until he finally said what they wanted."

"I've seen the police video. That's not really how it looks."

"They put that out!"

"Don't raise your voice," she said.

"I didn't—"

"You did. I'm not your sister. Or your girlfriend. And I'm certainly not Geri Bender."

When she said that, the first hint of doubt tickled the back of my throat. The hubris of my fame, however, immediately coated it. I leaned forward.

"Is this about what she does? How she looks? I'd expect better of you, Pepper. That's pretty catty."

I shouldn't have said that. When it came out later that I had called Pepper Thompson catty, it didn't look good at all. In the moment, I truly believed it. But that faith lasted no longer than a second. With a sharp smirk on her face, Pepper slid her iPad across the desk.

"Hit play, Theo," she said, her words rock hard.

"What's—"

"Hit play, please."

I didn't want to do what she said. I even thought it might be some kind of power play, her ordering me around. Curiosity, however, is a powerful motivator. My finger seemed to move of its own accord. I pressed the white triangle and could only stare. The shot was dark and grainy, obviously from a security camera. It took me only a second to recognize where it had been taken. The Wild Orchid on Hollywood Boulevard.

"Really . . ." I stammered, incensed.

Pepper didn't say anything. She just motioned toward the screen. And I watched Geri Bender step up onto the stage, gripping the shining pole as she did.

"So what, Pepper. She's a dancer."

That smirk stayed on her face. "Just watch."

That's when I knew. I slapped my hand on the screen, trying to stop the video before I showed up, bills in hand. Before Geri sauntered over to me. Before . . .

"This is how you treat the people you work with."

"This is how I protect my investments," she answered.

"I'm out of here!"

I got up so quickly that the chair almost tipped over. Before I could open the office door, Pepper barked out an order.

"You're not going anywhere," she said.

My fingers wrapping around the handle, I looked over my shoulder.

"You're going to stop me?"

"Sit back down, please. This is getting out of hand."

"You mean the part about you illegally videotaping me?"

"No, I mean the part about you having an affair with your subject's sister. Using her one-sided story to accuse the Tulsa Police Department of grossly mishandling her brother's case."

"Fuck you, Pepper," I snapped.

Her eyes slowly closed. "That was my last warning, Theo."

"Kiss my ass," I said, and stormed out.

*   *   *

Minutes after that meeting, I sat in traffic. The rage boiled up, escaping in random shouts and curses. I could not believe what had happened. That Pepper had somehow gotten video of Geri and me together. In the moment, I didn't question my behavior. Or my decisions. Maybe it was my meteoric rise, the effect fame had on me, but I saw myself as untouchable.

If you've never hit it big in Hollywood, if you've never walked into the swankest nightclub through the VIP entrance or if a bunch of rich people have never bid on your work, you might judge me. Certainly, a few people who fit that bill did. But looking back, after everything that's happened since, I still can't understand how I handled that situation. It was like I had gotten high on some drug, but the rush lasted weeks, maybe months. Worse, I'd become addicted to it.

I opened up my phone and posted the clip from my Bender film, the one I'd shown Pepper, to Twitter. As I inched up the ramp of a cloverleaf, I watched the number of likes racing upward. I hadn't traveled more than a mile before it had over a thousand retweets. I laughed. I felt vindicated. Until, as I scrolled through the comments, I saw someone had posted another video, the one Pepper had shown me. As my clip went viral, so did Pepper's. A messy lawsuit followed. She won, and I was told to return the advance her company had paid, most of which I'd already spent. Life after fame is expensive in so many ways.

CHAPTER

5

I HAD NO IDEA what time it was when I finally staggered out of the Ace Hotel restroom. I barely remember leaving the lobby. Somehow I headed in the right direction, across Twenty-Ninth and then up Eighth Avenue. As I meandered toward Hell's Kitchen, I pulled out my phone and tried to call Zora. She didn't pick up, so I left a message, not realizing how hard that single bourbon had hit me.

"It's me. Look, I didn't do anything wrong, you know. I mean, that whole Cassandra thing. I didn't know. I mean, she doesn't have to be such a . . . We are onto something here. The video . . . Oh my God, the video. This whole Miracle thing . . . You could have told me you were worried. And . . . I mean, I'm sorry if I got too personal. You're . . . I . . . It's all cool to me, you know. Anyway. Just call me. I mean . . . and I'm sorry. Yeah . . . call me."

I had to take a breath before continuing, and I sort of lost track again. "Oh, shit, I forgot . . . Jasper threatened me. Threatened to kill me. I couldn't believe it. He said if I didn't stay away from the girl, from Miracle Jones, that he'd kill me. I swear. It's crazy."

For a second, I was distracted by the light on Thirty-Second. I forgot I was leaving a message until I'd crossed.

"Yeah, okay. Call me. Soon. When you can. Okay? Yeah . . . 'bye."

For some reason, I just kept walking. Though I was in no condition to work, I started to put the pieces together. I laid out what I had. Something painting Jasper as on the edge. Something about the woman in that first story he'd told me. Walking on the beach. Like his first victim.

Full circle. It had to be Miracle, somehow. He must have stumbled across the daughter of his first victim. But what were the odds? That seemed impossible.

Had I been 100 percent, I would have stopped there. Like I said, I'm no novelist. No action movie director. I can't bend the lines of reality to make the story work. Plus, I just wasn't thinking straight. There was no way Miracle just randomly ended up on the beach in that exact second. Yet, in the moment, it fit so perfectly. So cosmically. It all made sense. Jasper needed to find Miracle. Kill her. And it would all be over. Full circle.

My brain kept churning. I storyboarded Jasper's life. I painted transitions and camera angles. I could hear gulls calling in the background as his mother talked about her divorce, about how much she didn't know. I framed shots of the moon and of bright-yellow daylilies. Morning fog shrouding a dark little cabin surrounded by the straight, thin trunks of white pines that jutted out of the soft earth like the devil's fingers. In my head, I scored the entire thing, a dark mix between *Requiem for a Dream* and the old *Halloween* movie.

Too much.

That's what Zora would say. I was pushing too hard. My eyes came up when her voice thrust itself into my head. And I realized I was way farther away from my building. In fact, I had to slow at the closest intersection and check the street signs like a lost tourist. I was shocked to find how far off I'd gone.

In that instant, an eerie feeling moved through me. It was like a shiver without the shake. As it passed, I looked left and right and back again, searching for eyes I knew were watching me. But I saw nothing out of the ordinary. Nothing more than the sparse crowd moving along the evening streets somewhere near Hell's Kitchen, I hoped.

My searching stopped on the glowing windows of the Starbucks across Forty-Third Street. I stared at the faces I could see through the glass. No one even paid attention. I doubted they could see me through the glare. But I couldn't shake the feeling. Someone was watching me.

Then, as if I remembered it for the first time, my conversation with Steph came back to me. The severity of what she'd said. The risk I was in. Cassandra could destroy me, especially considering the thin ice upon which my career lay. With a single word, her father could make sure that I never worked again in Hollywood. Or New York. Or Austin or Nashville or anywhere.

Hurrying, possibly a bit frantic, I headed north on Ninth Avenue. With every step, I fought the urge to look over my shoulder. At the same time, a cold sweet broke out on my forehead. I could feel perspiration soaking through my shirt too. Someone was watching me, someone out there in the darkness, following my every step. My throat tightened, like someone was trying to choke me, but going at it in agonizingly slow motion. I sped up, my heart racing even faster.

Ignoring the crosswalk, I stepped out onto the street, thinking I would head west. A cab swerved around me. The horn blared. A vivid image of the driver showed his face contorted in rage, transforming into Jasper's birdlike features. His piercing little eyes.

I stumbled up to the curb.

"You okay?" someone asked.

That's what got me to stop. I blinked and saw the man. He was short, probably five and a half feet, and built like a firefighter. He wore all black, which contrasted with his thick, styled salt-and-pepper hair. His eyes, as he watched me, were soft, concerned. I stared into them and felt strangely safe.

"Yeah," I said, between huffs. "I'm okay."

"You scared of something?"

"No, no." I put my hand up.

The guy smiled. "We all go a little mad sometimes."

"What?" I said, my tone sharp.

"Whoa, nothing, man," the guy said, taking a step back. "It's just an old movie quote. Take care of yourself, buddy. You don't look so good."

The guy shook his head before walking away. I took a deep breath and let out a soft laugh. The guy was actually right. I was going a little mad. No one was watching me. Everything would be okay. I just needed to speak with Kent—he would smooth over everything. That and get some sleep.

So I moved one block at a time, breathing in and out, keeping my head down and my eyes locked on the sidewalk in front of me. When I reached my building, I took the front steps as slowly and deliberately as I could. I pulled the handle, and the door opened.

Crossing my lobby, I honestly thought it was over. I thought it was all in my head. That I'd let the case get to me. Let it come close to pushing me off my already precarious ledge. I was debating whether or not to call Kent as I rose up the stairwell. Midthought, I opened the door to my floor and stepped out. My head turned and I looked down the hallway. That's when I saw it, a flash of bright yellow. And I knew, even from that distance, what it was. A yellow daylily circled into the shape of a perfect halo, sitting right outside my apartment door.

CHAPTER

6

"Theo?"

The voice came out of the void. Out of utter and total blackness. It drew me back like a harpoon through my temples. Like fire under my skin. For a second, I was nothing. Then I was painfully conscious. My eyes cracked open and the daylight made me blink. I saw Greg from the third floor. He stood over me, obviously concerned.

"How'd you get in?" I asked, the words like gravel stuck in my throat.

"What?"

Something seemed very off. My head turned. Despite the throbbing pain and the horrid taste in my mouth, I looked around and realized I wasn't in my apartment. No, I was lying on the ground in our building's lobby.

"Shit," I whispered, as the image of the halo came back to me.

"Have you been here all night?"

Trying to stay calm, I looked up at Greg. "Yeah . . . I guess. I . . . uh . . . got locked out."

"That sucks," he said. "I can call the super."

"No," I said quickly.

With my palms on the floor, I pushed myself up. Surprisingly, it wasn't too bad. I definitely felt better than the night before, at least until that flower flashed in my mind again. And the realization struck in full. Jasper had been to my apartment!

Panic surged, wiping away the last of my disorientation. He'd been there. He was out of prison. He was coming for me. I staggered back, away from Greg.

"You sure you're okay?"

"What? Yeah!" I stared at him. "Did you see the news this morning?"

He looked totally confused. "Some."

"Was there . . . did someone . . . break out of prison?"

"Huh?" Greg frowned. "Maybe I should call—"

"No," I said, throwing my hands up. "I'm cool. Just tired . . . I guess."

Greg backed toward the door. I smiled, trying to make him feel better. Once he left, I looked at the stairwell and felt very cold. I dreaded the idea, what I was thinking, but I had to know. So I forced myself to go up, one agonizing step at a time.

"It didn't happen," I kept telling myself.

But the memory was so real, so vivid. More so than anything else from the night before. I could have convinced myself that the meeting with Stephanie had never happened. I'd pushed myself way too hard. I was obviously exhausted.

At the door to my floor, I froze. I had to know, though. So I fought back the fear and pushed it open. Holding my breath, I leaned forward, stretching my neck so that only my eyes crested the doorframe. And there was no sign of the flower.

* * *

I sat down on my bed, focused solely on my breathing. In and out. In and out. There was no flower. It was all a hallucination. I could barely think straight. It was all in my head. The Halo Killer was in my head.

"Shit," I hissed.

With a spastic swipe, I fished out my phone. I saw the call I'd placed to Zora. Closing my eyes, I dug a finger into my temple. I vaguely remembered a rambling message I might have left.

"Reckless," I muttered, falling back onto the mattress.

It started with Geri Bender. That's what I told myself. I'd fallen for the wrong woman. An honest mistake. Nothing reckless about that.

Now, Cassandra. Zora was already nervous. Closing my eyes, I let the phone drop from heavy fingers. It rattled to the hardwood, but I didn't have the energy to check the screen, see if it had cracked. Instead,

I closed my eyes. With the briefest, maybe clearest, thought I'd had in over a year, I truly regretted every bit of my past success before falling into a fitful sleep, full of Jasper's shrill voice and eyes staring out of the darkness.

*   *   *

The ringing wouldn't stop. It pulled me out of the darkness, though it didn't touch the despair that clung to me as strongly as it had when I first shut my eyes. I needed to quit. Do something different. Normal.

"I should have been a barista," I said, leaning over the edge of the bed.

Grabbing the phone, I answered it without looking, trying to catch it before it went to voice mail. I was sure it was Zora. Calling to let me down easily. A laugh escaped my lips at that thought. She'd never do it easily.

"Hey," I said. "Sorry—"

"Hello?"

The voice was strong, firm, but definitely not Zora's. I bolted to my feet.

"Hello, uh . . . this is Theo Snyder."

"Mr. Snyder. This is Meg Jones. Miracle's—"

"Miracle Jones's mom," I blurted out.

"Yes," she said, properly. "I'm very sorry to be bothering you. My neighbor, Virginia Harris, gave me your card this morning."

"Yes, I was down there talking to her . . ." I had to pause to be sure exactly when I had been down there. "Yesterday. I'm so glad you called."

"Okay," Meg said. "I want to be clear here. I have no interest in taking part in your movie. And I hope my daughter will feel the same."

"Mrs. Jones—" I said, trying to protest.

"He doesn't deserve it, you know. The attention. You should just leave it alone. Have you thought about how the families are going to feel? How my daughter would feel?"

"I . . ."

My earlier doubts flared. I'd thought about it before, but as harsh as it may sound, it hadn't mattered to me. The work was more important than an individual's emotions. But hearing her words, piling them atop the doubts I'd felt before the call—they threatened to swallow me whole, weigh me down until I sank into the darkness of it all.

"That's not why I'm calling, however."

I blinked. "Excuse me?"

"I just wanted to ask you. Have you . . . seen my daughter?"

"Miracle?"

"Of course," she snapped. Then her voice returned to its business-like tone. "I'm sorry. I shouldn't have called. I just needed to know if you had spoken to her. Or seen her."

My heart missed a beat. "Is she missing?"

"I don't know if I'd say that."

"When was the last time you saw her?"

"It's been almost three days."

"That's not too long. Do you usually see her every day?"

Meg hesitated before answering. When she spoke, she seemed to choose her words with great care.

"She left her baby son with me. And said she'd only be gone for a couple of hours."

My eyes widened. "She left her baby?"

"It's not like her," Meg said defensively. "Not really."

"Do you have any idea where she might be?"

"No," she said. "Things have been . . . I don't know. Since they caught that man last year. Maybe even before that. I'm not sure. But I don't want to bother you with that. If you haven't spoken to her, I'll let you—"

"Meg," I said. "I don't mean to alarm you, but I think your daughter might be involved in something. I'm not sure what it is yet, but I think Jasper Ross-Johnson may have—"

"He's in prison, Mr. Snyder. I don't appreciate—"

"No, sorry. I just . . . look, I work with one of the best investigators in the country. If anyone can find your daughter, she can."

"I didn't mean to bother you. I'm sure you're busy."

"Ms. Jones, please. Let me help you."

I could hear her breathing for a moment. When she spoke again, that ironlike strength was gone.

"Could she be in trouble?"

"I'm not sure," I answered, hearing a baby in the background for the first time. "Why don't you tell me what's going on."

"Okay," Meg said, still sounding unsure.

Then she told me about her daughter. And, at the mention of Miracle's name, the camera in my head began to roll.

*　*　*

ACT TWO/SCENE 4

EXT. BAYSIDE HOME—DAY

MIRACLE JONES sits on the gentle rise of the roof, looking out over the water. She hugs her knees, her expression locked on some thought deep in her mind. The text notification on her phone sounds. She glances at the screen, then back at the sparkling bay. A CHYRON appears at the top of the screen: MAY 14, 2016.

At twenty, Miracle still lived close to home. She rented a room above Ginny Harris's garage. She was no longer that wiry, emaciated newborn with balled fists and a face red from screaming. There were still signs of her early trauma. She'd only grown to be an inch under five feet. Although the doctors had no way of knowing the height of her biological parents, they posited that her intense malnutrition might have had a lasting effect. Miracle could also eat nonstop for days and not put a pound on her frame. But most of all, to everyone who came across her as an adult, it was Miracle's eyes that hinted at the truth. Dark and large. A sharpness painted the edges of her pupils. A hardness seemed to reflect off their shining surface. Those who only saw her and had no idea who she really was might shy away, cringing with discomfort when she trained her unblinking attention in their direction. Those close to her saw it differently. The officer who had first responded the day she was found put it best. During his last visit, near her sixteenth birthday, he had said:

"She's looking for it to happen again."

On that clear spring morning, with the bay's briny finger gently touching the crisp, dry air, Miracle climbed out her kitchenette window. With the sun shining on her back, she sat near the peak above the garage, hugging her knees and looking out at the light as it danced across the soft current of Rehoboth Bay. As the moments stretch out slowly, the stillness was broken by her cell phone receiving a text. Miracle's hand moved like an afterthought, lifting the Samsung and turning the screen so she could read it.

Babe, where are you. I'm freaking out.

With the slightest shake of her head, she checked the time before slipping the phone into her back pocket. A lazy smile—brought on not by the text but by the thought of her dog—lifted the corner of her mouth as she rose to her feet. Max would be home in minutes. Crouching, she moved back to the window and slipped through.

* * *

The sound of his claws skittering up the cedar steps lifted Miracle from the couch. Before she reached her feet, something slammed into the storm door, rattling the metal panel and the chain dangling from the frame.

"Max!"

The door rattled again, this time more aggressively, as if it might fly out of its hinges and slam into her as she rushed to grab the handle. She threw the door open, and Max, Miracle's three-year-old Shar Pei, burst into the tiny apartment. His entire body seemed to vibrate with excitement as he headed straight for her. At the very last instant, he veered, only enough to avoid full impact. His stonelike skull struck Miracle's knee. She grunted in pain and Max froze on a dime. He twisted to look at her, as if he would attack anything that might hurt his Miracle.

"I'm okay," she said.

He remained frozen, his head tilted slightly. The folds of his face pressed over the tops of his eyes, giving him a comically serious expression.

"Maxy!" she said, kneeling.

That was enough. He decided Miracle was okay and returned to a barely contained chaos. His tail struck the lamp by the couch, and it fell to the thick carpet. His body clipped her, almost tipping her over. His bristly fur felt like sandpaper against her face as he tried to wriggle out of her hug and kiss her face.

"I missed you, buddy."

He moaned, an old-man sound he'd made since the day she brought him home from the shelter. Then he snorted, his wet jowls slapping her wrist and leaving behind a trail like a slug. She wiped it on her pants as her mother stepped through the open door.

"Hi, sweetheart," she said, excited. "I missed you."

"Was he good?" Miracle asked.

Her mother stood in the threshold, a hand on one hip. Her eyes, still soft, were undeniable. Miracle looked away, a recent habit, fiddling with the phone in her back pocket.

"Something's wrong," Meg said, matter-of-fact.

"What?" Miracle asked, too quickly.

Her mother's head tilted. "Something happened."

"Mom, come on!"

Meg's mouth opened, staying that way as she watched her daughter. Slowly her lips closed, but her eyes narrowed.

"You know we're here for you anytime. For anything."

Miracle looked up then, into those kind eyes. She smiled, but it was forced. And she knew her mother noticed.

"So, was he good?" she asked, changing the subject without much grace.

"Max is Max. He's offended by us, I think. So . . ." Meg paused, her eyes still narrow. "How was your trip?"

"Good," she says.

"Where'd you go?" Meg asked.

"To visit Gemma at her dad's place in Dover."

"Huh," Meg said, and paused. "I'll give you time. Come by when you want to talk. You can bring Max too, if you like. Your dad already misses him, I think."

Max took in the entire exchange as someone might have watched a significant moment in history. When Meg moved, he looked up to Miracle. Then the dog slipped on the wood floor as he scurried up to Meg. He did a quick circle, bowing his head as she tried to pat him. Then he was back at Miracle's side, panting and flopping to the ground as if it was all just a little too much.

* * *

The next morning, Max lay curled up in the perfect space created by Miracle's bent knees. His hooded eye cracked open as the sun peeked over the Atlantic. He yawned and licked his lips, his massive drooping jowls slapping against his teeth. Rising with a stretch, he padded up the bed and poked Miracle's eye with his wet, cold nose.

Still half-asleep, she reached out and swiped her Samsung off the bedside table. He had texted twice, both times waking her in the middle of the night but not enough for her to check the messages. As she sat up, the screen flashed on. She read the texts without unlocking the phone.

Text number one had come at 11:23 PM. It read:

Babe I miss you. Just want to make sure you made it home.

Text two came at 1:58 AM:

What did I do?

Shaking her head, she put her phone back on the nightstand, screen down. She looked up at the ceiling, letting the silence protect her for as long as she could. It didn't last, though. Within seconds, she vaulted off the bed and into the bathroom. Dropping to her knees, she dry-heaved twice. The second time, some of her long, dark hair dipped into the water of the bowl.

"Shit," she hissed, wringing it as she stood.

With a hand running along the wall, she moved to the kitchenette and swung open one of the cabinets. The motion sent another wave of nausea up from her stomach, but she swallowed it down. Pulling out a sleeve of saltines, she sat on the cold tile floor and forced herself to nibble one until her stomach settled.

With a groan that belied her youth, Miracle rose from the floor. She showered, got herself dressed, and drove her Honda Civic to the local CVS. She stood, alone, in the aisle with the pregnancy tests, chewing on the nub of a fingernail.

"Can I help you?" one of the employees asked suddenly.

"Nope," she answered as quickly.

Miracle's hand slashed out and she grabbed a box, identical to the one she'd bought two weeks earlier. Without making eye contact, she hurried to the front and handed the test to a cashier who looked like he couldn't be older than seventeen. The kid turned the box in his hand and frowned.

"We have digital tests that are easier to read," he said.

Her head down, she said, "I'll just take that one."

"The digital ones are cheaper."

"No thanks," she snapped.

The guy shook his head, like he knew so much better than she did. Her teeth grinding together, she paid $23.75 and nearly sprinted out to her car. Back at her apartment, she went straight to the bathroom. There was no need to read the directions. As she expected, the specimen collection wasn't the hard part. It was the three minutes after that, the waiting, that nearly did her in, again. She paced her tiny studio, counting steps. Ten from the bathroom to the bed. Fifteen to the oven. Five to the door. Three to the crappy couch her friend Gemma had saved from a dumpster three weeks ago. One to the picture of Max with a stuffed bear in his mouth on the coffee table.

When the timer on her phone sounded, she bolted back to the bathroom. She grabbed the stick from where it lay in the basin of the sink. Moisture touched the tip of her finger, but she barely cared. Instead, she stared at the two lines on the display. Yup . . . still pregnant.

* * *

Leashing Max, Miracle set off. For the first two miles, through neighborhoods and across the highway, Max went mad. He pulled at his tether, dragging her at times, his nose snorting along the ground as if he followed some nefarious trail. By mile three, he slowed, still leading but not tugging as he had. Eventually he glanced back at Miracle, like he was checking to see if they might turn back. She smiled at him but kept going.

Miracle made it to an upscale community with enormous homes right on the ocean side of the highway. She slipped under the lowered gate at the untended guard house and walked east down the deserted street. On Friday, they'd be back, the owners of these multi-million-dollar properties. Their young children would play on a nearly empty beach during the day. Preppy college kids just home from school would listen to bad rap music through Bose speaker systems way too loudly while playing beer pong on their spacious waterfront decks. An older neighbor might call the local police, who would come and ask nicely for the music to be turned down.

For now, however, she was alone. She slipped down one of the cedar-planked walks over the softly rising dune. The tall reeds of green grass swayed along with the breeze off the ocean as the sound of the surf surrounded her. Max found his second wind, his paws dancing as patiently as they could until Miracle was able to unclasp his leash. Once free, he bolted to the water, vaulting into the rounded foam of a small wave.

"Max!" she called out as she reached the flatter sand near the ocean and turned south.

His head whipped up. When he saw Miracle walking away, he leapt out of the water. He broke into a spastic sprint, his butt tucked under as his back legs outraced his front. He passed her and wheeled around. Still dancing, he stopped to look up at Miracle.

"Good boy," she said.

And he was off again to fight the surf, one eye on the water, one on Miracle.

*   *   *

As she neared the spot, her dog seemed to sense it. He left his fun and kept pace with her, looking up every few feet. Max whined once and Miracle reached down, scratching the bristly hackles above his shoulders.

Slowly she approached the crest of the dune. Below her, a small parking lot appeared, a single, lonely outhouse in the corner. She stopped, a chill bringing up gooseflesh on her arms. Max sat in the sand as she tried to keep her breathing steady. Without realizing it, Miracle let her hand slip past her waist, cupping her belly.

She stood there for a time, just staring and holding herself. Then, slowly, she moved, inch by inch. The closer she got to the outhouse, the more charge she felt. Her mouth dried. As did her eyes. But she pushed through it until she reached out. Her fingers touched the cool metal handle of the door. Her chest heaved as she swung it open and stepped inside.

Max followed her in. His nose lifted, taking in what to Miracle was a faint smell of urine and salt. Her eyes locked on to the sink. Everything else seemed to fade away. Her feet shuffled, moving her closer. Miracle touched the chipped porcelain, lightly, much like she had her own stomach. But it felt lifeless under her skin. Cold and harsh and lonely. Forgotten. Lost.

Her eyes closed. The pain seemed to enter her through that contact, rising up her forearm into her shoulders. It bunched there, sending tendrils along her spine and up into her neck. A throbbing started behind her eyes. Miracle blinked and her head lifted. She looked into the cracked mirror above the faucet. She saw a stranger staring back at her, someone she'd lost a long time ago.

7

"SHE LIED TO ME," Meg said over the phone, her voice cracking. I listened to her breathing change. I could hear the resolve. Even without meeting Meg, I had a sense of who she was. A rock; someone who never uttered a frivolous thought.

"What did she lie about?" I asked.

Meg paused before answering. "She didn't go see her friend Gemma."

"Was it her boyfriend . . . the father?"

"No," Meg said. "I've talked to them both since she left this time. She went somewhere else, somewhere she didn't want me to know about."

"Where?"

"That I don't know. But I'm pretty sure it has something to do with wherever she is now."

"What about Max?" I asked, feeling strangely concerned.

"Oh, he's here. She left him when she left her son."

"Wow," I said. "I have your number. I'm going to get off and call my investigator. She can help us. I'm sure of it."

"I need to ask you something, Mr. Snyder," Meg said in that tone of hers.

"Please, call me Theo. You can ask me anything."

"Why are you willing to help me?"

"What do you mean?"

"I mean, do you care about my daughter's safety? Or is this just about your documentary?"

I didn't answer right away. In fact, I thought about her question. In the past, I would have said it was all about her daughter. And it would have been an utter lie. Earlier that day, I would have given the same answer and convinced myself it was the truth. But there was something about that project, how crazy it had gotten. How lost I'd let myself get. In that moment, I felt like a different person. Someone who was far less sure about the future than I had been before I'd ever heard the name Miracle Jones.

"Both," I finally said. "To be honest. But . . . I'm in trouble." I laughed. "I've been in trouble for a while, actually. But it recently took a turn for the worst. This movie I'm working on, about Jasper . . . and your daughter, it's on very thin ice.

"If I was all in, if I only cared about the work, I don't think I would help you. I would want to find Miracle, but honestly, I don't need to. In fact, her being missing makes a more compelling story. No, I'm going to help you, really help you, because . . . I need to."

"Need to?" she asked, and I heard the suspicion in her voice.

"Maybe if I help you find her," I said, "it'll help me figure out exactly where I am."

She laughed. I heard it, though Meg tried to hide the sound behind a fake cough. And I realized how stupid I sounded. But for the first time in my life, I didn't care. Maybe I didn't even want to make this movie anymore. Maybe it wasn't too late to get a job at a coffee shop.

"Whatever the reason, I'm helping now," I said. "I'll call you back."

"I hope so," Meg said.

"You can count on it."

*   *   *

Honestly, I never imagined Zora would pick up. I could only guess what the voice mail I left might have sounded like. With what I'd learned from Steph hanging over our heads, I figured she was gone. I wasn't totally wrong, either, as I learned after she answered.

"You feeling better," she said in greeting.

"I'm really sorry," I said.

"About what part?"

I paused. "Definitely about what I said when we were walking back from the station. I just thought you were cool with—"

"You crossed the line, Theo," she said.

"I know . . . I know—"

"No, you don't. You think you do, but you don't. You can never know."

"I'm sorry. I really am."

"You know what," she said. "That's what he said to me. The one time my father talked about the whole thing. He said I couldn't understand, because of what I was. That's how he said it, too. What I *was*. He knew, I guess, even before I did. Because it took me years to really figure out what he meant. He meant that because I was gay, I couldn't understand why he had to have an affair. And why my mom had to just accept it."

I didn't know what to say. I felt like any response would be wrong. But that no response would be worse.

"That's fucked up," was what came out.

"Yeah," she said.

"And I understand . . . I mean, I . . . It won't happen again. I'll never ask you another question."

"Don't be a martyr," she said.

Crap. I just sat there, feeling dumber than I ever had before. After a few seconds, though, Zora continued as if nothing had been said at all.

"So why'd you call, anyway?"

"I . . . Why didn't you say something?" I asked. "Last night."

"About what?" Zora asked, sounding angry again.

"No . . . I mean about Cassandra. About how worried you are."

Zora laughed. "I don't get worried."

"That's fair," I said. "But Steph told me she heard from someone that you—"

"That's a pretty indirect source."

"But she told me she heard you were having second thoughts. About the project."

"If I was, you'd know. I don't hide things. I have no idea where she got that from."

"Kent, maybe," I said.

"Kent? Well . . ."

She had me there. Kent was certainly known to have a touch of the gossip in him. All good-natured, but he loved everyone's business.

"So . . . you're good," I asked.

"Of course I am."

"Thank God," I said. "Some crazy shit happened last night."

I told her about the flower. She didn't say anything for a few seconds.

"Do you still have it?" she asked.

"The flower . . . uh, no. It was gone when I came back upstairs."

"It just disappeared?"

"Um . . . . I guess so. But it doesn't matter. That's not really why I called. I need your help. Miracle Jones's mother just reached out."

The line was silent for a moment. I could hear her, and each breath felt laced with judgment.

"Are you there?" I asked.

"Yeah, I'm here," she said, her tone flat.

"You heard me, right? Meg called. She—"

"Who's Meg?" she interrupted.

"Oh, sorry," I said. "Miracle Jones's mother."

"So, you're buddies now?"

"No," I protested. "Well, I mean . . . she called. Her daughter is missing."

"And what does this have to do with me?"

"You're still mad. I can tell. This is about Cassandra, isn't it? You heard about the film she's working on."

"No," she said.

"It's on . . . Bender. And me, I guess."

She laughed again. "You?"

I wasn't sure if she was concerned or amused.

"I think she's just mad that I jumped her," I said. "Look, maybe the project's dead. Who cares? I just told Meg that we could help. And if you won't, then I will."

"You're diving a little deep here, Theo."

And there it was. Concern or judgment, I was sure I'd lost her. It dripped from her terse tone. To be honest, I couldn't even blame Zora. I'd become a pariah. Regardless, I waited, hopeful. The line remained silent. Shaking my head, I sighed a second time, a little louder.

"Okay," I said. "I understand."

"Theo, just listen to me for a minute," she said. "I really like you. And I don't say that very often. And . . . I can't believe you got *me* to talk. No one's ever done that. You have mad skill. I mean it. The best I've worked with. So please, take this as advice from someone that actually cares. Slow down."

"I hear you," I said. "And thanks."

I heard Zora. And in my own way, I listened. I thought about what she said. She might be right. But it didn't sway me. The funny thing is, I think she knew it wouldn't.

We ended the call. And I searched for the nearest rental car place and dialed that number.

"Yeah, I need a car. Right now."

* * *

Three hours later, I arrived at Meg Jones's home and knocked. A dog barked, then slammed into the closed door. When it opened, he bolted out, almost knocking me over, before rushing to the edge of the street. There, he sat, as if waiting for someone.

"He's done that since Miracle left."

I turned back around and saw Meg Jones for the first time, in her angler's vest and thick-soled hiking boots. She stood in her doorway, as solid a foundation as I had ever seen, with a fat little baby clinging to her neck.

"Is that . . . ?"

"This is my grandson, Owen. Miracle named him after the man that found her when she was a baby."

I stepped closer, staring at the child. For some reason, I felt overwhelmed. Like everything had taken on vastly more importance.

"I . . . I want to see what I can do."

"Did you speak with your investigator?" she asked.

"I did," I said. For some reason, I glanced over my shoulder. Max sat exactly where he had, but I saw Ginny Harris on her porch across the street, watching us. I waved, then turned back to Meg. "I'm not sure she's going to help."

"Why?"

"That's a long story," I said.

I half expected Meg to mention Bender or Cassandra. The way things were going for me, I might not have been shocked if she brought up Geri. Then again, I felt like she might be one of the first people I'd spoken to who had never heard of *The Basement*.

"What can we do?" she asked instead.

"Maybe if you tell me more about what happened. You mentioned that you knew something was wrong. That your daughter wasn't being truthful. When did you first notice that?"

A troubled look cracked her stoic facade. Meg stepped back into the house.

"Let's come inside. Away from the audience. And let me get Owen down for his nap. Because that's a long story too."

I laughed, despite myself. "I have the time." Then I looked back again. "What about the dog?"

She shook her head. "Max isn't going anywhere without his mom."

*   *   *

ACT TWO/SCENE 7

EXT. PARKING LOT—DAY

The sun bakes the same dark asphalt, those same faded white lines. The outhouse still juts from the corner of the lot. Miracle Jones steps out from behind it, her dog by her side. The weight of the entire world in her eyes.

From the day her mother handed her that article to the day Miracle took her first pregnancy test, her truth never rested more than a question away. At any time, all she had to do was ask. Her parents would have answered anything. She could have gotten on their desktop computer and used the dial-up connection to search the burgeoning internet for more news. Not long after that, all she would have had to do was pull the phone out of her pocket and surf for endless facts. Every detail was there for the taking. Yet she never dared look.

Maybe that doesn't seem realistic. How could someone fight that kind of temptation? Hold off those kinds of demons? For so long, all Miracle knew was the story she'd read, with its heartwarming photo and poetic flare. She was well aware that it hid a much darker truth. But she also knew that whatever that truth might be, it would define the rest of her life. No matter how much she wished it wouldn't. From that day in the sixth grade on, she was no miracle. And no Jones, either.

For years, she flirted with the edges. She wrote college papers diving deeply into the nature-versus-nurture debate. She marched for a woman's right to choose. She joined an adoptee support group but never attended the second meeting. When things got too close, she ran.

That second pregnancy test opened the door. There would be no more hiding. No more denying her past. Standing in that lonely outhouse, she got out her phone. After taking a deep breath of the late summer air, she finally did it. Miracle Googled herself.

Within the flood of initial search results, she found the article her mother had clipped from the newspaper. Staring at the other headlines, she opened that page first. Utterly alone, Miracle read that part of her story over and over again as the phone shook in her hand. Reality coiled around her, constricting her chest. The more she fought to leave that article and move to the others, the harder it became to breathe.

"Shit," she hissed.

The fire was lit. The future already in motion. Miracle hesitated only a moment. Then she dove into her story. She devoured every detail she could find, eating the tragedy as if she had starved her entire life. The ache inside her continued.

Abandoned her infant daughter in the filthy sink of a public restroom.
Doctors marvel at child's survival.
Who would do something like that?
What kind of mother . . . ?
Horror!
Miracle.

As tears rolled down the curves of her cheeks, she let the hand holding her phone drop. It rested at her side as she looked up at her cloudy reflection in the mirror. Her other hand slipped up to her shirt. Her fingers reached. But at the first touch of the fabric flowing over her stomach, she recoiled as if burned.

In uneven strides, she left that outhouse. Walking out onto the sand-dusted pavement of the lot, she lifted her phone again. She stared at the blank screen, her mind racing. She knew what she should do. She should call her mother. Tell her the truth, that she was pregnant. Meg Jones's desire to be a grandmother was epic. She had been bugging her brother for years. Her mother would be happy. She would be supportive. Maybe Miracle could tell her everything. Maybe, even, Meg would understand.

Her finger actually moved. Miracle nearly opened her phone and called her mother. But the gaping wound inside her might as well have severed the nerves in her hand. Clouded her mind. Shutting down one pathway and throwing open another.

Her head tilted upward as tears streamed down both cheeks. She screamed out at a life that she'd never asked for. At a world in which she could not exist.

"I can't do it!"

* * *

She was already tumbling through her past, gaining speed, careening toward something that she couldn't yet see. That she couldn't yet understand. There was no way of knowing how far the fall would take her. At some point, as surely as the force of gravity itself, the bottom would come. And the truth would obliterate her one way or another.

Honestly, she didn't think about her next action. Instead, lost in a tangle of forbidden thoughts, she called her mother. Meg answered with her usual excitement.

"Hi, baby."

"Hi, Mom."

Miracle paused. She had been about to ask Meg to pick her up. Then the reality of it dawned on her. If her mother came to this place, it would break her heart.

"Hi . . . hey, what's up?" The nervousness Miracle had heard the day before slipped back into her mother's voice. "Is everything okay?"

From where she sat, Miracle could see the highway. If she started walking, she might be able to get to Dewey before her mother. She looked down at Max, saw the foam around his lips and listened to his heavy panting. The thought of walking all the way home again was too much.

"Can you pick me up?"

"Where are you?"

"I . . . went for a walk with Max. Down to the ocean so he could play. We went a little too far."

"Where are you?" Meg repeated with the slightest edge of suspicion.

"Ah, Dewey. Indian Beach."

Meg paused on the other side of the line. "I'm just leaving Mrs. Hanson's house. We had a planning meeting this morning."

Miracle's eyes closed slowly. Mrs. Hanson lived on the south side of Dewey, one block from Indian Beach.

"I'm outside now," Meg said, her tone growing more suspicious. "Where are you exactly?"

With a sigh, Miracle told her. "We're at the state beach. Just south of you."

Mrs. Jones didn't answer right away. When she did, her tone was flat, unreadable.

"Just stay still. I'll be there in a minute."

*   *   *

The car ride was silent. Meg clutched the wheel and hummed to soft music from the radio. Miracle stared out the window, afraid to blink, because each time she did, a vision of the outhouse flashed on the backs of her lids, jagged lines and ominous sky, like a drive-in horror movie. The mood oppressed even Max, who lay curled in a tight ball on the back seat, moaning occasionally to remind everyone of his empathic discomfort.

Miracle had thought they were going home. She'd thought that was what she wanted. Instead, still humming, her mother turned onto Rehoboth Avenue. When she nosed into a parking spot, Miracle turned her head.

"Let's get lunch," Meg said, her tone impressively normal.

"Mom, you don't have to—"

Meg's eyes flared. "Oh, hush. We do."

"What about the dog?"

"We'll sit outside. It's nice."

The smile creeping across Miracle's own face surprised her. "Okay."

They walked down the main street. They even made small talk as Max trotted along beside them, his swagger returning with each step.

"I was going to take you to get oysters . . ."

Miracle stiffened. She wasn't sure, but she assumed pregnant women didn't eat raw shellfish. At the same time, the idea that she cared, considering her current mind-set, almost caused her to laugh out loud. A third thought popped into her head. Could her mother know?

"It's okay," Miracle said. "The café sounds good."

Her mother nodded. "It does, doesn't it?"

They sat outside and Max slipped under Miracle's chair, his jowls spreading out on the warm noon concrete. For a time, their lunch played out like all the others they'd had over the years. Then, out of nowhere, Meg's eyes took on the focus of a hunter.

"Are you still mad at me?" she asked.

Miracle's head did a quick shake. "What?"

"Are you still mad?"

"About what?" her daughter asked, genuinely confused.

"About not telling you. Before that little shit of a girl did."

A laugh burst from Miracle. "Mom!"

"What?"

"She was eleven . . . maybe twelve. You can't call her that!"

"Well, what would you call her?"

Miracle considered that for a moment, then shook her head. "A little shit."

"Exactly," Meg said, smiling proudly. "So, are you?"

"Of course not," she answered.

"You can be honest. Your father and I understand. We've talked about it so many times. I can remember that day I gave you the article like it was yesterday. Waiting for you to finish reading was like torture. All the questions you might ask just kept going through my head. Then . . . you came out and never asked a thing. Not once. Ever."

Miracle reached under the table and scratched Max's head. "I don't think I wanted to."

"I spoke to someone back then. A professional. And she told me that I should let you make the first move. It was so hard. I wanted to talk to you about it every day. But I . . ." Meg laughed, this time nervously. "Listen to me, saying how hard it was for me. That doesn't even matter. Not at all. All that matters is you. That's all that's ever mattered."

"Mom," Miracle protested, her cheeks flushed. "Don't worry about it. It's all good."

"I listened to that lady back then. And it felt wrong. Every day. Now, I . . . see it again."

Miracle's eyes narrowed. "What do you mean?"

"You're back in that place."

"I am not."

Meg's head shook. "You just happened to take a five-mile walk on your birthday? And you just happened to end up . . . there."

The air seemed to drain out of Miracle's body. She tried to look away. Tried to recoil from the rawness she felt burning inside her. But then she saw her mother, the concern on her face, the love in her heart. And she couldn't do it. Not this time, with the pregnancy and how she felt about it.

"I'm okay." She pushed the words out as if they had been lodged in her throat for over a decade. "I promise. I just . . . You're right. I never asked. I never wanted to know. I didn't want anything to . . . change."

"Oh, sweetie!"

Tears came to Meg's eyes. She rose, rushing to her daughter and wrapping her in an awkward hug. Max, disliking the sudden change in mood, sprung to his feet and tried to pry his way in between them. His efforts sent one of the wrought-iron chairs tumbling to the sidewalk. He jumped. Miracle jumped. And ever-pragmatic Meg let go of her daughter and lifted the chair back to its legs.

"Sorry," she said to the only other table of diners out there.

Miracle watched her mother return to her seat. She saw the tears. And she wondered where her own were. Why she felt so empty inside.

"Nothing will ever change. You're my daughter. I *chose* you!"

"I know. I do. When I have those thoughts, I just get mad, really. I feel like some stupid kid."

"Don't think that. Look, maybe I shouldn't say this. Or maybe I should have said it sooner. What happened to you . . . what you survived, it's real, Miracle. It happened, and it's big. It had to change you."

"I was a baby," she said. "All I remember is everything you and Dad did for me. That's all that matters."

Meg's head shook slowly. "I wish that was true. But what I do know is that we love you and we always will. You will always be with us. And you will always be Miracle Jones. All of you."

With a fierce determination painting the lines of her face, Meg leaned down. She pulled a neatly wrapped present from her bag and laid it on the table between them. It was about the size of a thick paperback book. But her mother's eyes told Miracle it was something far more important than that.

"Open it," she said.

Slowly, Miracle reached out and picked up the gift. It was surprisingly light, more like the pregnancy test she'd bought than a book. That thought set her on edge again. *What if it is?* The fear almost made her laugh. Maybe Meg knew. But she certainly wouldn't buy her a pregnancy test for her birthday. Her mom deserved far more credit than that.

Miracle's fingertips brushed the smooth paper, finding the seam. Always one to enjoy a good unwrapping, Max put his paws on the edge of her seat and thrust his nose under her forearm.

With a quick look at her mother, Miracle tore away. Within seconds, she saw the label on the box—*Ancestry*.

"It's a DNA test," Meg said, removing any last bit of uncertainty.

Miracle stared at it for a second in utter disbelief. She looked up at her mother. How could someone be so connected to her? How could Meg know that it was exactly Miracle's genes that weighed so heavily on her mind? It was as if she could sense every thought Miracle ever had.

Yet the box sat between them, the physical embodiment of their own unrelated DNA.

"I . . ." Meg's voice broke with emotion. "I've thought about this for a long time. I thought you might want to know. I mean, it would be a good idea, right? Even if you don't want to find your mother. That's up to you. But it's still good. See if you can find out your medical history . . . you know."

Miracle couldn't speak. She could barely think. Meg was motherhood as it should be. Someone who cared so deeply and understood her child so implicitly. Who put her child's needs above her own, no matter the cost.

But Miracle's biology hinted at something far different. Not something to pass on, like a beautiful bassinet or a lovingly knitted blanket. Maybe, instead, something that should have been left in a filthy sink to die. Forever.

"A GENETIC TEST?"

"Yes," Meg said.

"But didn't she already know about her mother—and what happened to her?"

"No," Meg said. "She knew nothing then, except that her biological mother had abandoned her. The ancestry test revealed her mother's name, at least—I think. It was a month after that when the article was published about the Halo Killer."

"Oh," I said, while something danced at the fringe of my thoughts. When it didn't strike right away, I stayed in the moment. "Weren't you afraid of what she'd find? That she'd . . . leave you?"

Meg laughed. "You don't have any children, do you?"

I shook my head. "Doubt I ever will."

"When you have them, when they are so little that you can fit them in your outstretched hands, you think they will be yours forever. When you take care of them, feed them, hold them when they cry, you think you'll be theirs forever, too. When they start school, you still make all the decisions—what they eat, what they watch, what they do. But then they grow. They change. It starts with opinions. Then defiance. But when they first ignore you, that's when it hits home. No matter how much you believed it when they were little, they were never *yours*. They are individuals, marching through life just as we did. And just like we saw our parents, they see us. Family, definitely. An annoyance . . . often. But when they turn into adults, we're mostly just an afterthought."

"That sounds sad," I said.

Her head shook slowly. "No, not really. I mean, maybe. But it's also the happiest feeling you can ever have. Because you know you did it. You succeeded in the most important job that exists. You got them to their starting line. Even though the rest is up to them, you hold this little thought—that without you, maybe they wouldn't have gotten there at all.

"The hard part, the part that hurts, is that . . . even though they forget, you don't. You are always *theirs*. That never changes. They have you no matter what. Whether they call you that week or not. Whether they send you a card on your birthday or not. That never changes.

"Now, that sounds sad, doesn't it? I don't mean it that way. I just . . . When I bought that test for her, I knew what she must have been feeling. She was pregnant. She was going to have her own child, one she would have to protect and raise. One that would be hers for a long time. I thought she had to feel afraid."

"Wait! So you did know she was pregnant."

Meg nodded. "Of course I did. I'm her mother."

"What did you think she was afraid of?"

"Not knowing. How can you raise your child if you don't really know who you are?"

"Oh," I said, leaning back on the couch in her front room. "I never thought . . ."

I didn't know what I was going to say next, but it never mattered. Because in that moment, someone pounded on the door. Meg startled and so did I. She got up to see who it was. Before she got there, though, I heard Ginny Harris's voice.

"Meg! Are you watching this! Meg!"

"Ginny, Jesus," Meg said. "You'll wake the baby."

She opened the door. Ginny already had the storm open, and Max burst into the house, his hackles raised. Standing in the threshold, Ginny looked past Miracle's mother, right at me.

"Did you see it?" she whispered excitedly.

"What?" I asked.

"He escaped!"

The world flipped upside down. I knew immediately who she was talking about. And the news paralyzed me. Ginny, for her part, watched my face like it was the best television show ever made.

"The Halo Killer," she said with great drama. "He's free."

9

I SHOULD HAVE BEEN thrilled. If it was true and Jasper had somehow escaped a maximum-security prison, my film had just become astronomically more marketable. Escapes were rare, certainly among the most high-profile inmates. Pure gold!

But sitting in Meg's living room watching the local news report on the prison break at Howard R. Young Correctional Institute in Wilmington, Delaware, I felt something very different. Numbing fear, if I were to be perfectly honest. I remembered the flower outside my apartment. I thought about just how skilled someone had to be to escape. And I could no longer blame my exhaustion. Instead, I heard Jasper's tinny voice in my head, threatening me over and over again to stay away from Miracle.

"Are you okay?" Ginny asked, a strange smile on her face.

"Huh." I blinked. "Yeah, definitely."

"Do you need something to drink?" Meg added.

"No, I'm good. Thanks . . . Why?"

"You look pale," Ginny said.

"I'm fine."

I ran a hand across my face. My skin felt clammy.

"Are you okay?" I asked Meg, turning my head so she wouldn't see the fear I suddenly felt.

"I think so, but looking at you, maybe I'm being foolish." I felt her hand on my shoulder, the surprising strength of her fingers. "Is Miracle in danger?"

I turned but couldn't look her in the eyes. Instead, I stared at the screen. The reporter stood outside the prison as he spoke.

Prison officials are claiming that there are no leads. No physical evidence. At this point, they are baffled, with little idea how this convicted serial killer escaped, only that he was logged in to his cell at the nine PM lights-out and that the cell was empty by six the next morning. But we have breaking news on this story. An exclusive source within the prison spoke to me on the condition I do not reveal their name. I was told that there are signs that Jasper Ross-Johnson was aided in his escape by at least one prison employee. Possibly more. We have uncovered documents authorizing the inmate's transfer to Sussex Correctional Institute in Georgetown, Delaware. At this time, it is believed that these documents were forged, but that a corrections officer used this paperwork to drive the inmate out of the prison. The whereabouts of both inmate and officer are unknown at this time. But an abandoned prison van was just found outside the city of Dover.

"Theo?"

"Sorry," I said, finally turning to her. I took a deep breath. "Yes, I believe she's in danger."

For the first time since I'd met her, Meg showed raw emotion. "Why? Wasn't murdering her mother enough!"

"That's the one thing I don't know. Not yet. But it's something. I believe Jasper may have had a run-in with your daughter. Although he made it sound like a coincidence, that's just not possible. So, I think he tried to find her. Probably not long after she was identified as the . . . biological daughter of his first victim."

"He contacted my daughter? You know that for certain?"

"Not for certain." I slowly shook my head. "There's something different about him. Like so many murderers, he experienced trauma when he was young. There was a head injury, and his home life was . . . difficult. I thought it was his father. But he said something last time, about a young boy he may have . . . killed . . . when Jasper was still a teenager. He said it was wrong. I think he meant the fact his victim was a boy, because every victim after was a woman. I believe most were mothers . . ."

"Oh, God. Miracle is a mother . . ."

"He can't know th—" The timeline started to take shape in my head. "When did you learn Miracle was pregnant?"

"It was about this time last year."

"Before the police identified her mother?" I asked, more to myself.

"Yes. That's what I said, didn't I?" she answered.

"Jasper was still at large. He would have followed the news. They all do. I read the articles. It wouldn't have been hard for him to find her. Especially down here. Everyone seems to remember the Miracle Baby."

"We need to find her," Meg said, standing up. "If he—"

"We will," I said firmly.

I rose and stood face-to-face with Meg.

"What should I do?" she asked.

"Let me make a call," I said. "Then we can go from there."

I pulled my phone out and dialed Zora's number. She answered on the first ring.

"Hey, it's me. Did you hear—"

"Where are you?" Zora asked calmly. "Don't answer that. Just say yes or no. Are you with Meg Jones?"

I felt my eyes narrow, even more surprised that she knew that. "Yes."

"Is she right there with you?"

"Um . . . yes."

"Listen to me, Theo. If you want to survive this, you need to leave. Now. Tell Mrs. Jones to go to a hotel, somewhere at least an hour away. But you need to leave immediately. Do you understand?"

"How do you know? He'll probably run off to Mexico or something."

"This isn't a movie," she snapped back.

"Well . . ."

She huffed. "Just get out of there. Now!"

"Hold on," I said.

I smiled at Meg and motioned to the front door. She looked suspicious but did not follow as I stepped out onto the porch. I glanced back to make sure Meg couldn't hear me before continuing.

"Are you serious?" I whispered.

"A friend of mine from the Department of Corrections called. He told me what happened."

"I heard. The news said he somehow forged transfer papers."

"That's bullshit," Zora said. "The story is that he almost killed the leader of the Aryan gang in the prison. Supposedly for no reason that anyone is aware of. She said the prison was about to explode. They needed to get him out. Fast."

"Are you serious?"

"Just listen to me," she snapped. "If he's coming for you, Theo, he'll know where you are. And he'll be close."

For me? "How can you—"

"Get out of there, now."

"What about Miracle? We need to—"

"I don't think that's important right now. I mean, if you want to stay alive."

"Come on, Zora." I laughed, but I knew it sounded forced. "He could be after her. I was just talking to Meg. There's something there. I think he found her, before he was caught. Or at least he was stalking her. She's in more danger than I am."

Zora didn't respond immediately. Then she made a frustrated sound.

"Fine. If I promise you that I'll find Miracle, will you get out of there?"

"Okay," I said, feeling strangely relieved.

"And warn her mother."

"Okay," I said. "Call me when you find her. I'll . . . where should I go?"

"Go to Kent's place. He'll never find you there."

"You really think it's that serious?"

"I know it is, Theo. And the sooner you do, the better your chances of surviving this shit storm."

10

K ENT LIVED ON the top floor of a building across from the park, between Eighty-Second and Eighty-Third. It took me over three hours to drive from Delaware to the car rental place and another twenty minutes to catch a subway to the closest station. During that time, I'd meant to text him. What was I supposed to say, though? *Hey, can I stay at your place? I'm sort of on the run from a notorious serial killer.*

When I got close, my mind was racing. I kept thinking about the flower. That it hadn't been there the next morning. It must have been in my head. The project—Cassandra—Bender—it just had gotten to me. I had been tired. Sort of drunk.

"Theo Snyder," someone said.

I startled. A large guy in a black overcoat and hat stepped in front of me.

"Yes," I said cautiously.

"Mr. Barre asked me to look for you. He's expecting you upstairs."

"Kent?"

"Yes, sir. Are you okay?"

"Yeah," I said, brushing a hand across my face. "Yeah, definitely."

"Great. Why don't you follow me? I'll have you up to the penthouse in no time."

*   *   *

"Thanks, Vincent," Kent said to the doorman as I stepped into his apartment. Then he looked in my direction and gave me the once-over. "Wow, you look like shit. You need a kombucha."

I barely heard him, utterly captivated by his place. I'd been to a few mansions on the island before. Kent's place felt like one of those, but floating up in the sky. All the walls and fixtures were pure white. The furniture, all white. The flooring, perfectly finished walnut and plush white carpets. Instead of a wall of windows looking out at the ocean, he had a wall of windows that sat perfectly balanced between the lush park below and the billowing clouds above.

"Sit," Kent said. "Before you pass out."

"I'm fine," I said for the hundredth time.

But I listened. Slipping out of my shoes, I walked softly to the closest couch. I sank into it, feeling it surround me like a warm hug. For a second, I felt dirty, like I was going to stain everything, but the exhaustion quieted that. When Kent came back with the tea, I could barely keep my eyes open.

"You look like you need a nap," he said.

"I feel like I need an IV."

He laughed. "Zora called me. She told me about that lunatic. Do you really think he's after you?"

"No," I said.

His head tilted. "Then why the hell do you look like you do?"

"It's a long story."

"I got time."

I looked into his eyes. They were mirrors to our friendship. I felt safe and whole sitting there, though I don't know why. I also felt more vulnerable than I ever had before. I told him everything. About Cassandra and Jasper. And most of all, about Miracle. He listened, asking only a few questions. When I was done, his head shook slowly.

"You're running yourself into the ground, Theo," he said. "I've seen it before. This project has your number."

"I think I'm starting to see that. But I can't stop. Not after getting this far."

He put his hand up, cutting me off. "Look, brother, I know what I'm talking about. You've put all your eggs into one basket. And from your point of view, they got smashed by Pepper"—he laughed—"of all people. Anyway, it's an addiction. No one wants to call it that, but it is. We're a generation of kids who grew up in front of the television.

Worshiped action stars and supermodels. We dressed like Michael Jackson as our parents elected an actor to be president. Believe me, I know. And I'm not saying I'm any better than you.

"But think of it like drinking. Almost everyone I know is an alcoholic. But most of them function. Most of them have families, show up for work, go to the gym, and raise kids. They can't do it without their nightly wine, or beer, or cocktail, but they do it. Then there are a few that can't. Drinking gets in the way of everything. They are the addicts, Theo. They are the ones that need an intervention."

"Are you calling me an alcoholic?" I asked, trying to deflect.

"No, I'm calling you a fame-aholic. Like the rest of us. But we're functional. We're not having panic attacks and driving so hard that we make ourselves sick. We're not on the run from serial killers or making unannounced visits to the adoptive mother of one of his victims—"

"She wasn't one of his victims," I protested.

"You know what I'm saying. And let me be frank. The rest of us aren't going out of our way to step on Cassandra's feet, either."

I had been leaning forward, listening to him. When he said that, I threw myself back and let the plush cushions swallow me whole. I moaned, but I'm not even sure he could hear it through the padding.

"Can you hear me, Theo?"

I nodded.

"Good, then listen. I don't tell people what to do. Ever. So, understand this is way out of character for me."

I looked up. Suddenly, Kent appeared nervous. He looked behind him as if afraid someone might overhear what he said next.

"It's time to cut bait. You're in too deep on this one."

"Why do people keep saying that? Zora, you . . . even Jasper. For that matter, why does everyone keep asking me if I'm okay?"

"Because we're worried," Kent said.

"Whatever," I said, absently rubbing at my face.

"Look, if you let it go, step away from this Halo Killer business, I can fix everything. In fact, I can get you funding for any other project you want to work on."

I poked my head up, my eyebrows raised. "Are you serious?"

"I am. I like you. More than most. And I want to see you okay. Can you do that for me? For you? Can you give this up? Start over. Together, we'll get you back to the top. But the right way." He stuck his hand out. "Deal?"

I stared at it for a second. My heart told me to refuse his generosity. My gut told me to leave, immediately. But my brain, it heard what Kent said. It listened. And it agreed. Slowly, I put my hand out. We shook.

"Great. Get some sleep. You can stay here until they catch that creep. Then we are going to make a movie."

"Awesome," I said, already groggy. "Awesome."

I fell asleep sometime between those two words, I think.

11

THE APARTMENT WAS as dark as my dreams. In them, something chased me. I thought it was Jasper. He was close. So close that I could hear the reptilian rasp of his breath in my ear. But when—in the dream—I turned, he wasn't there.

When I startled awake, still on Kent's couch, it took me a minute to get my bearings. When I realized where I was, my conversation with Kent came back. I recalled everything he'd said and everything I'd agreed to do. Or more accurately, not to do.

Sitting up, I rubbed my eyes and checked the time. I wanted to call Meg and make sure she was okay, but it was too late. Instead, I looked out the wall of windows at the silent park below. Although streetlamps burned among the towering trees, it felt so odd to be in a New York City apartment at night and not see a carpet of light out every window. In fact, the openness hung over me, an oppressive thickness that made my skin crawl. I felt eyes everywhere, boring into me. Threatening me.

I swear that, even in the moment, I knew how amazing Kent's offer had been. More importantly, I was 100 percent certain he would deliver. And I had shook his hand in good faith. Yet something moved me, like a primal urge. It tugged at my very center of reason. I sidled along the long, curved couch and toward the front door, careful to avoid making even the slightest sound. I slipped into my shoes, then grabbed the handle. My entire body vibrated with nerves, but I turned it. The sound of the latch disengaging might as well have rocked the entire building. I froze for just a beat, then swung the door open and hurried out.

"Mr. Snyder, can I help you?"

I hadn't seen Vincent standing outside the elevator. His question nearly ruptured my heart. He noticed when I jumped.

"Mr. Barre asked me to make sure no one came up or down tonight. I'm not supposed to—"

"Vincent," I said, my tone as smooth as I could make it. "Thank God you're out here. Something's wrong with Kent. He got up. I heard him walking out from his bedroom. Then a bang! He just fell. I can't get him up."

Vincent didn't hesitate. He rushed past me. Once he entered the apartment, I spun and ran to the elevator. I slammed my palm on the button, but nothing happened. Panicked, I looked over my shoulder at the door. I listened for Vincent. He would be back any second.

I pounded on the button again. Then I noticed the keys dangling from a lock beside the controls. I remembered Vincent using it downstairs to call the elevator. I turned it, and the doors swung silently open.

"Yes!"

"Mr. Snyder!"

Vincent's voice came from inside, but he was closing the distance fast. Without hesitating, I yanked the keys out of the lock and jumped into the carriage. I knew he'd get in trouble with Kent. And I felt bad, truly, but I hit the lobby button just as Vincent entered the hallway. The doors closed as smoothly as they'd opened. For a second I saw a slash of his angry, red face. Then I was on my way down. And he was stuck on the top floor.

* * *

Though it might not seem like it, I had second thoughts. Kent had been so generous. Logically, his offer solved all my problems. Not to mention Vincent. He seemed like a real decent guy. I regretted that I might have caused him trouble.

So, what made me do it? What was making me run away from my own perfect ending? Was it Meg? Some outdated need to help the woman?

I wanted to think it was that. That my motives were altruistic. But it just didn't ring true. It was far simpler than that. And more complicated. At the core, it was just the story. Though I could almost taste the danger I faced in the back of my throat, I couldn't leave it unfinished. I needed that ending. Not for me, but for the film. Otherwise, it would be a gaping hole inside me forever.

So, I moved through the night, staying close to the sides, to the darker shadows. Just after three AM, the streets were quiet but not empty. Other people passed by, mostly with their heads down and their pace quick. As I turned onto Sixtieth, I found myself alone. With a quick glance behind me, I pulled out my phone and thought about calling Zora, but I texted instead, due to the hour.

Hey, I'm heading over to my apartment. I need to get all of our stuff out of there. Just in case. We need to talk. I sort of agreed to give up on this project tonight. But I don't know if I can do that.

I typed more twice, erasing it each time. As I stared at the words that remained, I guess I knew. I wasn't giving up. I wasn't moving on. I don't think I'd had that exact thought, not when I snuck out, not when I got Vincent in trouble. Not until that very second. It was like my body had just moved me away from the safety and security. Kent had been so right. Nothing but an addiction can take over your body like it did that night. Like an addict, though, I had stopped calling the shots. Instead, the story drove me, as maybe it should.

I hit send and slipped my phone back into my pocket. It was a long walk to Hell's Kitchen and my apartment. I had no idea what I was going to do when I got there. What I would do with all the stuff. But I knew I wouldn't leave it behind. I was all in. No matter what. That ending was out there. And suddenly, undoubtedly, I needed to find it.

12

Almost an hour later, I slipped into my own building like some thief in the night. No one stirred. Alone, I crept up the stairs, hesitating only at the door to my floor. Before I stepped out, I pictured the flower I thought I had seen, and I almost turned back, ran to Kent, and hid myself inside his couch. Instead, I swallowed down the acid rising up my throat.

Nothing. The hallway was deathly still. I inched toward my door, holding my breath, expecting Jasper to jump out of every corner. Of course, that didn't happen. A smile stuck on my face when I realized what it actually meant to be home. I could get back to work.

My key slipped into the lock without a problem. The door opened. For a second I was lost in thought, planning my next moves. Then, when my first footstep echoed, I froze. My finger found the light switch. The overheads flashed on. I had to blink a few times before it registered. Before I realized my apartment was totally, completely empty.

I should have run, gotten the hell out of there. I couldn't, though. It felt like my shoes had rooted into my bare floor. Like the empty space before me had latched on to my bones, turning them into a solid, rigid mass. I just stood there and stared at where my bed had been, where my stools had sat beside the kitchen. Where my boxes, all my work, had littered the place as if hit by a sudden gust of wind. It was all gone now. Lost. Vanished. I stood alone, among nothing, and just stared.

"Where's all my stuff?" I whispered.

My voice bounced off every surface. I crept forward, into my own apartment. Slowly I closed the door behind me, my heart racing. I felt exposed. But I also felt, as with the flower, that this couldn't be real. I closed my eyes. Rubbed the lids into my skull until I saw stars. When I reopened them, though, still nothing.

I reached the counter, and something on the floor of my tiny kitchen caught my attention. It was a book with a dark jacket. My head tilted as I stared at it. Nothing about the pale type on the back or the grainy black-and-white author photo looked even a bit familiar to me. I moved closer, but the spine was turned away, toward the refrigerator, so I couldn't see the title. After another step, I could make out a few words on the back. One in particular made my stomach turn—*forensics*.

Somehow I forced myself to lean down, to put my fingers on that filthy thing, even though I knew already what it had to be. I jerked upward, flipping the book over. The title painted a scarlet path across the darkness—*Blood Stain Evidence*.

Still crouching, I shuffled away, falling to my backside. I slid out of the kitchen, around the counter so I couldn't see that thing any longer. My chest heaved. I couldn't breathe. But I pushed myself up and sprinted the short distance to the door. Slamming into it, I slashed the dead bolt home. Then the chain and the lock on the knob. Once it was secure, I fell back to the ground, huffing and sweating.

* * *

He was here.

I sat hunched over on the floor, violated and paranoid. Every noise I heard outside, I knew it had to be him. Stalking me. Waiting for me to step out. When my radiator hissed and creaked, I sprang up. I searched every inch of my place, which took only a second because there was nowhere left to hide. Then I returned to the door. As I sat on the hard floor, wrapping my knees in my arms, a second thought occurred to me.

Why?

If he'd wanted me dead, he could have lain in wait. Surprised me when I returned. He could have finished me off and slipped away, free and clear. That's not what he'd done. He'd broken into my apartment and taken everything. Not just my work, but my bed and my chairs. My clothes—everything but the crappy old phone charger I'd left plugged in behind where my bed used to be.

When I considered that, really thought about it, I laughed. He had done it for the same reason that he'd left that awful book behind for me. *To scare me away.* Jasper was trying to frighten me off because I was close to something. When I looked around at my bare apartment and thought about the effort it must have taken, I knew for sure that I was close to something *huge.*

In that moment, my fear vanished. Smiling ear to ear, crackling with excitement, I called Zora's number. Despite the hour, she answered.

"Where are you?" she asked immediately.

"At my apartment. You're not going—"

"Are you serious! Kent just called. He told me you snuck off. He also told me about the deal you walked out on. Are you crazy?"

"What?"

"He offered you the silver spoon. And you snuck out in the middle of the night. He told me you stole his doorman's elevator key."

"I left it downstairs. Look, it doesn't matter anyway."

"And why is that?" she asked.

"I'm at my apartment, Zora. And he was here. He took everything."

"What are you talking about?"

"Jasper broke in and took all my stuff. Not just our research either. Everything. He even left that book that Martino told me about. The one from his house. It was a message. He wants me to stay away."

"He was there?" she asked, her voice suddenly terse. "Are you sure?"

"You want me to text you a picture of the place?"

"This isn't normal," she said. "Look, I'm no quitter. Actually, I was thinking of giving you another chance, assuming this Cassandra thing gets smoothed over. But . . ."

"What?"

"You're not thinking straight. This isn't working out. You need to take care of yourself."

"And do what?" I asked.

She sighed. "Give it up. It's over. I can get you back to Kent's. You can lay low until they get that lunatic. Then move on. It's not too late."

I laughed. "Are you serious? Aren't you listening? This is huge! He's obviously hiding something. And he knows we're close. That's why he escaped. That's why he took everything.

"Move on? The one thing I know for sure is that that just isn't happening. I'm making this movie. And when it wins the Academy Award, Cassandra can suck it!"

I was out of breath when I finished that soliloquy. As I panted, the last part came back to me. I regretted it immediately. And the feeling grew with every second that Zora didn't say anything.

"Sorry, I—"

"Just be quiet for a second. I need you to understand something. Every morning, for a few seconds, sometimes even minutes, I can forget. But eventually I see them. The scars on my arm . . . the proof of how far I fell. I was lost, Theo. Done for. But then she showed up. She let me get involved. She let me lose myself in the story. And somehow, that's where I found it. My salvation. My strength. It was just enough. Just strong enough to give me purpose. I clung to that when I got clean. I held on with everything I had. And I made it.

"I see you, Theo. And I know the signs. Maybe it's karma. But I can't just abandon you. She stuck with me. Helped me when I needed it the most. And I am going to do the same thing for you. No matter what it looks like. How bad this gets. I'm not leaving you."

I didn't know what to say, not at first. It was beautiful, really, what she'd said to me. Maybe I didn't even realize that she was pointing out my own addiction. In the moment, it just sounded like she had my back. Strangely, though, I didn't know if I wanted that. A part of me just wanted to dive in, alone. Get lost in the film.

"I'm not sure—" I began, but she cut me off.

"Please! I see it, even if you don't. And I'm going to help you."

"What about Miracle?" I asked. "We need to talk to her. Keep her safe. He's probably—"

"I'll take care of it. Just stay still. Lock your doors and do not move."

"You think he's still in the building? I'll call the—"

"No," she said. "Just stay still. I'm coming."

The idea of Zora rescuing me seemed absurd at first. Then I thought about her, the way I acted around her, and it might sound childish, but it helped.

"Okay," I said. "When will you be here?"

"I'm almost there."

*   *   *

The knock on my door surprised me. I could have sworn only a couple of minutes had passed since I'd ended the call with Zora. Picturing Jasper on the other side, ready to pounce, I leaned closer.

"Who's there?"

"It's me. Open up."

I fumbled with the lock. Rubbing my clammy hands on the sides of my pants, I focused and got the door open.

"Thanks for—"

As the door opened, I saw her. Not Zora, but the young woman beside her. Her dark hair was pulled back, harshly, adding to the unbelievable intensity of her eyes. She was small, but in a way I'd never seen before. As if an average person had simply shrunk down by a third. Knowing her story, seeing her size and her eyes, I knew she had never truly recovered from her tragic beginning.

My mouth hung open as I took her in for the first time. The words stuck in my throat. All I could manage was her name.

"Miracle," I whispered, in awe.

She raised an eyebrow and turned to look at Zora, as if she couldn't quite figure me out. I imagined the expression that must be on my face. A reflection of the overwhelming yet unexplainable reverence I felt.

"Can we come in?" Zora asked, with a sigh.

I snapped my mouth shut. Blinked and swallowed. Then forced what I hoped looked like a normal smile onto my face.

"Yeah, sure." I awkwardly stuck a hand out. "It's so great to meet you."

Miracle Jones stared back at me. Those eyes, almost black and sharp as a surgical scalpel, peeled back my layers and laid my every intention at her feet. My hand dropped. I took a hesitant step backward. Then she smiled.

"You're Theo, right?"

"Um . . . yeah," I said. "I've met your mom."

Miracle snorted. "I heard. So . . . can we come in or not?"

"Oh, sorry."

I stepped aside, giving them plenty of room. As they entered, Zora looked around. Her tongue clicked off the roof of her mouth.

"I thought you were making this up."

"He was here," I insisted.

"I really doubt that," she said.

"Then how . . ."

I waved my arms around, frustrated. Then I grabbed her hand and led her into the kitchen. I felt almost childish as I pointed at the book.

"See!"

Before I could realize what she was doing, Zora bent at the waist and scooped the foul thing up.

"That's evidence," I screamed.

Miracle startled. Zora shook her head.

"Sorry," I muttered. "But you shouldn't touch that."

"It's just a book," she said.

"It's his!"

"How do you know that?"

"It's the exact book that Martino told me about. The one I saw at Jasper's house."

Zora frowned. "I don't know anything about that."

"I told you about that."

Her head shook slowly. "No, Theo. You didn't. You've been maverick since we started."

"Seriously?"

"Um, yeah," she said. "But let's worry about that later. You're sure this is his?"

"One hundred percent. He was here."

"He's not anymore," Zora said.

"How do you know that?"

"Because I know he's not stupid. Sick and a total weirdo, but not stupid."

When Zora said that, I noticed something strange. Miracle shot a look at her, the kind that would have made me apologize. Zora saw it and shrugged.

"We'll have to deal with him. Whether we like it or not."

Miracle's eyes narrowed for just a second; then she walked away, moving confidently around my apartment. She said something under her breath, but I couldn't hear it. Then she vaulted up to sit on my kitchen counter.

I still felt inexplicably overwhelmed by her presence. Maybe I knew she was the focal point of the ending I yearned to uncover. Or maybe it was something else. Something I just couldn't explain yet.

"Can I get you something to drink," I finally said.

Miracle smiled. There was something about it. Something natural. It reminded me that she was a real person, with real pain, real love, real loss. She was more than the story. And, in a way, less, maybe.

"Sure," she said. "Maybe water."

I nodded, feeling stupid for some reason. When I got to the kitchen, I threw open a cabinet and realized that Jasper had taken all of my glassware too. The absurdity actually made me laugh.

"Um, sorry, no glasses," I said. Then I turned to Miracle. "Hey, have you spoken to your mother?"

"Excuse me?" she said, her smile gone.

"Your mother. She thinks you're missing."

"I called her," Zora said. "Left a message right after I got ahold of Miracle."

My head tilted. "When was that?"

Zora rolled her eyes. "I knew where she was before all of this. I just thought you were going to drop this project the second you heard about Cassandra."

"So you did know about Cassandra too. Before me?"

"Yup," she answered, unabashed. "You know that already, Theo. Remember? But when Jasper got out of prison, I couldn't mess around. I went to get her."

"She saved me," Miracle said, mockingly.

"I didn't say that," Zora said softly.

"I know," Miracle said. "I just feel like my life has turned into a movie."

Zora shrugged. "It has."

To my surprise, Miracle laughed. "You're right. I guess it has."

My head was spinning. Our small gathering felt unnaturally familiar all of a sudden. I wanted to ask Miracle about her child. How she had just left him. But I stopped myself.

"You seem really relaxed, considering," I did say.

"God, Theo," Zora said. "You just can't stop yourself."

"I'm fine," Miracle said. "I mean, I'm pretty shaken. He's out there. I know he is. But he has no reason to be interested in me. He doesn't even know I exist."

"I'm not so sure about that," I said.

Miracle glanced at Zora before saying, "Maybe."

"Yeah," I said. "In fact, he threatened to kill me if I talked to you."

I saw the first flash of fear touch her eyes. A hint of vulnerability. And it helped center me. Bring me back to what was important.

"Can I ask you something?"

Zora interrupted before Miracle could respond.

"You two are going to stay right here, with the door locked. I'm going to the police. Let them know about what happened here. I have a contact that will take it seriously. I'll bring him back; then we'll go from there. Good?"

"Yeah," I said, then pointed at the book she still carried under her arm. "Are you taking that with you?"

"Yup. Otherwise, they'll never believe this one. You two behave while I'm gone."

My cheeks burned when she said that. Miracle just laughed, vaulting off the counter and locking the door after Zora left.

*   *   *

"Are you upset that your mother talked to me?" I asked.

It had been ten minutes since we were left alone. Although I took a seat on the counter across from her, by the sink, neither of us had said a word. I'd started to think Miracle was just a tough case. She'd been hurt at a young age. I saw it all the time. The walls had been built. And those eyes of hers were probably enough to keep everyone at a distance, unsure what she might do next.

When I spoke, she just stared through me. Then, Miracle blinked. When her eyes reopened, they had changed. Somehow those weapons had become windows. And I knew that her pain wasn't as far from the surface as I had first thought.

"No," she answered softly. "You're not the first, either. When they identified my mother, my biological mother, every reporter in the world called me. Called my mom. It was crazy."

"I guess . . . that's probably not cool."

"No, it's not."

For a second, I found myself soul searching, seeing my career in a new light. It sounds strange, but she had that way about her. With just a few words, she turned people inward. But not necessarily in a bad way. It was more like a shot of sudden honesty. Luckily for me, she let me off the hook immediately.

"I'm not saying that about what you do. I've had two people want me in their documentary. One back then, and someone right before Zora found me."

I leaned forward. "Seriously? What was her name?"

"I didn't say it was a woman," she said, smiling. "Anyway you guys are different. More professional. Less like vultures."

"Thanks," I said, still feeling sick.

I'd had no idea. I should have. Or, at the very least, Kent should have known. He should have told me someone had already worked on a piece of the story. But maybe, like me, he hadn't connected the dots.

Miracle smiled at me. "I mean it. But I guess it's all got me thinking. Since I . . . found out about my biological mother, I also found out what happened to her. I couldn't really accept that, I guess. I didn't know what to do with it. I'd wanted to know who she was. Why she . . . I don't know. But you want to know the worst part? I should have felt sad for her. About what happened to her. But I didn't." A nervous laugh burst out. "That probably sounds horrible."

"No," I said, feeling a little choked up. "Not at all."

Miracle watched me for a second. There was more to Miracle Jones. In that moment, I knew it for certain. Then she smiled again, and those kinds of thoughts seemed like nothing more than paranoia.

"How did you find out . . . who your real mother was?" I asked quietly.

A darkness crossed her face like a sudden storm. "She wasn't my real mother."

"Sorry, I meant—"

The cloud passed as quickly as it arrived, leaving behind sadness like a faded rainbow.

"It was Meg . . . my real mom," she said, interrupting me. "She gave me a DNA test."

"She mentioned that," I said.

"Wow. Did she tell you the rest?"

"No."

"Well, I guess I might as well."

* * *

ACT TWO/SCENE 10

INT. MIRACLE'S HOME—DAY

Miracle Jones stands alone, crying. Looking at herself in the mirror. Touching her stomach as if it represents both the hope of life and the damnation of the past. A knock sounds on the door. It is her baby's father.

Miracle spit into the plastic vial, no problem. She resealed the box and took it out to the mailbox without a second thought. The next day, her morning sickness was the worst to date. She knelt in the bathroom, dark hair sticking to her left cheek, and she cried. Alone, she sobbed as her dog scratched at the closed door.

She had read the internet. Articles about depression and hormones. Raising a child as a single mother. Her eyes ran along the page and the words simply merged into nonsense, neither touching her nor explaining away the crushing weight that only grew heavier every day.

Standing, she looked at herself in the mirror. Her face was pale, even for the season. Tears clung to her eyelashes, making them look even longer than usual. Her mother had very short, light lashes. Her father barely had them at all. She'd noticed that long ago. How different she was from them.

As if on cue, someone knocked on her door. Max went insane, his bark mixed with a deep growl as he scurried away from the bathroom to the front of the apartment. She heard his alert turn to a frantic whine. It was someone he knew. Her mother, probably.

After a pause while she considered cleaning herself up, Miracle simply shook her head. She moved to the front door, wondering why Meg had come to visit. Then she saw him through the clear glass panel of her storm, and her nausea flared back up.

"Hey," he said, just loud enough to hear over Max's racket. "You going to let me in?"

For a second she didn't say anything. Instead she stared at him, taking in his square jaw that jutted out in perpetual challenge. His light eyes that countered his dark hair and thick, perfectly groomed shadow. The way his lips curled up, the opposite of her resting frown. For a second she saw both herself as she had looked in the mirror a moment before and his face, merging, becoming one, becoming a new life, a life that still grew inside her.

"Hey, Eddie," she said finally, then added without opening the door, "I guess we need to talk."

*   *   *

Miracle had been dating Edwin Marcone for a little less than a year. He'd been the perfect match, exactly what she'd been looking for at the time. Fun, beautiful, tall, free, and living over an hour away. They saw each other on her terms, mostly. He'd come down a dozen times. They had met in Philadelphia more than that. Miracle had kept that fact from her mother the entire time. Meg Jones wasn't fond of her daughter visiting Wilmington. The idea of Miracle driving up to Philly, alone, not to mention meeting a boy there, would have given her a heart attack.

Max felt none of her trepidations. He bounced, all four paws leaving the floor, over and over in a frantic circle around Eddie. Miracle didn't move. Eddie tried to hug her, but the dog made that impossible.

So he gave in, dropping to his knees and letting Max unleash a proper greeting.

"It's good to see you too, buddy," he said, hands on the sides of Max's wrinkled face. "I missed you."

"You're the only one he acts like this with," she said. "Other than me."

"I told you I was a good guy," Eddie said.

"Yeah." Miracle moved away, back toward the bathroom. "Give me a second."

She stood in front of the mirror again. She could hear Eddie and the dog playing, his nails scratching up the hardwood even more. The sound gave her no joy. Instead, she stared into her own dark, unblinking eyes. The weight pressed even harder, like it might crush her soul.

He would stand by me.

He would be a good dad.

Meg would be an even better grandmother.

The thoughts peppered her like machine-gun fire. But they meant nothing compared to the other one. That one hung right behind her eyes, a throbbing cloud of pain and fear and confusion. No matter how hard she tried, she could not force together the pieces of that puzzle. She couldn't put it into words. Yet the more it pushed back on those other thoughts, the more it took over the basic commands of her life.

Like an automaton, she cleaned her face, brushed her teeth, put her hair up, and left the bathroom. Eddie had taken a seat on the couch, and Max took a seat atop Eddie. They were both all smiles and tail wags, but that lasted only a second. With one look at her, the mood changed to match her own.

"We need to talk."

Eddie frowned. "Yeah, you said that already."

"Let's go into town."

He nodded. Gently, Eddie slid the dog off his lap and got up. He followed Miracle outside and down the steps. When she headed toward her car, he paused.

"Am I coming with you?"

"We should probably both drive," she said.

"It's that bad, huh?"

Miracle didn't answer. Instead, she got behind the wheel and pulled off, alone.

* * *

"I'm pregnant."

Miracle dropped it like a bomb the second they took their seats outside the café. A woman at the table next to them stiffened, obviously overhearing. Eddie glanced at her, then at Miracle.

"I had a feeling," he said; then his expression turned very serious. "I'm excited. I think this is great. I—"

"I'm getting an abortion," she said flatly.

The woman behind them actually gasped. Eddie didn't. He froze, his mouth open, his eyes wide, his breath caught up by the sudden announcement. For her part, Miracle stared back, defiant, daring him to question her. That dark cloud had fully taken over. It called the shots, while she struggled against it like the bars of a prison cell.

"You're not serious," he said.

The storm raged inside her head. The real her tried to take it back. Tried to tell Eddie that she loved him. That she would have his baby. But the other thing was ready to fight, to push him away, forever. To be alone, like she'd been so long ago.

"Say something," he said.

But she couldn't. No words could escape that raging battle inside her.

A deep red spread across his face. "What gives you the right?"

"Just go, Eddie."

The words slipped out like shards of ice. He stared into her eyes and found nothing he recognized. As if in a daze, she rose, turned her back on him, and walked away.

"You can't do this," he called after her.

She didn't turn back. "Yes, I can."

*　　*　　*

Weeks ground by. Miracle noted ever passing minute as if it were a black *X* on a calendar. Every day she checked her email. Some days she didn't even know what she was waiting for. Other days, the anticipation, the need—it burned like fire.

On a Thursday, when time had finally turned into the kind of torture that she would not survive, she went on the internet. She searched on *abortion*. The responses broke her heart, but she scrolled through each. Then she searched on *abortion maximum weeks*. She clicked on the first link, and the tears started. With them came a helpless anger. If someone threatened her, she would fight. She would win. But how could Miracle defeat herself?

Max whined, but she didn't notice. Instead, she went to the web page for the genetic testing company and found a phone number. When she called, a very friendly representative answered.

"Can I help you?"

Miracle almost hung up.

"Hello?"

With effort, she broke through the pain and spoke. "Yeah, hi."

"Hi," the woman said. "How can I help you?"

"I . . . took a test. Three weeks ago. I know the instructions say it could take eight weeks, but . . ."

"Yeah," the woman said. "I understand. It's hard to wait. But we have a queue that—"

"I'm pregnant," Miracle blurted.

"Okay," the woman said, uncertain.

"I . . . I don't know how to explain this. But I . . . might need to . . . have an abortion."

"Oh! I don't know—"

"Please, wait. I know. This isn't your problem or anything, but . . ."

"Are you worried about the baby's health? Is that it?"

Miracle closed her eyes, seeing the truth within that darkness. "Yes . . . Yeah, that's it. I . . ."

"It's okay," the woman said. "I totally understand. Let me get your information."

Miracle gave her everything. Then she paused.

"I'm not asking for anything, really. I guess I just wanted to see if—"

"Miracle, I will do whatever it takes to save your baby. If that means I need to risk my job, I'll do it."

"I don't—"

"It's God's will, sweetie."

Miracle had no idea what to say. Therefore, she said nothing as the woman spoke to herself.

"Let's see what we have here . . . Yeah, here's your file. Your test has been processed, but the data hasn't been entered. You . . . Wait, I think there's a mistake. You only purchased the ancestry test, not the medical screening. . . . Miracle, are you there?"

"Yeah," she said, feeling dizzy. "I didn't know."

The woman didn't say anything for a moment. When she spoke, her voice sounded airy, almost ethereal.

"This is my time. I understand that now. I am going to upgrade this as our mistake. And rush the response. It will take a few days to get the sample reprocessed. But I'll check every day. You just hold off. Don't do anything you'll regret. Can you promise me that?"

The nausea threatened to double her over. Sweat dampened her face. Max licked her hand, manically.

"I will," she whispered. "Um, you said that the ancestry portion of the test has already been processed?"

"It has. But that won't have the information you need, sweetie."

"I just . . . it would help . . . to see that. . . . It would help me wait for the . . . rest."

"Oh," the woman said. "Okay, I guess. I can get that done. Today, maybe. If you think it would help."

"It would."

"Okay, then. Because all that matters is that beautiful baby of yours. Have you decided on a name?"

"I . . ."

"You need to give her a name. Mary would be nice. Your daughter, Mary."

"Yeah," Miracle said.

"God bless you, Miracle. And God bless Mary too."

"Thank you."

The call ended, and Miracle barely made it to the bathroom before she got sick.

*   *   *

The results showed up in Miracle's email less than an hour later. Her finger, which felt disembodied, hovered over the link to her identity. The moment dragged, as if her reality and the truth battled to a bloody stalemate. The protective wall her younger self had built, the barrier that had kept her questions at bay for so long, still stood. It still ruled. Yet a new force pushed against it. Something far bigger than Miracle could have summoned on her own. This power radiated from her core as her other hand gently cupped her stomach.

That was enough. It was everything. The pad of her index finger touched the screen. Like a flash of lightning, the page opened. Lost, she scrolled down, barely noticing the percentages of her heritage. Instead, her eyes searched for something else, something more real. When she saw the word RELATIVES, her heart nearly stopped. Regardless, the momentum of her search could not be dulled. She followed that link, and a list of names appeared on the screen.

Strangers. All strangers. Miracle swiped down. Names like Taylor and Crestworth. Henshaw and Foote. She scanned, her eyes burning. Jones was a common name. Almost as common as Smith. Even if it showed up on her list, it would mean nothing, statistically. Yet she needed it to be there. She needed one tether, no matter how thin, to tell her that maybe everything wouldn't change. That somehow she could be the person she wanted to be.

The distance of the relatives advanced. She passed third cousins, fourth, and still nothing. Tears clouded her vision, so much so that she could hardly see the screen. Still she searched, until the names ran out.

Miracle's hand shook more severely. She froze, staring through the screen, through time, back across an endless field of falsehood and lies. The list told her so little. It revealed an empty series of words. Nothing more. That was the truth of it. But to her, Miracle Jones died that day. At the same time, a new life came into existence. Like the birth of any newborn, however, this life remained blank, unwritten. As Miracle closed her eyes, she wondered if she had the strength to fill these new pages. She wondered if it was even worth it.

* * *

Hours later, she lay in bed, staring up at nothing, feeling nothing. The names clung to her, though she wished for a time that they wouldn't. She wondered what she had expected to find. What silver bullet could have appeared on that tiny screen that might have changed anything. Something that could have answered the questions that had burned a hole into her soul since the day she'd figured out she was pregnant.

Nothing. It showed nothing. It meant nothing. She rolled onto her side and Max groaned, shifting to press back up against the warmth of her body. When Miracle rose, he whimpered, as if sensing what was next.

The house was dark by then. She shuffled out to the couch, bending over to grab her phone off the floor. Miracle sat, her eyes intense and fixed, as she searched for the nearest clinic. Without a thought, she called the number. It went to a messaging service, and she hung up. Then she noticed the time: 2:34 AM.

"Shit," she hissed.

It was time. She didn't care about the test, about Eddie, or about Meg. Her decision was made.

No matter how much Miracle told herself that, some deeper instinct disagreed. She found herself opening the test results again, going to the list of relatives. This time she started at the top, focusing on the first name on the list: Roberta "Bunny" Henshaw. Opening another browser page, she Googled the name. Bunny lived no more than twenty miles away. The results said that Bunny was her aunt. Her mother's sister.

Miracle dug deeper, stalking Bunny as well as other genetic relatives. Maybe she dozed off. Maybe not. Eventually the sun came up. The clinic opened. But she didn't call back. Not that morning. Instead, still in the clothes she'd worn the day before, she grabbed her keys off the hook by the door and put Bunny's address in her GPS.

* * *

The trailer sat alone on a swampy lot adjacent to the Delaware-Maryland border. A rotting plank walk led from the gravel drive over the muddy pine needles to a front entrance painted a sun-faded pink. A pickup rested on three wheels and a stack of cinder blocks in the side yard, and a dog barked from where it was chained in the back. Miracle reached out to knock, but the door opened before she could. A woman stared out at her, defiant.

"What do you want?"

"I . . . I'm looking for Roberta Henshaw."

"You a bill collector?"

"No."

"That's the only folks who use that name."

Miracle dug her nails into the sides of her jeans. "I'm . . . my name is Miracle Jones. I—"

"What kinda name is . . ."

The woman trailed off. She stared at Miracle for a time, suspicion rearranging the deep lines of her face.

"You were that Miracle Baby?"

Miracle nodded. "Yeah."

Roberta's head tilted, but her eyes narrowed. "I read about you. A long time ago. Why'd you come around here?"

"I . . . I took a DNA test, and I . . ."

Without meaning to, Miracle looked around her. She took in the condition of the trailer, the truck. She heard the dog baying in the back.

She turned back to Roberta, noticing her frayed housedress. Her bare feet.

"I'm sorry," she said, backing up.

"Hold up," Roberta said, stepping out onto the planking. The look on her face had shifted, turning to an urgent need. "You took that test? And I showed up?"

"Yes," Miracle said. "I think . . ."

"Roberta 'Bunny' Henshaw?"

Miracle went still. "Yes."

"Ha! I never even seen my own test," she said. "When my sister went missing, a friend of the family, the lady our mamma cleaned houses for, paid for it. But I lost my job and had to move out of the house I was renting. Forgot all about it."

"Your sister went missing?"

"Yeah, Honey . . . I mean, Abbie Henshaw. She went missing a . . . long time back."

Miracle fought through her demons to ask, "How long ago . . . did she disappear?"

"Just over twenty years now."

They stared at each other for a moment. The pieces fell into place.

"I . . . I think you're my aunt."

"Seems I am."

"Do you know—"

"Honey," the woman said, shaking her head. "That's what we called your mamma. She was Honey and I was Bunny."

"She . . ."

"Come on in, child. We have a lot to talk about."

13

I LOOKED INTO MIRACLE'S eyes. "So, that was before you knew?"

Miracle laughed. It wasn't a bitter sound, not entirely. "Yeah."

"Have you, like, built a relationship with her?"

"I have," Miracle said, distantly. "It's weird. She's so different than I am. I try to find something. There has to be some trait that we share. But it's hard."

"Did she tell you about your mother?"

"She did."

I waited, needing way more than that. Miracle looked away, staring out through the window across from the counter. The questions built up inside me. But I kept them inside. Plotting the interview in my mind.

"At the time, all Bunny knew was that her sister went missing. She didn't even know about the pregnancy."

"How'd they find out . . . ?" I asked.

I meant to finish the question. Ask her what had led to the police identifying her mother as the Halo Killer's first victim. But I couldn't get those words out. Not sitting face-to-face with her. Instead, I slipped down to the floor and moved toward where my bed had once rested. Each footstep echoed. I touched the wall against which my corkboard used to lean. My eyes closed, and I could see it again. Along with the boxes of files I'd compiled. My hand patted the pocket with my phone. At least I had all the recordings. And all the footage. Everything wasn't lost, not yet.

"Have you met him?" Miracle asked.

I spun around and found those eyes trained on me.

"Jasper? Yes."

"Is he as scary as they say?"

I nodded. "Worse."

I felt uncomfortable again, so I moved to the window, laying my palms on the sill.

"Did Bunny help you decide to keep the baby?"

Silence. I turned, and Miracle's stare withered me.

"I didn't say that," she said, toneless.

"Sorry." I looked away. "I met your son. And I understand. I do. What happened to you is wrong. What Jasper did was—"

"He didn't do anything to me," she snapped. "I was already left behind. Tossed away. My mother coughed me out and spit me in a fucking sink."

I flinched. Her anger was so raw. So visceral. I wanted to apologize again. Hang my head in shame. But then, work took over. Something Jasper had said to me came back with a jolt.

"No," I said. "You don't know that. He told me about that night. When he . . . found your mother. She was on the beach, Miracle. Not a mile from where you were born. It was that night. Your mother had no chance to change her mind. Maybe she would—"

"He's lying," she said, the words cutting through the air between us. "That's all he does."

I blinked. "I thought you never met him."

"I haven't," she said.

I stared at Miracle, and it was her turn to look away under my scrutiny. My instincts fired across ever nerve of my body.

I was right!

From the very beginning, I'd known. She'd met Jasper and was lying about it. My gut had me certain. With that confirmed, it was easy to assume she had been that woman on the beach, the one from Jasper's first story. Her slipup proved it to me. Maybe Jasper had lied. Maybe that night had never happened. But he'd met her. I was sure of it now. I had to turn away to hide the smile on my face.

"I want to help you find your ending," I said.

And I waited. She would say something if I stayed quiet long enough. It's the oldest interview trick in the book. But that day it failed miserably. Not a minute after I put the bait out there, someone pounded on the door.

"Come on," Zora yelled from the other side. "We need to go. Now!"

14

"**H**URRY!"

Zora reached out for Miracle's hand as she passed me. They ran down the hallway, toward the exit. I watched for a second, confused by how familiar that gesture appeared.

"Come on!" Zora snapped at me.

Her tone forced me to move. I bounced off the doorjamb getting out of the empty apartment and caught up quickly as they reached the stairs.

"Are the police here?"

"No," Zora said.

Then she stopped on the steps. Her finger came up to her lips. My mouth opened, and she hissed at me.

"What?" I whispered.

Zora moved like a flash. One second she was a good ten feet away from me. The next, her face was so close to mine that I could smell her breath—coffee and Altos. She gripped my shoulder, pulling me so that her blazing eyes leveled with mine.

"This is serious," she said.

"Then tell me—"

A scream cut me off. I jumped. Zora spun around, focusing on the floor below us, where the sound seemed to have come from.

"Shit! Hurry."

Even I ran then. All my questions were gone as a second scream, definitely from the seventh floor, ripped into the stairwell. Grabbing the railing, I vaulted around that landing and left the sound behind.

"Is it Jasper?" I called out.

Zora kept running, Miracle right in front of her. We broke into the lobby and straight through it out onto the sidewalk. As the cool air hit my face, so did the whine of approaching sirens. I slowed, thinking that was a good thing. But Zora kept jogging down the block.

"The police," I said.

She didn't respond. Instead, she disappeared around the corner. I sprinted after them. When I reached the intersection, I saw them a distance ahead. I had no choice but to follow.

"What the hell," I muttered.

At the next crosswalk, Zora turned. She waited for me, which was something, at least.

"What is going on?"

"I was on the way to the Midtown precinct on Fifty-Fourth. I decided to listen to the police scanner. I wasn't four blocks away when someone in your building called the cops. They reported a suspicious man in the hallway. Short, with a shaved head and pale complexion."

"Oh God," I said.

"Yeah, so I came back for you two. I had to. We need to keep moving, though."

"Yeah," I said. "Definitely."

He's there. He was after Miracle. And he was close. The strange thing is, I didn't feel afraid. Not at all. I felt excited. A part of me wanted to turn around. Go back and find him. With Miracle. Be there for the confrontation. For the answers. Instead, I turned on my phone video camera, documenting our escape.

"Let's go," she ordered.

"Where?"

"Out of the city. Too many eyes here. We'll find somewhere random and safe, then plan our next move."

"We could go to the police," I said.

Miracle jumped into the conversation. "No."

"Why?" I asked, suspicious.

"Let's just get out of here. The police will think we're crazy."

"They just got a call that Jasper was seen in my building. They'll believe us."

Miracle's hands balled into fists at her side. For a second, before she turned away, I thought she might hit me. But Zora stepped in.

"We can do both. Let's get across the water. Then we'll decide."

"But—"

"You don't know everything, Theo."

"What's that supposed to mean?"

"Maybe she"—Zora nodded her head back toward Miracle—"doesn't want to go to the police because she doesn't want them to know where she is."

"That doesn't make any sense."

Zora rolled her eyes. "Her mother reported her missing. If they find her here, can you image the news stories? We need to figure out how to deal with all this . . . quietly. Are you in or not?"

"What's that supposed to mean?"

"Theo, we don't have time for this. Not in the middle of the street. If you want to go to the police, fine. Just don't mention her. Otherwise, come with us now. And we'll talk it all through once we find a safe spot."

I stared at her. That wasn't really a choice. There was no way I was leaving them now. Not until I had my ending. So I just kept filming.

15

"I GOT US ADJOINING rooms," Zora said, walking away from the front desk of the Residence Inn just across the river in New Jersey.

"Who's rooming?" I asked.

For a second, I thought she was going to say the two of us. That would have been awkward. But when she pointed at herself and Miracle, it somehow felt more so. It made perfect sense, in a way. But I remembered the way Zora had taken Miracle's hand.

"You two?" I asked.

"I'm not rooming with you," Zora said harshly.

"Yeah . . ." I let it go, for the moment. "What's that running us?"

"You can write it off."

I followed her to the elevator and to the room without saying another word. Honestly, a severe annoyance had been growing since we'd talked at the crosswalk. It wasn't just that conversation; it was everything. Things were out of control. In the silence, it was all piling up. Miracle, Zora, Cassandra. Bender and Pepper. I was on the run. That maniac had been in my building. Broken into my apartment. Stolen all my stuff. He'd left that damn book. Could one man, no matter how notorious, be behind all of that?

Then there was Miracle. Ever since we'd spoken, something had been gnawing at me. Maybe even before that. When she walked into my apartment, I had expected a victim. A scared, traumatized young woman. Instead she had seemed relaxed, or oblivious. Then there was what she'd said—*He was lying. That's all he does.* She knew Jasper. She'd spoken to him. Yet when I called her on it, she'd lied to me.

Lost in thought, I stepped through the door behind Miracle. Zora turned, a hand on her hip.

"You're next door," she said.

"Oh, I thought we were going to talk."

She smiled. "We will, but first you need to sleep."

"I do?"

"Look."

She pointed at the mirrored closet door. I took another step and turned. It would be totally cliché to say I didn't recognize the face that stared back at me. But I certainly looked awful. Even the bags under my eyes had turned a sickly gray. Veins nearly filled the whites of my eyes. For some reason, I stuck my tongue out. It seemed fine.

As I stood there, the exhaustion hit me, hard. I shuffled back toward the hallway.

"Yeah, that sounds like a plan."

Zora's head shook as she handed me the key card. "You'll need this."

*   *   *

The call tore me out of a deep, surprisingly dreamless sleep. My phone vibrated on the nightstand. I swiped at it, knocking it to the floor. I had to slide off the bed to find it. With a quick glance at the unfamiliar number, I answered.

"This is Theo Snyder."

I heard the hiss of breath before his voice filled my head. "Hello, Theodore."

"Jasper!" I scurried across the floor until my back pressed against the bed. "Where are you?"

"Now that's a strange question," he said.

My head spun. I pulled back the phone and checked the screen again. I'd never seen the number before, but it was a Manhattan exchange. At the same time, his voice sounded strange, distant.

"Are you on speaker?" I asked, distracted.

"Theodore, follow me, please."

"I want my stuff back! My files. My corkboard. I don't give a shit about the furniture."

Jasper didn't say anything right away. When he did, I swear he sounded concerned.

"You're not well," he said softly. "I think you've fallen down the rabbit hole."

"What's that supposed to mean?"

"I think you know," he said.

I rubbed at my eyes, digging into the sockets like I might mine the confusion from my head. Nothing made sense.

"I need my stuff, Jasper," I said instead.

"I don't have anything of yours," he said. "I owe you the conclusion to a story, however."

"What?" I asked, unable to hide the hunger I felt.

"Don't you remember our first conversation? I didn't finish that time. You'll find that I am a man of my word."

"Jasper, I—"

He didn't let me get another word out.

* * *

ACT TWO/SCENE 13

EXT. BEACH—NIGHT

We return to where our story began. The dark figure on the dune is the Halo Killer. His senses are keen, focused on his prey. Seemingly unaware, a woman moves along the surf, dangerously close to her fate. In the pale light of the moon, we see a neon yellow Sony Walkman on her head. A CHYRON appears on the screen: AUGUST 12, 2016.

Jasper stood among the daylilies at the top of the dune, watching her. The moon hung in the lightening sky, casting a pale shine around his long, dark shadow. The woman neared, moving along the surf line, her head down. He blinked, and as his eyes closed, Jasper could have sworn he heard the faint echo of classical music floating across the beach from her neon-yellow earphones.

In that moment, he forgot the other one. At the time, he didn't know her name was Barbara Yost. Nor did he care about that. But he'd never forgotten one in the middle of the process. Before the question was even asked. He'd never skipped a single step, no matter how minor. He needed to get back. Shape and freeze the daylily. Secure the building for the night. Incinerate the clothes he wore.

Instead, his intricate plans slipped away. Jasper took a step down the dune. He angled to cut this new target off, without even a thought of how he would take her. How unplanned it would be. How much evidence he would leave behind. Nothing seemed to matter. Nothing but an overwhelming need to lay his hands on her. To wrap his fingers around her wrist. To pull her out of her world and into his. To ask her. To hear her answer.

His pace quickened, and a new realization dawned. It came out of the darkest corners of his past. Like a crack of warm light under the door of a lonely closet. Like the soft whisper of a mother never heard. The feeling filled him at once with hope and searing need. After all the others, Jasper knew somehow that this one *had* the answer. Maybe it was finally over.

He stared at her. There was no subtlety to his hunt this time. Only a shining lust. And she never looked up. She never seemed to notice. She moved ever closer, oblivious to her starring role in the final act.

To his surprise, saliva filled Jasper's mouth. The muscles in both of his forearms cramped. He did not flinch. He didn't slow as she came to him. As she . . .

The woman stopped, carelessly turning and heading back the way she came. Her movement, so sudden yet so benign, startled him. He froze, his toes digging into the soft, pale sand. His body reacted first, spinning and following her, cutting the angle to intercept her. Speeding up. But his mind faltered.

Did she see me?

Does she know?

In all the years, Jasper had never questioned himself. He'd never doubted. His life churned like some faultless machine, ever forward, never changing. The questions that plagued him seemed so foreign. As if they belonged to someone else. As he closed the distance between them, he had time to consider it all. She was just a woman walking on the beach. Like all the others.

Then he saw it. Maybe he had before. It hung in a soft arc from her left hand, a freshly cut daylily. It was perfect. The yellow as bright as flame. The stem cut to the exact length. His heart seemed to stiffen behind his breastbone, like it might never beat again. The air left his lungs in a rush, and he couldn't find the strength to take more in to replace it. Jasper's step faltered, the tip of his sandal catching in the dry sand. He reached the edge of the surf, but she moved faster than he would have thought. He still wasn't close.

Overwhelmed, he stopped. The ocean hissed closer, reaching for his feet. He didn't move as the water kissed his skin. At the same time, the woman turned again. She moved up onto the drier sand, cutting across the beach toward a path over the dunes. The flower casually dangling at her side.

Jasper needed to follow. He needed to hurry. But he couldn't move. He couldn't believe it was real. That this woman existed. It had to be a dream. The flower had to be a figment of the past, an omen to the end. She had to be a ghost. The first. That woman, Abbie Henshaw, the one he had just read about in the news.

Impossible. He stood still as the cool water washed back over his feet. His eyes shut, and he kept them closed for a beat. Taking in a deep breath, he opened them again.

She was still there, still moving toward the winding path. He stared as her head turned. Through the predawn gloom, her eyes met his. Jasper was sure of it. She looked at him. And he saw her. He saw through her dark eyes. He saw inside her. And he needed more.

Jasper broke into an awkward sprint. His hands flapped at his side as he dug into the softening sand. Within a second, he was panting. His cheeks burned. Sweat dotted every inch of his smooth skin. He moaned, gasped, pushing himself, willing himself to move faster. To catch her. To have her.

The woman disappeared over the dune. Jasper stumbled, falling to his knees. But he sprang back up. Staggering, fighting to keep his balance. He cursed under his breath, something he never did. When he reached the dune, his heart beat painfully against his bones. Gasping, he reached the crest in time to see a nondescript sedan rolling out of the small parking lot.

Jasper stopped at the top of the rise. His eyes locked on to the car until it disappeared, heading north on the highway. Then he doubled over, almost falling to the ground. He heaved and groaned again. Unable to catch his breath, he sank to the sand. Sitting, hard, he hung his head between his knees. His vision swirled and darkened at the edges. For a minute, he was sure he would lose consciousness. That he would pass out, only to be awakened by the hand of a police officer. A stranger who would expose his world, lay it bare before everyone's judgement. And, for a flash, he had no fight left inside to stop it.

Jasper hurried down the dune and into the lot. Slowing, he walked to the spot from which he'd seen the car pull out. He knelt, even before he noticed the light from the rising sun striking the shining surface of a plastic card lying in the gravel like a calling card. His fingers pinched the corner and picked it up before he registered it as the key to a motel room. He read the name on the front in flowing script, and recognized it. Yet his brain made no connection, not at first. Instead, it drowned under the most basic of realizations—that nothing would ever be the same again.

16

"I KNEW IT," I blurted out, the phone pressed against my burning cheek. "The woman on the beach was Miracle, wasn't it?"

The phone line crackled. I heard static in the background as I held my breath, needing to know.

"A miracle," Jasper said, sounding lost.

"No, I mean the girl on the beach. It was Miracle Jones. The daughter of your first victim."

"You're not listening, Theodore."

"I am! I know she met you. I know she lied to me."

"Maybe she did," Jasper said. "Maybe I am."

"What does that even mean? Just tell me, was it her? Did you find her?"

There was a pause before Jasper spoke. In it, I could almost see his face, his birdlike eyes growing distant, vulnerable even.

"It's almost over. I've searched for so long. For so many years. For so many lives. And all I know, all I can tell you, is one thing. Some questions are better left unanswered."

The line went dead.

"Jasper! Jasper!"

There was no response. I dialed the number back, but no one picked up. As I ended the call, someone pounded on the adjoining door. I startled.

"What?"

"Open the door!" Zora called out.

I got up, cursing under my breath. It took me a minute to fiddle with the lock. When I got it, she burst into my room like some Wild West sheriff.

"What happened?"

"Huh?" I muttered.

"I heard you yelling his name. I thought he found us."

"Jasper?"

"Jesus, Theo. Yes. What is wrong with you?"

I tried to tell her about the call. Before my mouth could open, though, Miracle followed her into the room. Her dark eyes locked on to mine, and Jasper's words swarmed my head, but suspicion kept my mouth closed. Dark eyes . . . I knew she'd lied to me.

"I must have been dreaming."

Zora focused on me, into me, searching for something. I shivered, like a snake trying to free itself from its old skin. I swear she nodded. It was slight, barely a tip of the head, but I saw it. I know I did. And it gave me the strength for what I did next.

"I need to talk to you," I said, with a conspiratorial twitch of the eye. "Alone."

Zora blinked. "About what?"

"About the project."

"You really think we have time for that?"

"Jasper just called," I whispered.

She stared back at me for a second, then turned to Miracle.

"I'm sorry. Do you mind waiting for us in our room?"

"Sure," Miracle said, clearly uncomfortable. "But I think we should keep moving."

"We will," Zora said.

I just nodded. Once Miracle was gone and the door between the two rooms shut, I didn't hold back.

"She's lying to us," I blurted out.

Her jaw clenched. "Really?"

"I know she seems all innocent, but—"

"Do you ever think about anyone but yourself?"

Zora's words felt like a slap. I wavered, despite the confidence I had felt only a minute earlier.

"I . . . I'm not saying . . ."

"What are you saying, Theo?"

"I know she's been through a lot and all. With her mom. And—"

"You mean the part about being left in a sink for four days, or the part about her mother being murdered by a serial killer?"

I put my hands up. "Come on. I know that. I do. I just . . . She told me that she's never met him—Jasper. But it was a lie. I'm sure of it."

Zora stiffened. I had pushed her to an edge. I could feel the tension between us, and I knew I'd fractured her internal need to save me from myself.

"You're telling me that Miracle met the Halo Killer? And when do you think this happened? You think she visited him in prison? I can make a call, find out in a second, if that's really what you want me to do."

"No," I protested. "Not in prison."

"Jesus! When, last night, then?"

"Before," I said.

Zora moved so quickly. All of a sudden, she had thrust her face within an inch of mine. I startled, trying to move away, but my knees buckled on the mattress. I sat down, hard, and she leaned in closer, over me.

"How the hell would something like that happen? What, you think she hunted him? Who do you think this woman is? Another of your stories? Really, Theo, you're in the wrong business. You should be some two-bit thriller writer, the way your mind makes shit up."

"How dare you!" I sputtered, failing to sound as imposing as I wanted to.

"How dare I? You just accused this woman that we barely know of mysteriously tracking down the most elusive serial killer in history. Finding him. And what? Sitting down for a little chat? And then just walking away? That makes absolutely no sense."

"What if he found her?" I said.

"Why would he—"

"When they identified his first victim. When the article came out identifying his first victim as Abbie Henshaw, Miracle's mother. What if—stay with me here—when he read that, he felt . . . I don't know, threatened? Like she was stealing his attention?"

"Is that what he told you?"

"Um, no. He said he was out getting a flower for Barbara Yost and he saw her on the beach. He followed her to a car. And found a motel key card."

Zora hissed. "Quiet. Come on. That is total bullshit, and you know it. What, is your plan to march in there and confront her? Tell her that crap? Do you have any idea how that would make her *feel?* She's a person, not an actor from one of your reenactments."

"I don't use reenactments," I snapped, offended.

"Get ahold of yourself!"

I shot to my feet so fast that it was her turn to take a step back. "Stop saying that!"

"What?"

"You keep telling me that I don't look good. Telling me I'm diving too deep. That I'm reckless. That I need to get ahold of myself. You know what . . . fuck you!"

I'd finally done it. Zora was speechless. She stared into my eyes for a second. Then she turned and walked away. I was too full of adrenaline to follow. I thought I'd give us both a second to cool down. Then I heard a loud slam. I didn't move, not right away. Instead, I stood still and listened. But after that, there was just silence.

Slowly, I moved to the adjoining door. My hand hovered over the knob for a moment; then I turned it. My side opened. And so did theirs.

"Hello?" I called out softly.

No one answered. When I stepped into the room, it was empty. The only sign that Zora and Miracle had been there was the two key cards thrown on the desk. I knew, right away, that she was gone. That Zora was off the project. And I was alone.

PART THREE

THE QUESTION

1

THE SMILE BEGAN like a thin check mark. Slowly, it lifted one cheek, lightened the creases of my brow. My lips parted and an excited sound slipped out. Not a laugh. More a quiet snort. I was alone. And I felt free.

Like a bullet firing from the barrel of a smoking gun, I moved. In a beat, I had returned to my room. My fingers danced across the surface of the phone, redialing the number from which Jasper had called. The line rang and rang. I was about to give up when someone picked up.

"Hello?"

I didn't recognize the voice, but I could tell it belonged to an older woman, maybe in her seventies.

"Who is this?" I asked.

"This is Edith. Who are you?"

"Edith? Where am I calling?"

"The hallway phone. Look, who do ya want?"

She sounded strange to me. Almost as if she was pretending to have a Brooklyn accent.

"What? I . . . Someone just called me from this number."

"Wasn't me."

I paused. "Did you see anyone? A small guy with kind of orange, stubbly hair? Moves like a bird?"

"No idea. I gotta go."

"Wait. Where . . . what hallway?"

"Huh?"

"What building?"

"Look, this is gettin' weird."

I thought about telling her the truth. That a deadly man had stood exactly where she did moments before. I stopped, though, because she'd call the police. And that wasn't what I wanted. Not anymore.

"Is this Hell's Kitchen?" I paused, and told her the address of my building.

Edith sounded suspicious when she said, "Across da street."

"Shit," I said. "Really?"

"Yeah. Why? What's it to ya?"

"You might want to get out of there."

I ended the call. My eyes narrowed. A new resolve straightened my back. If I had been in my apartment and if Jasper hadn't stolen all of my stuff, I'd have dug into the *why*. Latched on to it and clawed even deeper. Because I felt it. Strong. Something big. I'd been lied to. Misdirected. But these people didn't know who they were dealing with. I was Theo fucking Snyder. I'd made *The Basement*. I'd been underestimated. Maybe used. I knew it. And now I was going to figure out why.

He thought he'd blinded me, but Jasper had made a mistake. I'd lost my papers, but not all the audio and video files on my phone. I lay back against the wall of pillows, slid my dirty shoes up onto the pure white duvet, and went to work.

CHAPTER

2

I DON'T KNOW HOW long I sat there, listening and watching everything. I know I went through most of it at least twice. Some, three times. As is usually the case, what bothered me came up early, in the first few minutes. At the time, I couldn't see it, though. I couldn't put my finger on exactly what it was. Not until I stopped for a moment, closing my eyes and feeling the air fill my chest and slip from my body.

"Too many coincidences," I whispered.

With a burst of action, I sprang to my feet, snatching the hotel notepad off the desk. The pen was a cheap ballpoint, but it worked. I needed to get organized, wrap my head around the complicated net that had draped over me and my life. So, I did what I always did when starting a project. The ballpoint seemed to dance across the page like I wasn't even in control.

TIMELINE
1996

- *Jasper records himself performing a forensics study at his home*
  The next day the Miracle Baby is born
  The Halo Killer takes his first victim

2012

- *A police officer links the 1996 killing of Jane Doe to the Halo Killer*

2016

- *Miracle finds out she is pregnant*
- *Meg gives Miracle a DNA test*
- *Miracle learns her mother's name—Abbie Henshaw*
- *Abbie Henshaw is identified as the Halo Killer's first victim*
- *Jasper is arrested*

I stared at the last two bullets. Something clicked. I grabbed my phone and searched the internet to find the article linking Abbie Henshaw to Jasper. I didn't reread it. Instead, I just checked the date: July 15, 2016. From memory, I knew that Jasper had been arrested August 14, 2016. A month later . . .

When my phone rang, I startled and sent the phone flopping to the mattress. I scooped it back up and saw the number. It was a New Jersey exchange. My heart beat in my chest as I tried to convince myself it was just Zora coming to her senses. Realizing she was being played. But even before I answered, I knew.

"Hello, Theodore," the raspy, thin voice of the Halo Killer greeted me.

I should have hung up. And run. I still wasn't sure how much time had passed, but he was in New Jersey. Closer.

My addiction called the shots, though. I just needed to know more.

"Was it the article that led you to Miracle?"

Jasper laughed. It sounded distant again, like he was holding the receiver away from his face.

"Really? That's your question for me?'

"I need to know," I said.

"We have more in common than you might think. It's a hunger, yes? You have to feed it. Or it will turn inward and devour you."

"The article, Jasper!"

He laughed softly. "You want to know about Abbie Henshaw? What it felt like to take her life?"

A cold sweat suddenly covered my body. "Jasper, I—"

His chilling voice interrupted me. "Then I'll tell you."

* * *

ACT THREE/SCENE 1

EXT. BEACH—NIGHT

Jasper Ross-Johnson stands over the battered, half-naked body of his first victim. In that moment, the HALO KILLER is born.

On that day, over twenty years earlier, Jasper Ross-Johnson became the Halo Killer. He stood over her, mesmerized by the frailty of her bone-thin arms. The way her knees bent almost backward. He'd never known eyes could grow that wide. That someone could fight for life with such determination. The hunger still rang between his ears. It filled his skull, sending undeniable pulses throughout his nervous system, directly to the tips of his fingers as he pressed harder, closing her airway. It could not be denied. He thought it couldn't be stopped. Then her lips parted in an odd way. Her tongue rolled in her mouth, as if she was attempting to make words out of the vacuum of deep space.

His head tilted. She attempted to speak. She had something to say. The urge battled his curiosity. Maybe the question had already formed in his head, without his realization. Whatever drove him in that moment, it didn't matter. His grip loosened and she coughed.

In her struggle, the string bikini top slipped from her chest. Some base instinct must have guided her fingers as they sought to cover her bare skin. He looked down, disinterested, until he saw the bloodstain on her tattered jean shorts.

"I didn't do that," he said, more to himself.

She gagged and gasped, clawing along the rocky surface of the jetty, trying to get away. Gently, almost lovingly, his fingers wrapped around her throat again. He felt the muscles of her neck tighten in protest, yet he didn't squeeze. Not yet.

"What did you say?" he asked.

"Please," she sputtered. "Please."

"No!" His voice rose.

She recoiled, her eyes even wider. His anger grew. With it, the hunger. His grip tightened.

"No . . . my . . . baby!"

"What?" he demanded.

"My . . . baby . . . I . . . need . . ."

"Toughen *up*!"

Spittle flew from his mouth as he screamed. Yanking back, he slammed her head against the stone. Her pupils rolled back.

"*No! No!*"

He shook her, violently. Her head struck again and again. At the same time, he cut off her air.

"Answer me!" A tear of exertion, not remorse, fell from his eye, onto the skin pressed tightly over her collarbone. "Did she love me?"

Maybe she lived long enough to hear his question. Maybe her mouth moved. He saw words there. He imagined how they would sound to his ears. She had the answer. He knew she did. Without a doubt. More so than any other would after that.

He lost time then. He traveled through it, back to his past, revisiting every moment. And each one tortured him. Tore at his heart, scrambled his brain, burned his smooth, red skin.

Eventually, long after she passed, he tore himself away, as if seared by fire. Panting, he staggered back. His eyes watered as he looked upon what he had done.

"Stupid," he muttered, scurrying like a crab on the dry sand.

He did not regret the loss of life he had so callously caused. Instead, he reprimanded himself. He had practiced for years. Perfected his craft. Yet the hunger had robbed him of his training. It ripped control from his mind. And it left this.

Rising to his feet, he took a step back toward her. He stopped, looking down at his footprint—evidence. The bruises on her neck—evidence. When he closed his eyes in frustration, he imagined the flecks of skin and the saliva he'd left behind for forensics to discover.

"Careless."

It was too late to do anything about it. He would never let it happen again. He would set a process, steps that would be followed, one at a time. Structure would be his defense. It would not quench his hunger but hold it at bay just long enough. They might have their evidence, but he'd never give them more to match with it.

"Patience, practice, purpose."

Nodding, Jasper caught sight of the Walkman. It had come to rest on the rock above her head, the neon-yellow strip like a halo. The sight burned into him, latching on to a memory of his recently passed father. And he smiled. He would leave a calling card. Not a Walkman—that would tie him back to this sloppy mess. But something just similar enough. Something dramatic. Something beautiful.

Two victims were left on the beach that night. One would have remained outside this story had a detective not happened upon the file of Jane Doe and glanced at the crime scene photo. By then, sixteen murders had been attributed to the Halo Killer. But not that one. Not until that detective noticed the way the Walkman rested by Jane Doe's head. The way it looked like a halo. When he checked the date and did the math, he realized it had to be the first attempt. The papers agreed. So did his supervisors. And he was rewarded with a nice promotion.

The second victim would never be identified. His name had been Jasper Ross-Johnson. A quirky man with an unsettling past. The Halo Killer took him as he did the others. Jasper died that day, yet unlike Abbie Henshaw, there would be no freedom in his passing. Instead, he would haunt the night from that moment forward. His only chance at escape—a Miracle.

3

"AND THEN THE article came out," I almost screamed at him. "They identified Abbie Henshaw a month before they captured you. Why? What—"

"You're still not listening, are you?" Jasper said.

"How did they stop you?" I needed to get him talking. So I played to his ego. "You were perfect. An expert. Like you said: patience, practice, purpose. Was it evidence from that case?"

But that made no sense. They had linked the two cases four years before that. If they'd learned anything useful, they would have caught him long before. Identifying Abbie Henshaw should not have mattered.

"Jasper! What happened? How did they get you? How did they find that woman in your cabin?"

"Cabin?"

"Yes! Cabin!"

"Passion leads to mistakes," he said, pausing while he continued to laugh softly. Then his voice expanded with anger. "And *they* never found that woman. I told them where she was."

My heart missed a beat. "What?"

"They would have never found her. And she would have died of dehydration. I could never let that happen."

"Wait! You told them where she was?"

"Of course."

"Why would you do that?"

"Because I failed. I gave in to the hunger, just like that first night after my father's death. I thought I could control it. I thought I was in control. I got careless, and they caught me."

I felt so light-headed. None of what he said made sense. I ignored the glaring irony of it. That he'd saved Barbara Yost from certain death. Instead, the high coursed through my veins. I had been right. I'd known something didn't add up.

"If you had to tell them where she was, then they didn't find you at the cabin. And they didn't find her first."

"Of course they didn't," he said, offended. "No one was going to find that cabin unless I showed them where it was. I'm about to hang up, Theodore. I told you, after the first . . . one, I never made a mistake. I planned everything. I was a hundred steps ahead of them. I had them focusing on all the wrong things. Not just the flower. I planted DNA. I wore oversized shoes. I was astronomically better at their jobs than they were. Always."

"But they captured you."

The line went silent. I could not even hear the sound of his breathing.

"Jasper? Are you there?"

"They didn't do anything," he said, pronouncing each syllable like it burned his mouth.

His words came back. The ending of his little story.

"It was a Miracle!"

"Good-bye, Theodore. I'll see you soon."

The line went dead. My fingers gripped the phone so tightly that I thought it might snap in two.

"*Jasper!*"

But there was nothing. Though I didn't know it at the time, soon we would stand face-to-face, and I'd feel the Halo Killer's fingers around my throat.

4

WHEN I FINALLY looked at the screen, I stared at the number from which Jasper had called. It was a 210 exchange, and I knew what that meant. He was in northern New Jersey. Near the river. He could be down the street. In my hotel.

I didn't wait to find out. His words haunted me.

I'll see you soon.

I flew from the edge of my bed, fumbling with the lock for only a moment. Sprinting down the hallway, I bumped a man rolling a bag in the opposite direction.

"Watch it," the guy snapped.

I ignored him, pushing past two women to get into an elevator carriage that had just opened. One of them called me rude, but I didn't apologize. I couldn't speak. If they'd known what I knew, they wouldn't have been able to either.

When the doors opened, I crossed the lobby quickly, heading straight out the entrance. Standing under a light, I looked up and down the street. No cabs sat outside the hotel, so I stepped onto the darkened sidewalk, staying close to the side of the building. At the corner, I saw one rolling toward the intersection. The light was off, but I made a move toward it. Then I noticed a small shadow in the back seat. Maybe it was a woman. Or a child. In the night, it could have been anyone. But I stopped, shuffling backward.

Whoever sat in that cab turned his head. He looked right at me. And I felt the Halo Killer's eyes meet mine. Or at least, that's what I convinced myself. Without a thought, I spun on my heels and darted back toward the hotel. The light above the entrance felt like fire on my skin. Exposed, vulnerable, I veered away, running down the sidewalk. I had certainly visited northern New Jersey, but the darkness made it seem like an alien world. Suddenly I was running through the thick humidity of a dangerous jungle, some predator at my heels.

I spent nearly an hour swerving down unfamiliar alleys and sidling along poorly lit streets. As I passed a shady bar, my head swiveled. Glancing over my shoulder, I saw another cab approaching, fast. I ducked inside the door of the bar, holding it open just a crack. The cab didn't slow, but I swear I saw him in the back seat, again. Stalking me.

I slipped inside. The bartender and an older couple sitting across from him just stared at me. I let the door close behind me.

"You okay, buddy?"

"Yeah," I said.

I just wanted to leave. But I couldn't. He was out there. I was sure of it. Instead, I took a seat as far away from the other patrons as I could and fished my wallet out.

"Scotch with ice," I said.

"Sure."

As the guy fixed my drink, the couple lost interest. Slowly, my breathing returned to normal. He slid the Scotch across the oak surface, and I took a quick hit.

"You look familiar," the guy said.

"Have you seen *The Basement*?" I asked with a sigh.

"Is that a band?"

My eyes narrowed. "No."

"Huh. My name's Brad."

"Theo."

"Have you been here before?"

"Nah," I said.

"Damn. That's going to drive me crazy. You live nearby?"

"No, I—"

"Oh, shit!" Brad said, drawing the interest of the couple again. "You're that documentary guy."

Annoyed, I said, "Um, yeah. *The Basement*."

"From the news," the guy said.

I froze. I swear the old guy slid closer, his face thirsty for drama. The inside of my mouth turned to sandpaper.

"The news?"

"Yeah," Brad said. "That prison break in Maryland."

"Delaware," the old guy slurred.

"Right, Delaware. Dude, they're looking for you."

"Who is?"

"Like, everyone. The police."

"Why?"

The guy laughed. "You don't know why? That's crazy, man. I guess that serial killer guy is after you."

"That was on the news?"

Brad nodded, way too excited about everything. "They found some note he wrote. In his cell. It was all about you. They're not saying what it said, exactly. But they said you need to go to the police, man. Like right away."

The bartender jerked over to the television set and turned it on. The screen flashed to a news report already in progress. A young man stood outside the prison, microphone in hand.

A documentarian, known for his film The Basement, *had recently visited the convicted serial killer. Authorities are asking Mr. Snyder to contact the Delaware State Police immediately. For his own safety.*

Once again, the infamous Halo Killer is believed to be on the loose, somewhere in Sussex County, Delaware. Residents are asked to be vigilant but to avoid any confrontation.

"He might be coming here," the old guy at the bar said.

"Oh, shit," the bartender said through a throaty laugh. "Coming here? That's fucking gnarly. But they just said he's in Delaware."

I got up off the stool, taking a step backward. "They're wrong."

"What?" the bartender asked. "You hear that! He might be here. You can stay, man. It's cool. We're not scared."

Their heads pivoted like they were all watching a tennis match, from me to the TV and back.

"I gotta go," I stammered, backing into a table.

Spinning, I hit the door, hard. It swung open far enough to slam into a stone planter. The glass panes rattled, echoing down the street.

"Dude," Brad said from inside.

Then I was gone. In that moment, I realized I had only one chance to get out of this. I had to stop being the hunted. And be the hunter instead.

5

I WAS ON THE run. Maybe on the lam. But it just didn't matter. Instead, my thoughts were like the jaws of a pit bull. No matter how hard I tried, I could not tear them away from what Jasper had said. A Miracle! He knew I was close.

I had to switch buses four times, but by nine in the morning, I stepped out onto the streets of Georgetown, Delaware. It was a different world. I wandered along a grass-lined sidewalk in front of the stark white pillars of the town hall building, staring across a well-manicured traffic circle at an ornate fountain. Mist rose from the spray, casting a rainbow over a passing pickup. As I searched for a street sign, I must have passed a dozen small flower gardens, each punctuated with a small American flag planted in the soil.

On the bus, I had Googled the address of the police station, the one that had sent the officers that captured the Halo Killer. I found Race Street and tried to decide if I should take a left or a right. I must have looked lost, because a patrol car rolled to a stop aside the curb.

"Hey there, can I . . ." The officer stared at me for a second; then recognition dawned. "You're Theo Snyder."

I took a step back. I don't think I considered running, but my need to dig deeper, to uncover the true story, surged far more powerfully than common sense.

"How'd you get down here?" the woman asked, tipping her mirrored sunglasses.

"Bus," I said, taking another step back.

"You know you're in danger, right?"

"That might be a little overblown," I said.

"Either way, I need to take you in to the station."

"On Race Street," I said. "That's where I'm going."

She squinted at me. With a choppy nod to herself, the officer put the car in park and got out. She approached, thumbs tucked into her belt.

"You were heading to the station?"

"Yeah," I said. "I was hoping to interview one of the officers that arrested Jasper Ross-Johnson."

"The guy that's after you?" she said, looking bemused.

"He's not . . . I'm sure this is all some kind of misunderstanding. I'm working on a documentary. They probably found notes from one of the interviews I conducted with Jasper in the prison."

"Jasper, huh?"

"Um, yeah."

"You know he escaped, right?"

"Sure. Sounds like an inside job to me."

She shook her head, like I had no idea what I was talking about.

"Look, I need to take you to the state police, out on the highway. They'll be able to help you."

"But I need—"

She put a hand up. "Sir, they can help you. Why don't you come with me."

"I . . . Are you arresting me?"

"Should I?" she asked.

"No. I didn't . . ."

"Climb in the back. I'll drive you over."

I hesitated. "Okay."

A minute later I found myself in the back of the police cruiser. The officer slowly maneuvered through the old colonial town. I stared out the window for a moment, then leaned forward.

"So, you're town police?"

"Yes, sir," she said.

"And the state police arrested Jasper?"

"Yes."

"Did you—"

I saw her glasses tilt up in the rearview mirror before she said, "He murdered one of my friend's sister."

"Oh . . . I . . ."

She said nothing more. Silently, she pulled into the parking lot of the state police station. I tried to open the back door, but obviously, it was locked. When she let me out, I followed her.

"Look, sorry," I said. "I didn't mean—"

The officer never turned. She walked up to the front desk and spoke with her back to me. I couldn't make out her words, but I saw the dispatcher crane her neck to look at me. Then the Georgetown officer was gone, and I was told to take a seat.

6

"Can I record our conversation?"

The state police detective just stared at me. We sat in an interview room. I had hoped he would offer me something to drink. Or eat, even. I'd grabbed lukewarm coffee and a stale cookie at the hotel before leaving New Jersey, but I was starving. Instead, he'd just walked in and sat down across from me.

"Mr. Snyder, this isn't a part of your movie."

"Of course it is," I said.

"You're in real danger."

"I don't see it like that."

"Why not?"

Because he's after her.

That's what I wanted to say. But I couldn't put the police onto Miracle yet. That could ruin the story. As I sat in the waiting room for over an hour, I started to picture an ending. I knew I shouldn't. It broke every rule of documentary making. But I couldn't stop it. I just kept picturing Miracle and Jasper coming face-to-face.

"He's long gone," I lied.

"How could you know that?"

"Because, he told me."

"What?"

"After the camera was off one day. He leaned close to the glass and said if he ever got out, he planned to go to some backwoods town in Mexico. No one would ever find him there."

"Do you have a recording of that?"

I shook my head.

"Excuse me," he said.

The detective left the room. As soon as the door closed, it dawned on me what I had just done. I'd broken the law. I'd lied to the police. Led them to a false trail. So that I could find the truth before they found him.

Leaning forward, I covered my face with my hands. A second later, I realized I was probably on camera, so I sat up straight. Tried to act normal. My heart was beating like mad. I felt like I was riding a roller coaster in the dark, like I would never see the next turn coming. I knew I needed sleep more than anything else. Every time I had tried to rest, something had happened that got me up and running again and again. When I closed my eyes, frustrated, the exhaustion tried to take hold. But the picture came back. Jasper and Miracle. Face-to-face.

*　*　*

"So, were you in on the arrest?" I asked.

The detective, having returned moments later, had taken his seat across from me. He looked utterly distracted.

"Excuse me?"

"When Jasper was—"

"You mean the serial killer," he said.

"Well, yeah, sure. Were you there when he was arrested?"

"We all were," he said.

"Really. Let me ask you something."

"Mr. Snyder, I really don't think you understand. There is a massive manhunt for the escapee. You're now a part of it. We're going to ask you to stay in the station, at least for the time being."

My body tingled with the need to get out of there. But I stayed calm.

"No problem," I said. "I want to help. But can I just ask you a couple of questions? It might help me gauge how much of what he told me was actually true. Like that whole Mexico thing. He could have been playing with me."

The detective leaned forward. "Why would you think that?"

"I've spoken to him. A lot. He's crafty. And he's hiding something. That's why I'm here. One question. Please." He nodded, so I continued. "Was he arrested at the cabin? Where he had Barbara Yost?"

"Is that what he told you?" the detective asked.

I paused, thinking about how to respond. I needed to play the man correctly if I had any chance of getting out of there.

"No," I said slowly. "He told me that he was arrested somewhere else."

"That's correct. He was apprehended twenty feet off Coastal Highway, between mile markers seventeen and eighteen."

That meant nothing to me, especially considering I'd read it on the report during my research.

"On the highway?"

He nodded.

I thought about the key card Jasper had mentioned.

"Outside a motel?" I asked.

"No, sir."

"How did you find him?"

The detective's eyes locked with mine. His head shook, but he told me.

"We had an anonymous tip."

"Someone called you? Was it a woman?"

"Our tip line is confidential, Mr. Snyder."

"What was the tip?"

"I can't tell you that."

"So, you caught him. Then he told you about the cabin. And about Ms. Yost?"

He didn't answer. I could tell I was losing him. So I continued.

"He told me that he did. He said that it wouldn't be right if she died out there. I think he meant it would be wrong unless he did it."

"That man is a lunatic," the detective said, losing his calm.

"I agree. The worst I've seen."

He glared at me. "That man murdered innocent young ladies. Daughters, sisters, mothers. He took so many people from our community. Brutally ending their lives. And you find this interesting. Maybe you should just move on, Mr. Snyder. Go back to Hollywood."

"Okay," I said.

I stood up, reaching for the door handle. The suddenness of it startled the man. I had the door open before he reached his feet.

"Where are you going?" he demanded.

I stepped out into the hallway, sending my response back to him as casually as I could.

"I'm leaving."

"No, you're—"

"Are you arresting me?"

The detective just stood there. He stared at me like he wanted to rip my head off my shoulders.

"No," he said. "I'm trying to protect you."

"Thank you," I said.

And I hurried out of the station.

7

I WAS GETTING CLOSE. I could feel it. I knew I needed to get away from the police. I had the feeling that they would follow me. Maybe even bring me in for jaywalking or something. Anything to get me off the street. Or, if they were smart and they truly believed Jasper was after me, they could tail my every move. Follow me until he found me. Kill two birds, so to speak.

He wasn't after me, though. The deeper I fell, the more and more I believed that. There was something else. Something bigger. And Miracle was a part of it. She was probably the anonymous caller. She'd turned her mother's killer in to the police. Ended his reign of horror.

It all added up. But as I put distance between myself and the station, the itch began. I knew that Miracle had lied. I knew she was involved. But something felt off. I didn't know what, though.

I needed help. Not yet knowing who I intended to call, I pulled out my phone. I decided on Jessica. I would need a camera operator. When I tried to dial her number, however, it wouldn't go through. I looked at the screen, and it said I had no cellular service.

"Really!"

When I looked up, though, I could see a massive cell tower up ahead, one that looked vaguely like a pine tree. I checked again, but nothing. When I tried to go to the internet, I had no connection.

"Come on!"

I turned, looking back at the massive white manor housing the state police. I could go back. They might even let me use the phone. But that would be crazy, so I sped up. I was in a rural area, so it took me about ten minutes to reach a tiny clapboard farmhouse that sat back off the road. Slowly I moved up the walk, feeling more and more like someone might point a shotgun at me with every step.

I knocked tentatively. When a young guy with a thick beard and Buddy Holly glasses answered the door, it surprised me.

"Oh, hi . . . um, do you think I could use your phone?"

The guy nodded, pursing his lips as if the answer required a good bit of thought.

"Is it local?"

"Uh . . . no."

"You can use mine, then."

He opened the storm door, and I noticed the tool belt around his waist. When I stepped into the small foyer, he handed me a specimen of the newest iPhone in an ombré case.

"I'd let you use the landline, but it's not my house. I'm just here doing some work."

"Okay," I said. "Thanks."

He opened the phone and handed it to me. Then he just walked away, leaving me alone. I imagined someone acting like this back in the city, or in Los Angeles, for that matter, and it made me laugh out loud.

"You okay?" he called from the other room.

"Yeah."

I stared at the screen for a second, then decided to call my own number first. It rang once, and a message played.

We're sorry. You have reached a number that has been disconnected or is no longer in service.

"What the hell?" I whispered.

That couldn't be possible. I had my bill paid automatically. Next, I called the provider, entering my number when prompted. As soon as I did, the call ended. A jolt of suspicion caused me to look over my shoulder. I tried a second time, and the same thing happened.

I had to concentrate to keep my hand from shaking. Something was very wrong. The only thing I could think to do was what I had originally planned. I called Jessica.

"Someone disconnected my phone," I blurted out.

"Who is this?"

"Jessica?" I asked, confused. Then I remembered I had called from a strange number. "Oh, it's me, Theo. I just borrowed someone's phone."

"Where are you?"

"I'm in Delaware. I need you—"

"The police came by yesterday, looking for me."

"To your apartment?"

"Yeah," she said. "Then they asked me a bunch of questions about that guy. The . . . Jesus, am I in danger?"

"No way. You're fine."

"Look, I'm sorry. I really am. But—"

"No," I snapped. "No way. You can't leave now. I need you. This is huge. Bigger than you can imagine. When we get this finished, when we tell this story, you'll get any job you want. Shit, they'll offer you a million to do your own film, if that's something you're interested in. Just stick with me. Trust me."

Either the line crackled or she scoffed. "I can't—"

"Okay, I'll tell you the truth. But you can't tell anyone else. Not the police. Anyone." I took a deep breath. "You know that young woman, Miracle? She isn't what she appears. She's using us to get to Jasper. I think she plans on killing him. Getting revenge for her mother or something. I'm not sure yet. But I know she's been playing us . . . Playing us all."

"All of us?" Jessica asked.

"All of us."

"Even Zora?"

"Even her."

"And how do you know this?"

"I just left the police station in Delaware. They said that when they arrested Jasper, he wasn't at home. He was near the beach. Someone had called in an anonymous tip. It had to be that woman from the story. I think it was Miracle."

"Okay . . ." she said. "I don't know what you're talking about. But you need help. I'm out of here. I don't get paid enough to . . ."

Her voice trailed off. There was a harsh rustle against her speaker. Then Jessica ended the call. I stood there, staring at the screen, until the guy came into the foyer. Smiling, I handed him the phone.

"Thanks, man," I said.

"No worries. I have an unlimited plan."

As I turned for the door, one thing Jessica had said struck me. She'd asked if Miracle was playing all of us—even Zora. Before that moment, I'd never thought to be concerned. Zora could obviously handle herself. But if she was with Miracle, maybe she didn't know. Maybe she wasn't safe.

"Can I make one more call?"

"Um, yeah. Hey, are you sure you're okay? You don't look too good."

"I'm fine," I answered, annoyed.

He handed me the phone, and I dialed. With a soft laugh and a shake of the head, he headed back to the kitchen just as Zora answered.

"Hey," I said.

"Who is this?"

I'd forgotten about the number again. "It's Theo."

"Where are you?"

"I'm in Delaware. But listen. We need to talk."

She sighed. "I thought I made it clear when we left you in New Jersey."

"Are you still with her?"

"With who?"

"Miracle, for Christ's sake."

"No," Zora said. "I got her on a train this morning. She's heading to her boyfriend's house in Philadelphia. I'm out, Theo. Totally and completely."

"Thank God. I'm onto something. Something huge. You sure you're making the right decision?"

"Oh, I'm sure."

"Okay. But do you want to hear what I've learned?"

"Sure," she said, sounding more interested than I had expected.

"She found him, Zora. Not the police. And she tried to set him up. Something about a hotel key card. That's how he was arrested."

"Who's she?"

"Miracle!"

"Wow," she said. "You're telling me that someone without any experience hunted down one of the most notorious and elusive killers in history, beating every detective in the country. And she did all of that without telling anyone. Come on. Just listen to yourself. It makes no sense."

"Yes, it does," I answered, sounding more petulant than I'd intended.

"No, Theo, it doesn't. What's your evidence?"

"I . . ." Suddenly, my head felt cloudy. I couldn't organize my thoughts. "The article! And she disconnected my phone . . . somehow."

"I have to go," Zora said.

"But—"

"Get some help. You need it."

Zora ended the call. I stared at the screen until it relocked.

Evidence.

Evidence.

Maybe she was right.

"Hey, buddy," I called out.

The guy came back, still smiling at me. He put his hand out, and I gave him the phone.

"Does this place have Wi-Fi?"

"Sure," the guy said. "But I don't know the password."

"Is there a Starbucks nearby?"

"The library has free Wi-Fi."

"Cool." I paused. "You think you could give me a lift?"

The guy actually laughed out loud. When I just watched him for a moment, he stopped.

"You're testing my Christian kindness," he said.

"Sorry," I muttered. Then added, "But can I get that ride?"

CHAPTER

8

I SAT IN A comfy chair under a window, trying to concentrate. It didn't work. It seemed as if every word that had been spoken to me over the past few days blew through my thoughts like lights from a disco ball. Frustrated, I rose from my seat and found the nearest bathroom. Pushing the door open, I moved to stand in front of the mirror. I stared at my reflection. Deep circles hung under overly wide eyes. Sallow skin looked all the paler under dirty black hair. My clothes looked as if they had been slept in by multiple people. My stomach growled loudly. And my mouth was so dry that my tongue stuck to the roof.

I was a mess. But I wasn't crazy. Not like they thought I was. In fact, if it hadn't been for Bender, no one would ever have dreamed of thinking it. They would have seen the truth. That I was on a hunt. And that my ending inched closer and closer every minute.

I splashed cold water on my face and did what I could with my hair. Tucking in my shirt, I looked at myself again. With a grunt, I left the bathroom and saw a vending machine nestled in the corner. My mouth watered. I hit it up, but the best I could do was some Lance crackers. Stuffing two in my mouth, I returned to the same seat. I intended to use the Wi-Fi on my phone and search the internet with a new eye. When I'd done my research earlier, I'd never imagined that this story would grow so spectacular.

For some reason, I checked my email first. As I scanned through the junk, I noticed a message from my mother. I'd almost forgotten that she even had an account. I expected it to be some innocuous note about a little-known third cousin, but I was horribly wrong.

Dear Theodore,

Where are you? I called you five times now but the recording said your phone has been disconnected. I saw the news on Fox 5. The police are looking for you. And a woman came to my apartment. I thought she might be a detective but she didn't look like it. She started asking me questions about you. And that Bender woman. That dancer. I told you to stay away from her. I don't know what else I can do. I need to know that you're okay. Call me, please.

Love, Your Mother

"Nononono."

I reread the note three times before responding.

Mom, I can't call right now. My phone is out of charge. Everything's fine. I promise. But I need to know who the woman was that came to your house. What was her name? Please get back to me immediately.

I hit send and realized I had been holding my breath. When I exhaled, I guess I started to talk to myself.

"What the hell?"

"Shhhh," someone hissed.

I turned and saw a guy, who looked homeless, sitting at the desktop computers nearby. I hadn't noticed him before, but now he was glaring at me.

"Sorry," I muttered.

It was Cassandra, or someone working with her. She'd started working on her documentary. Honestly, I'd thought it was a warning, a threat. I'd never imagined she'd really make a movie about me. Strangely, for just a second, it felt sort of . . . exciting. An entire documentary about me. That thought vanished quickly.

I leaned in and hit refresh on my email. There was no response. I hit it again and again and again, for how long I have no idea. Maybe a minute. Maybe an hour. Time seemed to have both stopped and careened forward.

Finally, her response popped onto the screen. I opened it, and it was even worse than I could have expected.

Dear Theo,

I'm glad that you're well. Please call me as soon as you can. I don't know if she gave me her name, but she was a tall woman, like a man. Had this giant bunch of yellow hair on top of her head. Like someone from the islands. I think she was lying, because she told me she was working for that famous director. You know the one? Or maybe it was his daughter. Yeah, that was it. That famous director's daughter. Once she said that, I asked her to leave. She was probably one of those crazy hackers that watch the news and try to take advantage of the elderly. Please call me. I'm worried.

Love, Your Mother.

I couldn't move. It had been Zora. She'd interviewed my mother. She was investigating me. For Cassandra. My eyes closed, and I remembered what she'd said on the phone. That she had moved on already.

"Shit," I whispered.

And the homeless guy growled.

CHAPTER

9

EARLY IN MY career, I worked on a piece for the local news. It was about a boy—I won't use his name—but he had a horrible illness. The kind that parents won't even explain to their other children for fear that they will never sleep again. I read up on it before the interview. Even as an adult, I wasn't the same for days.

When it came time for our meeting, I felt sick to my stomach. Driving to his home, I thought about turning around at every single intersection. I didn't, though. When I arrived, his mother walked me into their sun-room. The boy sat in his wheelchair, his eyes bright but his body ravaged. I took the seat across from him and cleared my throat nervously.

"It's okay," the kid said in a voice at once frail and indomitable. "It's not contagious."

I laughed. He smiled. We talked for over an hour. I felt amazing when I left his house. As I drove back to my place, one thing he'd said stuck with me. When I'd asked him how he remained so happy, the boy answered:

"Who said I'm happy? It's just life. I wake up. I face what I have to face. And I go to sleep. People always tell me how strong I am. I never really understand that. I can't even lift a sheet of paper. I need help going to the bathroom. The truth is that I'm just who I am. I have what I have. I've never known anything different."

I stood in that library and let his words straighten my back.

"I am who I am," I announced.

A smiled crept up my face. And I went back to work.

*   *   *

I imagined I was that kid. That I confronted the mountain of madness that seemed to be crumbling all around me. Zora was working with Cassandra. She was going to tear my life apart. Or at least she was going to try. In the face of that possibility, I rose like a phoenix. My fingers flew across the keyboard, possessed with a new energy, a new determination, one that would never be dampened. I had a head start, and I intended to use it.

She thought she was so damned special. That she was the best investigator out there. But Zora had forgotten something. I'm a filmmaker. A damned good one. I'd canned half a dozen lesser known films and *The Basement* without her.

Smiling, I dove deep. I'd already spent hours parsing through Jasper's life, not to mention the lives of his victims. When I had, though, I had been looking for something else. The perfect hook. With fresh eyes, I let my gut feeling guide me, and I searched for every article on Jasper's arrest that I could find.

I read everything I came across, some of it material I'd seen and considered before. Like the story about Barbara Yost's rescue. Someone at the station must have tipped off a local reporter. She was at the cabin when they rescued Barbara Yost. Video of the moment had gone viral: an emaciated woman covered in a thick blanket, crying as she was led through the darkness into the light of the camera. A perfect shot, really. One that solidified the crime scene in the minds of every American. One I would get for my film.

Then I dug deeper. I searched harder, smaller, more local. As that video played on every national news program, someone would tell the real story. The more intimate one. And there would be a detail that wasn't as "sexy." One that would slip into the ever-expanding ether of the American news cycle, the endless drone of the less popular, the less viewed, the less liked. The anti-viral.

That's where I found it. Searching through the *Daily Whale*, I came across a front-page article. The reporter, on a ride-around with the Rehoboth Beach Police, had happened to be in a cruiser when the all-points came out on Jasper. Right after an anonymous call. The officer raced to the scene, arriving moments after the state troopers, too late to be a part of the headline news. The reporter took a single, grainy phone shot through the window. It was no wonder the image never caught on. Not only was it out of focus, but the subject, Jasper Ross-Johnson, the infamous Halo Killer, had a jacket thrown over his head. As the police ushered him into a patrol car, he could have been anyone. Male, female, maybe even a teenager.

That photo, however, nearly took my breath away. I stared for a second without realizing why. Then, in the corner of the shot, I noticed it. A small, blockish concrete building. An outhouse.

Frantic, I opened a new window and searched for stories about Miracle. I found the one I was looking for immediately. The first story to break. One showing the tiny outhouse within which a tinier newborn somehow survived four days in a cracked, dirty sink. I moved the two pictures next to each other on the screen.

"How'd I miss this?" I muttered.

There was no doubt. The scenes were identical. Jasper had been arrested in the very parking lot of Miracle Jones's birth. A coincidence? That thought made me laugh. Not a chance. As I sat there, staring at the screen, the part of my brain that told stories took over. I imagined that night, the fall of the Halo Killer at the hands of Miracle Jones.

*   *   *

In my imagination, I pictured Miracle kneeing in the shadows, inches from the apex of her nightmare. When she closed her eyes, took the briny air in through her nose, the aroma triggered something deep in the primitive parts of her brain. She felt an overwhelming need to flee from that place. From the ghosts of her past. Her own infant screams echoed between her ears.

The agony of Miracle's truth, however, had never been enough to stop her. She'd survived. She was famous for that trait, known across the Delmarva Peninsula. The steel of her spine straightened. She took in a deep breath, and a hand slipped into the front pocket of her jeans. Her fingertips brushed against the piano wire and electricians' tape of a homemade garrote. She pulled it out, absent-mindedly admiring her work. Over the course of a few weeks, she'd watched videos on how to make it. Then she'd sat down with her supplies: eight thin metal rods, a roll of tape, and a length of translucent string. She tied one end to the center of a rod, then taped three to that, making a handle and grip. She did the same with the other side. And, like on the videos, she practiced on fruit, wrapping the wire around an orange, crossing the handles, pulling them apart. That first time, as the wire cut the fruit cleanly in two, she nodded. She had her tool.

Miracle's boyfriend lived in Philadelphia. If she had wanted a handgun, it would have been no problem. He would have gladly contacted a friend of a friend. In fact, with her driving into the city alone to visit him, he would have thought nothing of it. She'd considered it, but a gun wasn't enough. It was too good for the man that stole her mother away. No, she intended to loop the line around the man's neck and pull him close as he thrashed and died. She wanted to feel him leave this world in pain and fear. Just as he'd done to so many others.

The time ticked close. He would be there in moments. She was sure of that. Her plans had been meticulous and perfect. Every step led to that parking lot, to the end of the Halo Killer at the hands of Miracle Jones.

Slowly, she lifted the garrote, held it out in the dim light from the one overhead lamp. Staring at the smooth surface of the line, she wrapped it around her own neck. Crossing the handles behind her back, Miracle closed her eyes and tugged. The wire bit into her skin. Her yelp of pain cut off as the pressure closed her airways. She jerked, then whipped the cord from around her throat, letting one handle fall to the ground. She bent at the waist, coughing, as her hand touched her skin. She felt the warm dampness of her blood and nodded. Just enough to look like self-defense.

As if on cue, a single light appeared, moving north on Coastal Highway. She froze, listening, picking up the soft rumble of a moped. It was him. He'd taken the bait she had left at the hotel room. Miracle crouched, her every muscle tensing. Her pupils stretched, turning her eyes black as she peered through the night. Slowly, silently, she picked up the other handle, savoring the weight of it in her dry palm.

He pulled into the lot as if it meant nothing. His indifference infuriated her, breaking down any last stitch of guilt associated with what she would do. He deserved a million deaths. And she deserved to deal every one.

The Halo Killer slipped off the seat of his scooter like a bird hopping on a ledge. Slowly, he moved closer, into the light. For the first time, she saw his face up close. She saw the weakness of his chin. The sallowness of his cheeks. The frailty of his fingers. Then the lamp illuminated his eyes, far darker than even hers. In them, she saw his truth as much as she saw her own.

Miracle rose out of the shadows. She had no intention of skulking like him. Lying in wait and pouncing on the helpless. No, she would come face-to-face with his evil, and watch as it burned.

He saw her immediately. His eyes widened, but he did not slow. Nor did he lunge forward. Instead, he moved like a long-lost lover, shy but unstoppable. The distance between Miracle and the Hallo Killer shrank. She lifted her garrote. He smiled.

In a flash, however, the intimacy of this final moment exploded in flashes of red and blue. Engines roared. Gravel sprayed. Without a thought, Miracle slipped back into the darkness as Jasper stared into the oncoming lights of a half-dozen squad cars.

10

"Too early," I said.

The man hissed at me again, but I ignored him. That had to be it. The police had arrived too early. Her plan, at least how I imagined it, had failed. But, as I should have known, nothing could stop someone like Miracle Jones, someone who had already danced with the devil and survived, seemingly unmarked. Her hunt had never ended, only paused, while the Halo Killer was in prison.

How'd she find him?

The question lodged in my head, suffocating everything else. Could Miracle Jones have done what no one else could? Lure him out of hiding? I closed my eyes and pictured the woman sitting on the counter in my empty kitchen. I saw her dark, intense eyes. The strength somehow hidden behind her wiry, short frame. Was it enough? Maybe . . . Maybe not.

Once again, I dove, switching from the small screen of my phone to one of the desktops. The library around me disappeared. I entered my research as if floating through the internet. I gave my fingers freedom as they guided my way, driving the search until it focused on Cassandra. The daughter of a prominent filmmaker. A prominent director in her own right. She had been on this story before me—allegedly. She would have come across that name, Miracle Jones. Coincidence? It surely could be.

But to turn on me? Investigate me?

That was emotional. Illogical. Sure, she had the bigger name. She could act with impunity. That fact, however, made her involvement in all this even more suspect. Why would she waste her time doing a story on me? The Bender story had very short legs. *The Basement* was huge, a household name. I, however, was not. Who would watch a movie about me?

No one. Though it hurt, thinking that, my ego could not cloud the truth. Not any longer. Maybe that was why I hadn't seen it before. In that moment, it seemed utterly clear.

It took me less than two seconds to find the next clue. One look at IMDb and the connection hit me like a stone to the face. Cassandra had a movie in development. It was the story of a well-known crime blogger. Her work had led to the arrest of a man who had killed forty-three young men in San Francisco. But that wasn't what grabbed me. It was how the blogger had done it. She'd convinced local authorities to submit unidentified DNA from the crime scene to a local ancestry company. The sample identified a fifty-four-year-old woman from Los Angles as a sibling. It took the police less than a week to identify her only brother and obtain a DNA sample from his home. It was a match, and the story of the crime blogger's part in solving the crime hit national media.

At first blush, the project read like any other. One that I might have been interested in myself, for that matter. When I saw it, though, the connection was made. I knew for certain that I was being played.

Since meeting Miracle that first day, something had gnawed at me. I couldn't imagine her using a DNA test and tracking down her mother, then somehow identifying her as the Jane Doe. She didn't have that kind of experience. But Cassandra did. She had used it to solve the unsolvable case. Miracle alone could not have found Jasper. But Cassandra had already proven she could. She had been the anonymous tip. Miracle had shared her DNA results with Cassandra. And I would wager that they had approached Bunny Henshaw together. Cassandra was a pro. She could have convinced the police to run Miracle's DNA results against their database. And that sample had led to Miracle's truth. Her connection to the Halo Killer.

11

I WALKED UP TO the first librarian I could find. She smiled at me.

"Can I help you?"

"I was wondering if I could borrow your phone to call my cellular provider. I'm having a problem with my service."

"Sure," she said. "Which one?"

"Um, AT&T."

She dialed the number from memory and handed me the receiver.

"Wow," I muttered.

When the computer answered, I gave it all my information and eventually got connected to a real person. When I told him the situation, he checked my account.

"Huh," he said. "You're right. This shouldn't have happened. For some reason, your account was suspended."

"Suspended," I said. "Why?"

"I have no idea, actually. You're paid up, with no history of delinquency. All I can say is that it shouldn't have."

"Could I have been hacked or something?"

"I guess," he said.

"Huge," I muttered to myself.

"Excuse me?"

"Oh, nothing . . . You can't tell me any more about it?"

"Not really. Oh, wait, there are notes. It says here that a relative of yours called and said you were in a coma. She asked if your account could be suspended."

"And you would allow a relative to do that," I asked.

"It seems she had all your information, including your four-digit pin number." He paused. "Uh, I guess you're not in a coma."

"Nope," I said. "Did my relative give a name?"

"Yeah, it says it was your mother's sister. Her first name was Cassandra."

I felt like every nerve in my body caught fire when I heard that. I wanted to jump up and down like a child. But I stayed stone-cold calm.

"Thank you," I said. "Can you just make sure my service is back on? And can you put a note in there to make sure that this can't happen again?"

"Definitely, Mr. Snyder. I'm sorry about the inconvenience."

I laughed, by accident. "I'm not."

With a nod to the librarian, I left. Within minutes, I had an Uber on the way to pick me up and take me to Baltimore-Washington airport. It took even less time to find Cassandra's office number. I dialed, smiling.

"Hi, this is Theo Snyder. I'd like to set a meeting with Cassandra for tomorrow."

"You said your name was Theo—"

"I made *The Basement*," I said.

"O-o-oh. Sorry, sir. Let me check—"

I cleared my throat. "You'll fit me in. It's about her . . . *involvement* with the Halo Killer."

After a pause, the officer assistant said, "I'm sorry. I'm not sure I understand what you're saying. Is that a project you're working on?"

"It's one we both are," I said.

"Okay . . . Can you hold for a second?"

I nodded, feeling satisfied. "Sure."

My car rolled to the curb, a black SUV. Jumping in, I leaned back, feeling at once exhausted and strangely content. I was close now. I could feel it. And I was sure I had caught Cassandra off guard.

"Hi," the assistant said, after taking me off hold. "Cassandra can meet up for coffee at ten AM tomorrow. Does that work for you?"

"Definitely," I said.

She gave me an address, and I put it in my phone.

"I'll be there."

When I checked for flights, the only one that could get me to Los Angeles in time cost over a thousand dollars. Timing was tight, but I booked it. I would confront Cassandra and end this charade. Then, for fucking with my mother, I would ruin her.

CHAPTER

12

I BURST THROUGH THE door of the juice bar on Rodeo Boulevard, feeling like I didn't really exist. The flight out had been awful. Picture the most nightmarish passenger you could have sitting next to you on a plane. The sounds, the smells, the heat, the inadvertent touching. I had one of those to the left of me. And the one to the right was even worse. He was an elderly gentleman with a forked beard and tinted glasses. He felt the need to talk all night, to me, about the stupidest crap imaginable. When he recognized me, it got worse. Story after story about his local theater group and their numerous amateur productions. No matter what I did, he wouldn't stop. Eventually, while he was midsentence, I put my earbuds in. He actually asked to share one. I almost killed him.

I tried to get some sleep on the car ride over, but the driver had a repeat of the Stern Show on the entire way. I gave him a high rating because I never asked him to turn it down. But when I stepped out onto the sidewalk, I swear it swayed. I had to reach out and grab the door or I would have fallen.

"You okay?" the driver asked.

"I hate that fucking question," I replied.

Cassandra wasn't there, so I walked up to the cashier, staring up at the menu.

"You have coffee, right?"

"Tea," she said with a warm smile. "Naturally decaffeinated."

I rubbed my eyes, igniting sparks on the backs of my closed lids. "Energy drink?"

"We have a matcha cold brew."

"I'll take a large," I mumbled.

When she handed me the drink, I just stared at the emerald-green color. My stomach turned a little, but I took a sip.

"Hi, Theo," someone said.

I spun toward the door and found Cassandra standing two feet away. I had to tilt my head up to meet her eyes. That made me look right back down to see if she was wearing heels. She wasn't.

"Yeah, I'm tall," she said.

"I'm short," I said, trying to smile.

I fought the urge to take a step back. She had that kind of persona, the type that took over an interaction before it could start. Maybe it was the intensity in her eyes. Or the power she knew she had in the business.

"Bad flight?" she asked.

"Yeah . . . how'd you know?"

She laughed, like I had been joking. Then she stepped past me and up to the counter.

"Shit," I blurted out. "I should have waited . . ."

"Red-eyes go first," she said.

I stood there, stupidly, as she ordered. Her choice looked no better than mine, so at least there was that. Some of the energy that had brought me there returned. I stood up straighter. And I summoned my most fatherly tone.

"Should we sit?"

"I think we should."

Cassandra let out a soft laugh, and I followed her to a seat in the corner. Unlike in New York, we had a little space to talk, which was for the best, considering.

"Can I start?" she asked.

I paused, still squatting over my seat, completely taken aback. Was she going to admit it all? That she was using Miracle Jones to fabricate the most amazing documentary ever? One with the kind of draw-dropping ending that would shake up the entire industry?

Or maybe she would say that I'd gotten too close. And she was going to do whatever was needed to stop me. As I hovered above the pink plastic, I really thought about it. And, I have to admit, I felt a little impressed. Or maybe jealous. A bold plan.

"How'd you get him out of jail?" I blurted out before she could continue.

Cassandra just stared at me with those eyes. Like tractor beams, they lowered me to the seat. Her reaction steeled my resolve, though. I had never been surer of myself than in that moment.

"Sorry, go ahead," I said.

Her head shook. "You know, I watched *The Basement* with my father. He's a tough critic." She laughed. "Even to me. But he loved your film. I mean, really loved it. To the point that it made me . . . uncomfortable. Maybe I shouldn't say this, but I've been jealous of you since."

My jaw almost dropped. Maybe it was that simple. A rival's move to take me down. Maybe the film wasn't even the top priority.

"Really?" I asked.

"Yeah." She leaned forward. "But I'm worried about you. When my assistant said you sounded strange, I gave Steph a call."

"You know Steph?"

"Of course I do," she said.

"Working with Miracle, I get it. Good story. But you shouldn't have gone after my mother," I snapped.

Her eyes widened. "Excuse me?"

I noticed the confusion on her face. Yet I pushed through it, even though my gut screamed out to stop. To take a breath and reassess the situation.

"I get the rest. Even more now. But sending Zora to my mother's place? That was low. I mean, fucked up, really."

Something changed in that moment. I had sensed a camaraderie when we first stood across from each other. A level of shared respect. When I said that last part, any lingering regard vanished. She watched me through iron eyes, and I suddenly wanted to apologize.

"I have no idea what you are talking about," she said flatly.

"This whole Miracle and the Halo Killer thing. If I had known you were interested, I would have given you a call. I'm no vulture."

"Miracle? Are you talking about that serial killer with the flowers? I'm not interested in that story. Not at all."

My vision lost focus for a second as my brain tried to comprehend what she was saying. She was lying! But my instincts countered that accusation immediately.

"You weren't working on that story?"

"Nope," she said.

"What about me?" I asked.

She laughed uncomfortably. "What about you?"

"Are you doing a story on Bender . . . and me?"

That's when she got angry. Cassandra gripped the edge of the table and nearly stood up.

"Really? You think I would do something like that?" Her head shook, but the tension in her arms disappeared. "I'm going to take one more minute of my time to tell you something, Theo Snyder. You have it. More than most. But whatever *this* is—drugs, drinking, whatever— you need to get a handle on it, and fast.

"I'm going to walk out now. And I'm going to act like this little conversation never happened. If I hear my name come out of your mouth again before you get your shit together, I'll finish you. Understand?"

All I could do was nod. So did she. Then Cassandra got up, grabbed her drink, and left. I just sat there, my mouth hanging open. I'm sure she thought her threat had caused my reaction. But it had nothing to do with that.

It wasn't her. She didn't even know who Miracle was.

That just couldn't be true. My digging could not have been wrong. The impossibility of that left me frozen, agape, and overwhelmed like a blown circuit. I don't even think I was breathing. Then my phone rang. And I neared the bottom of the rabbit hole.

13

"HELLO, THEODORE."
        I jumped to my feet, whipping the phone away from my ear. Turning the screen, I expected to see a Los Angeles exchange. Instead, the call originated in Delaware. I let out a breath and lifted the phone back up.

"Hello, Jasper."

I was wrong.

I couldn't get that thought out of my head. I had been so sure that somehow Miracle and Cassandra were connected. That Cassandra had helped Miracle find her mother's killer.

But that didn't make sense. I had been wrong. Confused. Before the DNA test, Miracle had had no connection to the Halo Killer. No reason for revenge. No reason for Cassandra to give a damn. That chicken, the test, had to come before the egg, Miracle's connection to the Halo Killer. I had made a mistake. I had been reckless.

With my free hand, I pressed a finger into my temple, hard. I needed to clear my head. I couldn't think straight.

"How do you keep calling me? You just escaped!"

"I'm resourceful. Where are you?" Jasper asked.

"In LA," I said.

"Why would you do that?"

"What?"

I wanted to assume Cassandra was lying. But that was impossible. In my head, I started to repeat a mantra:

Chicken before egg.
Chicken before—

"It's almost over," Jasper said.

My head throbbed. I felt sweat rolling down my side and back. I needed to sit down before I fell.

"What are you talking about?" I whispered.

"Our film, of course."

The corners of my vision turned to fog. The entire place spun. "What?"

"You need to get home, Theodore. It's almost—"

*   *   *

Something cold and wet pressed against the skin of my face. It pulled me from the most utter blackness I've ever known. My hand moved before my eyes opened. I felt the dampness around my head.

I'm dead.

I don't know where that thought came from. When my fingers came together and stuck, I decided it had to be blood. That I'd been shot. My heart thumped against my ribs and inside my skull. I tried to open my eyes, but only the left one listened. The lashes matted together before snapping apart. The brightness cranked up the volume of my headache, and I winced.

"He's awake," someone said.

I tried to look up, see who was talking, but everything appeared thick and green, like I'd been abducted into some alien flying saucer.

"Somebody should clean his face. He might choke . . . or something."

A napkin ran across my cheek and came away that same sickly green. My mouth opened, and I tasted green tea. The drink I'd bought. Groaning, I slapped a hand down on the floor and tried to push myself up. Something touched my shoulder. Blinking, I cleared my vision enough to see that it was the woman from behind the counter.

"Don't move," she said. "An ambulance is on the way."

"Ambulance?"

"You passed out."

"Where's Cassandra?"

"I don't know. Is that your wife? Do you want me to call her?"

My eyes rolled back, and I lowered my head to the floor. Matcha cold brew stuck my hair together in thick clumps, but I didn't care. I felt so weird.

"Am I alive?" I asked.

"Oh, shit," someone else whispered.

"Yes, of course," the woman said, touching my arm. "You're okay. Everything is going to be okay."

Time passed as if in a dream. I heard the sirens. They grew louder and louder. Closer and closer. The door swung open. Then came the sound of metal wheels clanking against the patterned tile floor. A new voice spoke to me.

"Sir, what's your name?"

I opened my eyes again and saw the paramedic. She knelt on the floor, her fingers touching me below the chin.

"We need to get him cleaned up," she said, over her shoulder. "Sir, can you tell me your name?"

"Theo," I said.

"Your last name. Do you know that?"

It seemed like such an inane question that I didn't answer it right away. But she was insistent.

"Sir, your last name."

A strange suspicion mixed with the malaise.

"Why?" I asked.

She turned away from me and started asking the woman from the counter questions. She spoke quickly, too fast for me to follow. I tried to stand up, and she turned her attention back to me.

"You passed out," the paramedic said. "Can you tell me your last name."

"Snyder," I finally said.

"What day is it?"

"It . . ."

I blinked. I had no idea what day it was. Friday, maybe. I tried to picture my boarding pass from the plane the night before. Or this morning. Whenever.

"Do you know where you are?" she asked.

"New York?" I said, then realized I was wrong. "No, Los Angeles. I got a tea."

"We can see that," she said.

The paramedic took my blood pressure. Then she unbuttoned my shirt. It was weird, but I couldn't stop her. I suddenly felt so tired. Like even the act of speaking might be too much. So I didn't fight. I just let them work on me for what felt like an hour.

"We're going to get you up onto the gurney," she said.

For some reason, that statement slapped me back to reality. I sat all the way up so quickly that she couldn't stop it. The room spun, but I fought through it.

"No, I'm fine."

"Your blood pressure is dangerously low, Mr. Snyder. And your resting pulse is in the one twenties. We ran an EKG. It looks okay, but we can't let you go with your BP that low."

"Take it again," I said. "I'm fine."

"Mr.—"

"Please."

She shook her head and wrapped the cuff back around my arm. I focused, meditating, trying to get my heart rate down. Trying to stay calm.

"It's better, but—"

"I'm okay. Just a little tired."

"You're dehydrated too."

"Yeah," I said. "Probably."

"We should take you to the hospital. Get you on an IV drip. They can monitor you."

He called.

I tried to get my phone out, but that made me even more dizzy. Pausing, I took a deep breath and tried again.

"Sir, I—"

"I just need my phone."

I got it and opened the recent calls. The top number was a 302 exchange. That had happened. Jasper had called me again. And he'd said it was time to end the story. I needed to get back.

"I can just sit for a minute; then I'll be fine."

"You're an adult, Mr. Snyder. And you're not incapacitated. We can't force you. But it is in your best interest to—"

"Thank you so much," I said.

Somehow, I rose without any help. Concentrating with everything I had, I managed not to sway.

"I'm a mess," I said with a laugh, brushing at the green dampness that seemed to stain every inch of my upper half.

"You are," she said, but I think she meant way more than the drink.

14

To get back, I had to take another red-eye. I landed in Philadelphia at around five thirty AM. The airport was empty in an eerie sort of way. I moved with the other passengers in a bunch until most peeled off to go to parking or baggage claim. I slipped outside and stood on the curb.

To be honest, I felt almost exactly as I had in that juice bar. I moved through a thick, clinging haze, like someone had engulfed the real world in Bubble Wrap. Somehow I arranged an Uber. I failed to notice the make or model of the car. Nor would I ever be able to describe the driver. I simply slumped into the back seat and closed my eyes.

"Hey, buddy, wake up."

I startled. When my eyes opened, I saw Miracle Jones's childhood home out the side window. My vision blurry, sort of floating through time, I reached out and pulled the door handle. It swung open and I stepped out.

The driver muttered something, but I didn't hear him. I shuffled up the walk toward the front porch. When I glanced back over my shoulder, I saw the neighbor. She waved, and I wanted to say hello, but I couldn't remember her name. I just lifted my hand up. When I turned back, Meg Jones leaned against her railing, watching me.

"Thank you," Meg said.

I blinked. Those two words might have been the most heartfelt I'd ever heard. For the life of me, I had no idea why she said them, though.

"Is Miracle here?" I asked, feeling very confused.

"No," she said. "But she called. And told me how you found her. And that you're keeping her safe."

I could see the relief she felt as if it were a third person standing between us. Vaguely I remembered sitting in her living room, watching the news. Learning that Jasper had escaped. Learning that her daughter was in terrible danger.

In that moment, I felt dirty. I had been a vulture, sensing the pain and fear in others from hundreds of miles away. Circling over their lives as if their loved ones were already carrion. I saw. I understood. I even humanized. Yet I still stole their souls without care or compassion.

"I'm sorry," I whispered, looking up at Meg.

"For what? You saved her. You protected her. I never thought . . ."

"What?"

She took a breath. "I just thought you were another of those news reporters. That you'd take what you wanted from me and leave without even thinking about my daughter again. Then she called! And she told me you found her. That you and your partner were going to keep her safe until this was all over."

"Where did she call from?" I asked.

Meg frowned. "A New York number. I think it was a cell phone . . . Weren't you with her?"

I almost laughed. "I probably was. My investigator actually found her. Her name is Zora. Your daughter is safe."

I said that last part with confidence. For I did believe Miracle would be safe. Strangely, if I worried for anyone, it was Jasper.

Meg would never have dreamt what I thought. She moved down from the porch and engulfed me in a businesslike hug. I let her hold me for a second, then pulled back.

"Did she say where they were?" I asked.

"No, just that she was safe. Can I ask you something?"

"Sure."

"I'm trying to stay calm, but . . . Miracle would never just leave her baby for four days. He means everything to her. And . . . after what happened to her, even the thought of abandoning him . . ."

Unless she was trapped in a very dangerous game. One that put her son's life in peril.

The realization struck so hard that I almost said it out loud. But I stopped myself. Spared her that kind of worry.

"I don't know," I offered instead, though I was pretty sure I did.

"I guess I just have to trust her," Meg said. "She said it was almost over."

"She did!"

Meg arched an eyebrow. "Yes. Does that mean something?"

"No," I said. "I hope she's right."

As if a chain snapped inside my head, I remembered. Jasper had called me. He had told me that the end was near, too. And he wondered why I had left. He expected me there. He needed me there.

"One last question," I said carefully.

Meg sensed my trepidation. She took a step back. "Go ahead."

"Can you tell me where your daughter was born?"

15

NOT ONLY DID Meg give me directions to the state beach parking lot, but she let me borrow her car. On top of that, after telling me that I looked like I was running on fumes, she sent me off with a freshly made ham sandwich and a travel mug of the best coffee I'd ever tasted. I tried to refuse. She was the salt of the earth. A truly good and honest person. In the end, she was insistent. I told her nothing of my suspicions. She never asked me why I needed to go to that place. All she did was hand me the keys and remain steadfast. Eventually, I caved in. I got behind the wheel and drove.

It didn't take long to find the spot. Since it was off-season, the lot was empty. I rolled into the first stop and killed the engine. Then I called Jessica.

"Are you in Delaware?" I asked.

"Uh, no," she said.

"I need you here! It's happening. Now."

"Look, Mr. Snyder. I . . . Zora told me to tell you that you're not to call me again."

"Zora told you to say that?"

"Um, yeah."

"Let me guess," I snapped, slapping a hand on the steering wheel of Meg's car. "You just happened to get an offer from Cassandra. Maybe DP? Is that it?"

"What?" Jessica said, but she sounded entirely guilty.

"Whatever. You'll regret it," I said. "I mean, not in a threating way or anything. I'm not crazy. I just mean that when this hits, and it is *huge*, you'll wish you hadn't been such a . . . Oh, whatever!"

I ended the call, pounding on the wheel again. Then my phone rang. I figured it was Jessica calling back, coming to her senses. But it was Zora. I took a deep breath before answering.

"Hello, Zora," I said.

"Theo. Are you in LA?"

"Excuse me?"

"I heard from a friend that you're in LA. I think that's great."

I frowned. "Why would that be great . . . exactly?"

"You're finally taking this seriously. When we left, I was worried you'd do something crazy, like try to find him. I'm just happy that—"

"I'm not in LA."

"Yes, you are. I just—"

"I got back a few hours ago. I know everything now. The pieces all fit together. It's going to end, Zora. And I'm going to be here for it. With or without your little friend Jessica."

"What the hell, Theo?"

"What does she have on you? Why are you lying for her?"

"Who?"

I smiled to myself. "Miracle."

Zora paused for a few seconds. "Where are you?"

"I'm at the beach. In the parking lot. You know the one."

There was a pause. I think I heard her hand cover the mic. Then she was back.

"Theo, stay there. Don't move. I'll be there in twenty minutes."

I laughed. "I knew you were close."

"You don't know shit."

*   *   *

I moved along the edges of the lot, gauging the sunlight through my phone. A real camera would be ideal, but the more I thought about it, the more I liked the idea of a raw, gritty quality to this scene. A beautiful film, stunning and thoughtful, yet culminating in the kind of frantic imperfection that provides the very foundation of the social media generation. It would be groundbreaking and viral. Coppola meets Kardashian. The concept made me giddy.

"It is going to be huge," I chattered to myself as I strutted along the sandy edge.

My eyes lifted off the screen, and I noticed the sun dipping low, toward the sparkling surface of the bay across the highway. It would be dark soon. I reimagined the entire moment, but in the pale greens and black of a night-vision lens. Too contrived, I thought. Too intentional.

When the car pulled into the lot, my heart raced. But it was only Zora, driving some small foreign sedan that I'd never seen before. She pulled to a stop, parking close to Meg's car. I took a step toward her, but the door swung open.

"Get in!" she snapped.

"No way," I said. "He's coming here. I'm sure—"

"You are such a fucking idiot!" she hissed.

Zora jumped out of the car and grabbed my arm.

"Let go of me," I demanded.

I ripped her hand away. Spinning, I sprinted to the outhouse. I had to see it. To truly understand where my story began. I kicked the door open and entered, Zora following close behind. I ignored her and took it all in. My eyes caught the cracked, graying sink. I moved to it, ran my hand along the smooth but grimy surface. I took air in through my nose, smelling the brine and musk. A chill rose the hairs on my arm.

"This is where it started," I whispered reverently.

"What are you talking about!?"

I focused my camera.

"Miracle Jones was born in this very building," I said. "In this very spot."

Before I'd finished the sentence, she grabbed me. Turning me roughly, Zora yanked me close. Our noses almost touched. The fury radiating from her hard eyes burned the skin of my cheeks.

"What the hell are you doing? Don't you get it? He's been playing you all along. Have you been talking to him? Did he lead you here?"

"I . . ."

My eyes crossed. My legs turned soft. I blinked, but I couldn't refocus.

He's been playing me?

My brain tried to comprehend that. It tried to deny it. It tried to fit those pieces together. Something clicked. I started to shake.

"He's playing me," I whispered.

A caring smile overshadowed the anger on her face. Zora loosened her grip on me.

"Yes, Theo. He is. For whatever reason, he is."

"Why? It doesn't . . ."

Maybe it did. Maybe it made perfect sense. He'd started it, hadn't he? He'd hinted at Miracle's existence during that first call. He'd led me to find her. To bring her into the story. Into his web.

"He's after her, isn't he? He's been using me to find her."

She watched me.

"Why, though?"

God, my head hurt so much. For the first time, standing in that awful restroom, I realized just how sick and tired I was. I hadn't slept more than an hour straight for a week. I hadn't eaten a real meal until Meg's sandwich. I'd existed on caffeine and sugar. The paramedic had warned me. She'd told me about my heart rate, my blood pressure. She'd told me I was dehydrated, but I hadn't listened. Like an addict, I'd pushed through it all. Only caring about one thing. Maybe it was all part of his plan. Maybe he'd run me ragged. Kept me off-balance so I wouldn't notice. In my exhaustion, I would be a good little puppet on the end of his strings and serve up his victim on a shining gold platter.

Though my thoughts refused to straighten, one loose end rattled against my temples. I swallowed the dry lump in my throat and looked Zora in the eyes as clearly as I could.

"What about Cassandra?" I whispered.

"Cassandra? What about her?"

"Her movie. On me."

"What are you talking about? Why would anyone do a movie on *you*?"

"You went to my mother's apartment." Somehow I found the energy for anger again. "You questioned her."

She looked incredulous. "I did no such thing. Jesus!"

"She told me," I sputtered.

"I have no idea what you're talking about. Look, I heard Cassandra was annoyed that you beat her to the story, but that happens all the time. Though I don't know her well, she's a professional. She wouldn't waste her time on some kind of stupid revenge project." Her fingers tightened on my shoulders. "You know that. I know you do."

"My mom wouldn't lie," I said, straightening my back. "Someone came to her."

For just a second, I saw it. A flash of concern. A hint of uncertainty. Zora was a person who thought she knew everything. Usually, she did. But something clicked in that moment. I was sure of it, so I pressed.

"You know these guys as well as I do," I said. "I'm starting to believe you. That he's playing me. And I think you're right that he's trying to get me to bring him Miracle. But . . . someone is helping him."

She let go of me and stepped back. Her eyes narrowed.

"Could it be Miracle?"

A laugh burst from Zora. It erupted in that confined space, a clap of judgment right in my face.

"Do I need to spell it out? He *killed her mother!*"

"I know . . . I know."

The air left my body. She was right. That made no sense. And in that realization, it dawned on me just how horribly I had been used.

"Is she safe?" I managed to ask, softly.

Zora nodded. At the same instant, I heard the soft rumble of a moped engine pulling into the parking lot outside. Lights panned across the slit-like windows just below the ceiling, casting Zora's face in a cascade of eerie shadow and brightness. Her head turned, and a hand slipped into the front pocket of her denim jacket.

"It's too late," she said. "He's here."

"Jasper?" I asked, though I already knew the answer.

As his name slipped between my dry lips, I felt the thrill. It crackled along my back, down my arms and legs, settling in the hollow of my stomach. At the same time, something triggered in the deeper shelves of my brain. A message was sent. It fought its way across channels storming with adrenaline. *Danger*, it pulsed, over and over again. Though even it knew I was powerless to heed my own warning.

"Take this," Zora said.

My eyes focused on her hand as it pulled free from the pocket. Shining silver flashed between nails painted a red so deep it almost appeared black. Like a puzzle coming together, shapes merged. A trigger guard. A snub-nosed muzzle. Shadowed dimples along a jutting cylinder. I just stared as the word *gun* slowly formed in my charged brain.

I had never in my life held one. In fact, I had emphatically claimed I never would. My hesitation, however, set the rage off in Zora's eyes again.

"No you fucking don't, Theo. You got us into this. Take it!"

"I—"

"*Take it!*"

My hand shot out. My fingers encircled the warm metal.

"Careful," she hissed. "Jesus."

I let go. Quickly, Zora adjusted her grip, holding it by the barrel, which pointed at the floor.

"Have you ever—"

I shook my head. She motioned, and I took the gun by its black handle, making sure my finger stayed away from the trigger. From outside, I heard the scuffle of shoes across pavement.

"You take it," I whispered, my voice quaking.

Zora ignored me. She squared off, facing the doorway. Every muscle in her body seemed to tense at once. I found myself slipping to the left, just a hair, so that her body rested between me and where, I assumed, he would enter.

"Theodore?"

The whisper filtered into the tiny outhouse, and I felt the hairs on my arm stand straight. It was him. I had no doubt. In just the utterance of my name, I heard his high-pitched lilt. I saw his birdlike face. The Halo Killer had come for us.

"You're not alone," he added.

Zora put a finger to her mouth. Like a stalking leopard, she padded closer to the door. She pressed her back against the wall beside it and nodded to me, making a gesture toward the gun. I held it up like some kind of 1980s television cop, a cheap imitation of T. J. Hooker.

His footsteps inched closer. I held my breath. Zora waved a hand at me, telling me to take aim at the doorway.

"Is she here with you?" Jasper whispered.

My head shook. The door rattled softly. Without intending to, I shuffled back a step. Then it swung open so suddenly that I startled. The gun swung upward as I slipped on the tile floor.

At the exact moment, Zora pounced. She leapt through the swinging door. Leveling the pistol, I looked out. No one was there. Just Zora, lunging from the outhouse, disappearing in a flash around the side of the building.

"Zora!"

In response, I heard more footsteps, this time slapping madly against the surface of the parking lot.

"Zora!"

A sound shattered the stillness. Like the call of a fox. Or the scream of a dying rabbit. Impotent, I swung the gun around, pointing it directly at the mirror above the sink. The shriek echoed in the tiny space, bouncing off the thick cinder block walls, off the inside of my skull. The pistol swung wildly in my shaking hands.

Then something hit the other side of the wall, like a wet thump. I jumped back. More footsteps, this time running off.

"Zora?" I pleaded.

But there was still no answer. Holding my breath, I pushed through the numbness of panic. And I stepped out into the growing darkness.

CHAPTER

17

WHEN THE SOLE of my shoe scuffed the pavement, I froze. In my ears, the sound might as well have been an avalanche.

"Zora?" I whispered.

Frozen, I heard nothing. I inched further out of the scant cover provided by the outhouse. I felt exposed, like I stood under a burning spotlight. But the sun had set, and thick gloom hung over the asphalt. Through the panic I felt, I somehow found the wherewithal to keep filming.

"Zora?"

I rounded the corner of the building and saw her. She lay in a crumpled heap against the cinder block wall. I panned the shot, slowly, framing her perfectly.

"Zora!"

The shot bounced as I scurried to her side, I dropped to a knee, the pistol falling to the ground beside me. Zora's head turned at an odd angle and her dreadlocked hair shrouded her face. My free hand shook as I gently lifted her limp wrist. It felt frighteningly cold.

"You're okay."

My fingers fumbled, slipping under the sleeve, trying to find a pulse. My head swiveled left and right, as if someone might suddenly arrive to help. Or the opposite. As I looked east, toward the ocean, I saw a shadow slip away among the high yellow reeds.

Zora's hand fell from mine. It flopped to the pavement, lifeless. He'd killed her. I was sure of it. Then, nearly stopping my heart, she moaned.

"Stop him," she pleaded, her voice thin and labored.

"I need to get you help. I—"

"Stop him," she whispered. "It's the only way to save her."

"Who? Miracle? You brought her here? You put her in—"

"Just protect her!"

Without another thought, I scooped the pistol off the ground. A strange courage, something I had never truly felt before, filled me with an unstoppable strength. I sprinted up the sand to where I had seen him disappear. Gun in one hand, camera phone in the other.

Sucking in air, I crested the rise. The ocean appeared below me, cast in deep purple and inky black. The rumble of the surface hung in the air, thickening it somehow, as if the water might rise up and take us all.

I stood, bent slightly at the waist, the pistol by my side. From that vantage point, I could see for miles. I should have spotted him immediately. Then I could give chase. I would catch him; I was sure of it. I had to protect Miracle. Make up for what I'd let Jasper do to me. The risk I had already put her in.

My eyes slipped down and took in the revolver in my hand. The weight of it begged me to let go, let it tumble down and bury into the soft sand. I had no intention of using it. I could not dream of shooting anyone. Particularly . . . Jasper.

That thought turned my stomach, but there was no doubting its veracity. I didn't want to hurt him. Nor did I want him hurt. Instead, I felt drawn to the Halo Killer, like an addict to his drug of choice. I wanted to be near him. Talk to him. Learn from him. I wanted to mine his story. Craft it. And release it to the world. At some point the desire had become a deep and dire need. A hunger.

"*Jasper!*" I called out, shattering the stillness.

As if in response, a feral scream tore into the night, coming from the parking lot behind me.

CHAPTER

18

I SPUN. THE FAST-APPROACHING night covered my vision in a thick, hazy glare. Tearing back down the rise, I lifted my hand up, shading my eyes with the gun, as if that would help, trying to see Zora. Just as I started to make out a darker shadow against the wall, something swiped at my leg midstride. I stumbled, falling forward. My arm shot out, trying to break my fall, and the pistol sank into the dune.

Before I could process what had happened, he was on me. Like a striking snake, Jasper's smaller frame somehow coiled around mine. I heard a grunt, then a strange keening laugh, as I fought for my life.

Together, we rolled down the dune. His fingers felt like ice-cold nails boring into my flesh, one set on the bicep of my right arm, the other digging into the corded flesh of my neck. As my airway slowly thinned, I sucked in a desperate breath. With it came a plume of sand. The crystals coated my mouth and tore at my esophagus. I coughed and sputtered as his grip tightened.

Somehow, I still held the gun. Laughing, he slid his hand down my forearm, reaching for it. Unable to get a breath, I panicked. I knew I could not let him reach it. If I did, I would be dead. A part of my brain that had been dormant fired to life. It drowned out the rest, forcing its will over every muscle in my body. It had one purpose. One drive. To keep me alive.

A sound rumbled up from my chest but caught in my throat. With it came a burst of strength. I twisted my body, using my weight to manhandle Jasper. His laughter rose, piercing the night. I twisted my shoulders, and his grip on my neck broke. Folding in on myself, I tried to push up to my feet.

Jasper just kept laughing. The sound held no mania. No anger. Not even effort. Instead, he sounded like a child struck by something novel, like a baby seeing his mother sneeze for the first time. It would have unnerved me, but that kind of thought did not exist. Instead, I fought.

Somehow I circled my left arm around his head. Twisting again, he rolled over my body, his back slamming into the sand. His laughter broke for just an instant, then came back with double the intensity.

"Zora!" I screamed, my voice tinny and frantic. "Help!"

Jasper moved like lightning. Somehow he was atop me again. Both hands slammed into the pistol. He grabbed a finger and pulled it back. I heard a crack and grunted in pain.

The gun flipped through the air, landing softly on the sand a few feet away. I clawed at it, but Jasper didn't. Instead, his knees pinned my shoulders and his viselike grip took my throat again.

"Nononono," I pleaded.

Then, I could not make a sound. I could not breathe. I felt my muscles fading. A strange, dangerous heat sparkled up and down my spine. Forgetting the gun, I thrashed, mauled at Jasper, yet somehow he controlled me. This birdlike man, twenty years my senior, half my weight, held. Firm as stone.

I tried to beg. To cry. To talk my death away. Instead, powerless, immobile, I looked up into his face. I saw the serenity. I felt his hot, predatory breath as he moved closer to me. His sickening smile threatened to draw my soul into him, to feed on my very existence. Then his lips parted. And he spoke, loudly, almost theatrically.

"Did she love me?"

My lips parted, but I barely heard his words. All that would have come out was more pleads to spare my life. But Jasper reacted. His head tilted. A look of hunger crossed his face, unlike what had been there before. His face lowered, moving even closer.

"Did she love me?" he asked again.

His voice changed. As the words slipped from his mouth, he sounded younger and younger and younger. I tried to scream. To rage against my own end.

Like a jolt of electricity had suddenly run through his body, Jasper shuddered. His eyes seemed to reboot. A clarity slipped across the rictus that had been his face. Miraculously, his grip on my throat loosened.

I didn't hesitate. As oxygen filled my lungs to bursting, I lunged. My grasping fingers found the revolver's handle. The gun moved quickly, flashing toward Jasper's head. He turned, but that content expression never faltered. Even as the barrel struck him in the dip between his nose and forehead. Even as I pulled the trigger, sending a single bullet into his orbital, through his brain, and shattering the back of his skull.

A red mist shot from Jasper's ruined eye. He never made a sound. In a shocking instant, his body went utterly limp. Not even a flinch. One beat of my heart and he had been trying to kill me. The next, he floated to the sand like a sheet of paper.

Though Jasper never made a sound, I cried out. Not in words. Instead, a sound I could never have imagined came up from deep in my core. It rang out across the sand, over the rumble of the ocean. It emptied me, leaving me as lifeless as the Halo Killer.

PART FOUR

THE HERO

1

IN A VERY corporal way, Theo Snyder died that night, alongside Jasper Ross-Johnson. As I lay frozen on the soft sand, ten yards away from Miracle's outhouse, I was reborn. Alone, abandoned by reason and innocence, I felt the cruelty of the world surrounding me like the kind of cold that reaches inside and wraps its fingers around every bone. And I thought of her.

Miracle Jones.

For a long time after that evening, I wondered. Why would her name come to me then? I'd faced death. I'd tasted it. And to survive, I'd dealt it. A man lay murdered beside me. I could still feel his clawing fingers on my throat, his filth on my conscience. When my mind reached for some anchor, some slice of reality that would begin the process of rebuilding what had been taken from me, I thought of her.

Maybe Abbie Henshaw haunted that place. Maybe Miracle herself did. The will of a tiny, innocent child. One who knew nothing but suffering. How could she have expected anything different from life? How did she push through each day knowing that her birth, her abandonment, had happened? That senseless pain and crushing loneliness existed and could be called down on anyone, at any time, pure and tarnished alike?

As hard as it may be to believe, I did not pat myself on the back. I didn't consider the possibility that my horrible action hid a greater good: The Halo Killer no longer hunted. Miracle could move forward, safe for once. Safe forever. We all could.

I heard a voice in response, like the call of an angel beckoning me to follow, to leave the weight of existence for something greater and something less, all at once.

"He's alive."

I blinked again. Red and blue lights flashed against the night sky. A kind face looked down at me. Fingers touched my neck as another hand lowered a clear oxygen mask over my mouth.

"Labored breathing. Contusions, deep. Maybe swelling. No full obstruction."

Some clarity returned. The moments before I'd killed a killer. The chase. The pounding of the ocean. That scream.

"Zora!"

I tried to call out. To shout her name as if my voice could protect her somehow. Instead, it came out a pitiful, damaged croak.

"Easy," the woman said, her fingers moving across the skin of my throat. "You shouldn't try to talk."

"Zora!" I rasped.

"Everything's okay." She smiled down at me, as if I was a hero. "They are both safe now."

2

THEY TOOK ME to the hospital. X-rays were performed. I was told to keep my talking to a minimum. Then a familiar face entered my room. The detective from the Georgetown station of the state police. When I saw him, my throat tightened again, but it was only nerves.

"Hello, Mr. Snyder. How are you feeling?"

We were alone, so I ignored the doctor's suggestion and spoke.

"I'm okay," I said. "Can I . . . uh, help you?"

"I was wondering if I could ask you a couple of questions."

When I tensed, it caused a pretty good coughing fit. A nurse rushed into the room and checked my throat. She checked my splinted finger too. I wasn't sure why.

"I'm not sure visitors are such a good idea," she said to the detective.

He flashed his badge, and she looked at me. I said nothing, still worried about what he would ask. I wondered if I needed an attorney present. If I asked, though, I would look pretty guilty.

"Okay, this can wait," he said, turning toward the exit.

"No," I blurted out.

"Mr. Snyder," the nurse said.

"I'm fine," I said, and I think my voice sounded stronger than it had. "I'd like to do this now."

Reluctantly, the nurse left us alone again. I stared up at the detective, trying to keep my eyes from closing.

"Am I in trouble?" I asked.

He laughed. "Should you be?"

"No," I said, halfheartedly. "Then why do you want to ask me questions?"

"I just need you to go through what happened this evening. I've already interviewed Zora Monroe."

I leaned forward and coughed again.

"Is she okay?" I managed to get out.

"She's fine," he said, smiling. "And very thankful."

"Really," I said.

"Shouldn't she be?"

I shrugged. "She's a tough one."

"I could see that. Can you just tell me what happened?"

I paused, thinking for only a second. Then I told him everything, from the time I'd arrived at the parking lot to the moment I looked at Jasper's ruined face. He took notes, and as I wound down, he nodded.

"Okay," he said. "Would you mind if I took a photo of your neck?"

"Uh, sure."

He snapped a shot using his phone.

"Was Zora hurt?" I asked.

"Not bad."

"Is she here?"

"No," he said. "She refused treatment at the scene. Let me ask you one thing, Mr. Snyder. How did he find you?"

I didn't answer immediately. He slipped his phone into a pocket and moved a few steps away. I swallowed, and it felt like I had a bird caught in my throat.

"He didn't," I said carefully.

"Then how—"

My eyes fluttered. "I'm not feeling well. Can we do this another time?"

His eyes narrowed. A beat later, his smiled returned.

"I understand."

The detective left. I tried to close my eyes, but it felt like the lids were connected to an exposed power line. I knew it was nerves, anxiety, whatever someone might call it. I didn't, however, know why. I could have just told him some of the truth. That Jasper had used me. That he had been hunting Miracle. It was all innocent. For some reason, however, I didn't feel that way. Innocent, I mean.

After an hour of fidgeting in my bed, I fell asleep. I don't think they needed to keep me in the hospital, but some of my vitals were still off. Thankfully, they left me alone. And I slept for over thirty hours. It wasn't until I woke up that I realized just how big it had all become. How much my life had literally changed overnight.

3

My EYES CRACKED open again. Soft light played against the dark-ness of my hospital room. I sensed someone there with me, but after so many hours of sleep, I felt detached. As if I was waiting for an elevator that would lift me back into the real world.

"Wow," a man's voice whispered.

My head turned, and I saw him. Dressed in deep blue scrubs, his silhouette darkening most of the television mounted on the wall. I could see the gentle rise of a dune in one corner of the shot, the long reeds gently swaying in the breeze. The scene changed, showing a weathered newspaper headline. I read the first four letters of the word—*Mira*—around the nurse's head.

He turned and noticed I was awake. Like the snap of a finger, he transformed into the perfect professional.

"Mr. Snyder, how are feeling?"

When he moved, the entire screen came into view. It was the head-line from after Miracle found out that Jasper had murdered her mother. Though the sound was muted, the closed caption ran across the bot-tom. My eyes strained, but I caught the gist of the news report as the nurse checked my vitals.

"I just want to say," the nurse began, holding my arm at the wrist. "You're a hero."

I barely heard him, because as the news informed the world of that very fact, how I had single-handedly saved them all, not to mention Miracle Jones, from the Halo Killer, Zora's face appeared.

"Can you turn that up?" I snapped.

"Um, sure," he said, sounding hurt.

I just couldn't believe what I was seeing. It wasn't until I actually heard her voice that I did.

"We had been working on a documentary," Zora said. "Theo had met the man a few times, interviewing him in prison. I believe it was when Ross-Johnson learned that we had found Miracle Jones, the daughter of his first victim, that something happened. We want to see him as a monster. Or a nightmare. But it's simpler than all of that. He was a predator. And that information, Miracle's existence, was like a flash of movement to him. It triggered the hunt. And he would either succeed or die trying."

"But he was in prison," the reporter said dramatically. "How did he get out?"

"I have no idea," she said. "But I'm sure the police are looking into that. Once he did, though, he had one goal. One target. And that was Ms. Jones. We tried to hide her, but he would not be stopped. It was Theo who figured it out. That he was baiting us, trying to lure us back to where Ms. Jones was born. For him, I think that mattered. The idea that it could end where it began.

"Once we realized it, we called the police. But he got there first. If it . . . wasn't for Theo, I'd be dead. And I truly believe Ms. Jones would have been next."

The reporter's eyes shined with practiced emotion. "Would it have ended there?"

Zora's head shook slowly. "From what we learned about him, I don't think he would have ever been caught again. There's really no way of even guessing just how many people Theo saved. It's overwhelming to even think about it."

"Wow," the nurse said. "Thank you."

He sounded so sincere. I had no idea how to react.

"Um . . . thanks. Can you turn that off?"

"Sure," he said. "Are you feeling okay?"

"I'm starving," I said.

He smiled. "I can fix that."

The nurse switched off the television and turned to leave. In that instant, my phone rang. I looked for it, but he was faster. He raced around the bed and snatched it off the rolling table. He handed it to me with another smile.

"That's been ringing nonstop," he said. "I can't believe you slept through it."

I took the phone and tried to smile. He backed away and I glanced at the caller ID. It was my agent, Steph, and my stomach did a flip.

"Hey," I said, feeling very vulnerable lying in that bed, a pale blanket covering my paler legs. "Look, I was really not well. I can't even remember what I said to her. I—"

"Who?" Steph asked, sounding utterly confused.

"Cassandra," I said. "I met with her in LA. I should have told you. I just . . . things got so . . ."

"Are you okay?" she asked.

"Um, yeah," I said. "I mean, I feel a million times better. Way clearer. I didn't realize how bad it got."

She laughed. "You were being played by a master, Theo. He knew exactly what he was doing."

"Who?" I asked, strangely unsure.

"The Halo Killer. He ran you ragged. It's wild, really. People can't stop talking."

I ran a hand through my hair. "Great . . ."

"No! Are you kidding? Have you been asleep or something?"

"Um, yeah. For a couple of days, I think."

"You're a fucking *star*, Theo. The news cycle can't get enough of you. And when people in the business heard what Zora had to say, come on. She might be the most respected person out there. If he played her too, that's something special."

"What are you saying?" I asked.

"You're a hero."

"Yeah, I just heard that."

"You haven't checked your email?"

"No."

"Let me put it this way. While you've been asleep, your movie's been knee-deep in a bidding war."

"Seriously?"

"Ha," she said. "Are you sitting down?"

"Well . . . kind of."

"We're talking eight figures."

The phone fell from my hand. It clattered to the floor, and I made no effort to retrieve it. Instead, I just lay back and laughed until my throat seized shut.

CHAPTER

4

A TORRENT OF NEWS outlets waited at the hospital exit. More met me at Penn Station. A few followed me home. The next morning, a single crew remained outside my building. I bought them coffee from the bodega on the corner and let slip that I was on my way to meet with Zora. The reporter looked like she might hug me, then offered to give me a lift to Brooklyn. I accepted, though I wondered how appropriate it might be.

It felt surreal stepping into the same coffee shop in which we'd first met. Like a lifetime had passed in the span of less than a week. Adding to the overall effect, I found Zora waiting for *me*. She waved, then glanced over my shoulder at the reporter and camera operator following me in. I shrugged, as if to say it was my cross to bear now. She nodded and rose. I almost fell over when she gave me a hug.

"You okay?" I asked her.

"Why?"

"I don't know. You seem different."

She smiled like I'd never seen her smile before. "We all have a part to play."

That confused me. I sat, slowly, looking into her eyes. I leaned forward. I wasn't sure if the camera was rolling, so I spoke softly.

"I wonder. Was he playing me from the beginning?"

"Jasper?"

I nodded. "I'm trying to remember. I know he led me on a wild chase. He kept me off-balance on purpose. But . . . did I feel okay, even then? I wasn't myself, definitely. That whole Bender thing . . ."

"Did he know about that?"

A hiss escaped my lips. "He mentioned it the second time we spoke."

Her head shook. "I think he chose you. He knew you were on the ropes. More pliable. More likely to take chances. Follow his lead without vetting every step. He's the worst I've seen."

"Yeah," I said. "He marked me right away, didn't he? Saw me as an easy target. He already had the strings attached." I lowered my head to the table. "I feel so stupid."

"Theo, he played me too."

I almost laughed. In many ways, Zora was my opposite. Her confidence hovered between us like a giant magnet. At once it drew me into her influence yet repulsed any good feelings I might have been harboring about myself.

"Yeah," I muttered. "I guess he did."

Casually, I looked over my shoulder. The reporter and her crew were being ushered out of the café. I let out a sigh, then turned back to Zora.

"Are they on you still?" I asked.

"Not since you were released."

"It's unbearable—"

"Stop it," she snapped. "You know you love this. You know this is what you've always wanted. Feed on it, Theo. Because, tomorrow, it might all be gone."

"Wow," I said. "I guess the real Zora just woke up."

"Look, I've laid it on thick. I've hoisted you up into the stratosphere. You're a hero now. A genius." She shook her head as if the very idea repulsed her. "You saved our lives. I'll give you that. And I owed you. That's why I played their game. I told them the story they wanted to hear. That you figured it all out. You got Miracle to safety and faced Jasper to protect her. The perfect promo for your film."

Zora's words, both on the TV and as I sat across from her, were not adding up.

"She was there. At the outhouse."

She did not blink when she said, "No, she wasn't."

"But you said—"

"I said nothing. Theo, it's all good now. Let it go. Let it all go. Your story has basically written itself. Put it in the can and you're set for life."

"Are you forgetting something?" I leaned forward. "There's someone still out there. Someone had to be helping him. Not just the escape, but everything else. Planting that Cassandra story. Disconnecting my phone. He couldn't have done all of that alone. We—"

"Not my problem," she said.

"What?"

"I'm done."

"Come on," I said, incredulous. "You have to be joking. You can't walk away from this kind of money."

"Look, I think you're right. Someone was helping him. There are a lot of batshit crazy people out there. A lot of prison trolls. Fame chasers. Star fuckers."

"Wow," I said.

"Am I wrong? It's the oldest story out there. Some woman falling in love with an inmate. Getting caught up in a dangerous plot that they misread as a romance novel. Or maybe it was a guy . . . who knows? But I do know one thing for certain. Those whackos are utterly harmless without Jasper pulling the strings.

"The Halo Killer is dead. His story is finished. And I'm finished with it."

"Come on," I said. "I know you've heard. About the deal with Netflix. It's the top story on Variety right now."

She sighed. "I thought you of all people would understand that this was never about the money. You won, Theo. Enjoy it. But it's time for me to set out. Get back to work. On something else."

"On something for Cassandra?"

Her eyes closed slowly. "Please take this as me trying to help you. That comment is exactly why no money in the world would ever, ever convince me to work with you again. Good-bye." She rose from her seat. "And good luck."

All I could do was stare, dumbfounded, as she walked out of the café.

CHAPTER

5

WEEKS PASSED AS I buried myself in work. Jessica returned, apologizing for the misunderstanding. I took her back immediately, making her my partner on the project. There was plenty of work to go around, and it was good to feel like I wasn't alone anymore.

We made amazing progress together. The film pieced itself together just as I had imagined, and it looked like we would make the deadline set by our new producer. Until it came time for the ending.

"Let's see that part again, but with his voice isolated."

I leaned over Jessica's shoulder, staring at the screen as the picture wound in reverse. Jasper's thin lips unsaid his slick, penetrating words. I could almost hear them in my head, each syllable like a tug on the puppet strings.

"Have we gotten the score samples Evan said he'd send over?" I asked.

Still working the dials on the editing table, Jessica shook her head.

"I saw the storyboard for your ending," she mentioned. "The stuff at the beach with you and . . . him."

"I gave it to you," I said, sounding defensive.

"Uh, I don't have any of those shots," she said.

"I know. I have them. They're on my phone."

"I'm not trying to give you a hard time," she said. "I just . . . I know we're on deadline now. I . . . it would help."

"I've done this before."

I knew I sounded petulant. I was also well aware that my slacking caused her trouble. For some reason, though, I'd been unable to put together the footage from that night. I couldn't bring myself to watch it.

"Sorry," I muttered. "I—"

A loud knock sounded against my apartment door. I jumped. Sudden noises had done that to me since that night.

"Theo!" a voice boomed from outside.

"That's Kent," I said.

"Oh, shit," Jessica whispered.

"No, it's cool. He doesn't really work for his dad."

When the dust had settled on the bidding war for my film, Kent's father had come out the winner. He was our executive producer. The one waiting to see the first cut. Unlike Jessica, though, I had no worries about Kent. He flew with the breeze. If anyone understood delays, it would be him. In fact, I'd known he was coming. We were going out for lunch.

I opened the door, and he stormed into my newly furnished apartment. As he took in the leather couch and the new editing table, he whistled.

"My dad's paying you well, I see," he said.

"Insurance," I lied for some reason.

"Yeah," he said, smiling. "Guess where we're going."

"Nobu," I answered.

"How'd you—"

"You've always liked symmetry," I said.

He squinted, looking like he might scratch his head. Then the smile returned.

"You know, I really do. I just never thought of that before. Let's go."

* * *

As I moved through the restaurant, every eye seemed to follow me. That day, Kent got us a table in the middle of the dining room. Within minutes of sitting down, four people visited us—a literary agent, two producers, and an extremely rich Upper West Side gentleman who threw star-studded parties frequented by Kent. After that guy left us, my friend smiled across the table at me.

"Different, huh?" Kent asked.

"Uh, yeah."

"Someone's been watching you since we walked in," he said.

"Who?"

Kent used his eyes to point out the direction, then whispered, "Subtle."

Pretending to stretch my legs, I looked over my left shoulder. I saw her in the corner. When our eyes met, she smiled. I smiled back, but I could barely breathe. When I turned back to Kent, he laughed at how red my cheeks had turned.

"Is that really her?" I asked.

"Yup, she has a concert at the Garden tonight. An intimate little gathering. You should go say hello."

"No fucking way," I said.

My hands were shaking. Kent could not stop laughing.

"Get used to it," he said. "Just wait until the film finally comes out."

* * *

When I got back to my apartment, Jessica was gone. Locking up behind me, I sat down, hard, on the couch. The soft leather felt cool against the back of my neck. Slipping out my phone, I checked my social media. The iconic pop star from Nobu had slipped into my DMs. I stared at the notification, unable to open the message.

"What the hell?" I said softly.

My voice echoed off the wall, giving me a chill, reminding me of when my apartment had been utterly empty. The hand holding my phone slowly lowered. I leaned back, letting myself sink deeper into the seat, like I might slip through it, through the very floor, and never stop.

My thoughts spun in a dangerous direction. I asked myself, shouldn't the DM represent the apex? The top of the mountain? I pictured myself as a boy of twelve or thirteen. Dreaming of the perfect life while staring up at some poster on my bedroom wall. I could not have even imagined that the woman on that poster would reach out to me. Would chase me!

I'd made it. Closing my eyes, I pictured everyone in Nobu that day, all of them watching me. Visiting our table. Shaking my hand. I thought about my schedule, filled with prestigious events. The entire city had seemed to suddenly notice me.

"Who cares?" I whispered.

Because, for some reason, I didn't. In fact, I felt a strange sadness. Like a hole had opened inside me. Not a new one; more like one I'd thought I'd filled. I'd shoveled and shoveled, dedicating every ounce of myself to what I'd thought I needed. Success, money, fame—I'd stopped at nothing to reach it. To grab all I could. But the more I pulled it in, the more I dumped it into that empty space inside me, the wider it grew.

I lay back, thinking of that pop star. She had everything I thought I wanted. I wondered if her note to me was just part of the same vicious circle. The same endless dance. A call for help. Because once we possessed everything, all of our dreams, maybe we realized we had been looking for our salvation in all the wrong places.

I stared up at the ceiling. My mouth opened and closed like a hungry fish. Then the words slipped out, shining a light on this new truth.

"Why do I feel so empty?"

I had it all. And, for some reason, I felt nothing. I felt no different. I was still Theo Snyder. Nothing more. Maybe, since killing a man, I was actually something less.

6

I KNEW WHAT I had to do. Like a flash, my phone came up. I found the video file and hit play before the revulsion growing in my stomach reached a point of no return. With my eyes burning, I relived the night I'd killed the Halo Killer.

I stared, transfixed by the screen. The shot jostled as I moved through the parking lot. Zora arrived. I pulled away from her and ran. We stood in the cloistering outhouse. The sound of Jasper's moped was clear. The tension of Zora's face was clear. The entire scene was utter gold.

Zora raced from the outhouse. I didn't move right away. Seeing that embarrassed me, but it could be edited out. I'd keep the part when I heard the noise outside and pointed the gun in that direction, at the old cracked mirror. When I finally exited the bathroom, the camera panned down to Zora, her face shrouded in shadow. Somehow I lifted the phone up and caught the flash of movement on the dune. Though out of focus, I knew it to be Jasper, baiting me, drawing me away from her. He searched for Miracle. That had to be it.

Zora's scream stopped my heart for a second time. The shot swung wildly. Then Jasper attacked. The phone fell to the sand, faceup. The moon stared down like an unfocused eye. Grunts. Pleads. Then, to end it, a gunshot.

There was more to follow. It played on my phone, but I had left. I had returned to that night. I relived it over and over for I don't know how long. Eventually I returned to the real world to find the battery on my phone near dead and a trail of dried tears on both cheeks.

* * *

I fell into a fitful sleep on the couch. In the middle of the night, though, my eyes snapped open.

Protect her!

I fell off the seat, snatching my phone so quickly that I tore the charger from the wall. Kneeling on the cold hardwood floor, I accessed the recording a second time. My fingers spun like fine silk, cuing the shot to the moment Jasper arrived on the scene. With it on pause, I cranked up the volume. My finger shaking, I took a deep breath and hit play.

Zora convinced me to take the gun again. She slipped out of the outhouse to confront him. Frustrated, I stopped the video.

"Shit," I hissed.

It could not have been a dream. I'd heard it. I knew I had. But I replayed that moment over and over, four times, and still nothing.

I slammed the phone on the ground, harder than I'd meant to. As those two words swirled in my head, other memories slipped in beside them. Cassandra's reaction. Miracle's lie. Jasper had toyed with me. He had run me ragged. I was sick. Dehydrated. Hallucinating. Or . . .

On the fifth replay, I let the clip run. I heard Zora's body slam into the wall. I went outside, knelt at her side. And it was then that she whispered it to me.

"Just protect her," Zora whispered.

I skipped back thirty seconds. Watched it again.

"Stop him," she said. "It's the only way to save her."

I slapped the screen, pausing the video. My heart raced. A sweat broke out again, but this time it was different. Not the cold, cloying fingers of fear and anxiety. No PTSD. This was adrenaline.

It didn't add up. Zora had told me at the café that Miracle wasn't there. I played the clip again. Listened to her plea. I had to stop Jasper. It was the only way to save Miracle, who wasn't even close by. Then I rewound the scene back to the time when Zora handed me the pistol. I saw how I'd fumbled it. I'd probably almost shot myself. Or her.

That's when the inconsistency seemed crystal clear. If she was worried about Miracle and she was sure that stopping Jasper was the only way to save her—in that very moment, when our lives hung in the balance—why would she hand *me* the gun? Why not keep it herself? Face Jasper armed?

That's when I realized a simple truth, something that had been bothering me for days. It wasn't PTSD that kept me from finishing the film's ending. Instead, I suddenly knew that there was more to the story. That the true ending hadn't been written yet.

7

THE NEXT MORNING I sat in Steph's lobby, my legs stretched out under an amorphous glass-topped table. A young guy in the back office kept glancing over his laptop screen at me. I fidgeted until my agent appeared suddenly.

With a wry smile, she asked, "What, your phone not working again?"

"It is."

"Too big to call first?"

"Come on—"

"I'm just kidding. You've never just shown up before. Come to think of it, you've never even called me." Her head tilted. "You look . . . different."

I tried to protest, but she cut me off.

"No, I mean in a good way. Confident. I guess a couple million can do that for someone."

"Maybe," I said.

That's when her eyes narrowed. I knew she saw it. She'd worked with me long enough to recognize the look in my eyes. I was back on the hunt. Her head just shook knowingly, and she led me into a small adjacent conference room. Shutting the glass door behind her, she took a seat.

"You're up to something," she said.

"I just have a question for you, really."

She put a hand up. "Before you even ask, I think it is my job to say, just deliver your film and take the money. Then move on to the next one."

I ignored her and asked, "Who told you about the Cassandra thing?"

"Cassandra thing? You mean about her coming after you?"

"Yeah," I blurted out. "That she was going to do a movie on me and that Bender crap."

Steph shook her head and laughed. "I think that was all noise."

"How do you mean?"

"I think people got nervous. You weren't acting like yourself, you know? I mean, you looked like shit, really."

"Thanks," I muttered.

"No, I mean it. In hindsight, it all makes sense, right? Jasper had been manipulating you. To get to that young lady . . . what's her name?"

"Miracle Jones."

"Yeah, that's it. To be honest, when I saw you that night, I didn't think things were going to work out. You looked—"

"Who got nervous?" I asked.

"I think I told you. It was that investigator, Zora."

"You spoke to her? She told you that directly?"

"No." She squinted. "I heard it from Kent. But, maybe . . ."

"What?"

"I promised him I wouldn't say," Steph said. She looked out the window, as I had before. "At the time, it made sense. He and Zora go way back. If she was nervous, he'd—"

"Zora? He and Zora go way back?"

"Sure," she said. "I think she's his half sister or cousin. Something on his mom's side. Or maybe they went to grade school or something."

"Are you shitting me?"

"Um, no, I'm not."

"So, could Zora have had Kent tell you that stuff?"

Steph nodded. "Maybe. Look, I've spoken to Cassandra since. She said there was nothing to it. Like I said . . . noise. But she was glad to know that's what brought you out there. She was a little worried about you."

"There was nothing to it? At all? Cassandra was never upset with me?"

"Not one bit. She's the one that called me, to see if you were okay. I guess she's a big fan. But it's all cool now, Theo. You're great. She's great. All clear. She did ask me about something you said to her. About harassing your mother?"

"Oh, yeah," I said, sheepishly. "I thought she had Zora . . ."

Zora.

I just sat there, staring at Steph without actually seeing her. Another piece fell into place. Then the memory hit me so quickly that I said it out loud.

"She told me she had a friend at a big cellular provider. That's how she found Barbara Yost."

Steph frowned at me. "What?"

"Oh, nothing," I said, still distracted.

She patted me on the knee. "You just need to finish up that film of yours on time. That's not going to be a problem, is it?"

"Oh, no," I said, as more pieces clicked together in my head. "Not a problem at all."

CHAPTER

8

So MANY THOUGHTS. Sitting alone in my apartment, reality struck like lightning. Kent had never told me he was related to Zora, somehow. He'd talked to Stephanie. Zora had lied to me. Miracle had told me she had never met Jasper before. So many lies.

There had to be a connection. And I would find it. I pulled out my phone and opened my IMDb app. I typed her name in the search field, relishing every letter—ZORA MONROE. When I hit enter, I knew it was a long shot. Detectives and investigators never got credit on a film. Not in the database, at least. Unless they showed up on-screen. Something I could not imagine Zora agreeing to.

There were two hits for Zora as herself. Somehow, despite my doubts, I'd known they'd be there. I opened the first and dismissed it as a student film immediately. The second, however, nearly took my breath away. The short synopsis gave away the connection even before I saw Cassandra's name as the director. It was the same project I'd found earlier. The one where a writer had used commercial DNA evidence to track down a serial killer.

"Wow," I whispered.

Cassandra wasn't the only one with experience using DNA to locate someone. I needed to search for one last connection. I could feel it even before I Googled *"Zora Monroe" "Miracle Jones"*.

My teeth ground together when page after page of results showed. I hadn't considered their tie-in to the reports of Jasper's ending. Sighing, I scrolled. Despite the deadline, I had all the time in the world.

* * *

"Zora" "Miracle Baby".

It was the fifth variant I'd tried. When I hit enter, something immediately caught my eye. In the small slice of text below one link, a name stood out, just barely jogging my memory. Holding my breath, I switched back to my IMDb app and Zora's results. The name from the search matched the director's name on the student film I'd dismissed earlier.

Returning to Google, I opened the link. It led to an old screenwriters' forum. The director had posted about a project he wanted to develop regarding the infamous "Miracle Baby." In the post, the guy said that his friend Zora Monroe would be working on the story with him. He was asking if anyone had a medical contact he could use to discuss the baby's miraculous survival. I didn't care about that, though. Instead, almost salivating, I checked the date of the post. It was two years before Miracle Jones learned her mother's identity.

For a while, I had thought that the other documentarian Miracle mentioned, the one who had contacted her before I ever did, was Cassandra. It wasn't. But Zora had worked with the guy it really was.

I remembered that first night I'd met Miracle. The way Zora took her hand. The familiar looks that passed between them. I hadn't missed it. At the time, it just didn't fit. Now I knew. Zora had known Miracle long before all of this. Long before her pregnancy.

"I got you," I said, laughing loudly.

9

THE LIST SLOWLY began to take form.

She had Kent introduce us.
She set up the interviews.
She ran me ragged.
She disconnected my phone service.
She had Kent tell Steph that I had upset Cassandra.

What else could she have done? Could she have been the reason I felt like someone was watching me? Could she have placed the flower outside my door? Cleaned my apartment out?

One thing she had done, without a doubt. She had handed me the fateful gun that killed the Halo Killer.

How had I not seen it before? How could I have thought Jasper was playing me? When all along, it had been someone else. She had led me on a wild chase. Kept me off-balance for weeks. Played on my recklessness, exaggerating it until it became predictable. She could have done it all.

Zora.

Motive may be the most important tool in storytelling. A person can do anything, anytime. History has surely taught us that. But any action that can't simply answer a singular question will ring untrue, unbelievable. And that question is—*why?*

Maybe that was how Zora had fooled me for so long. My gut might have hinted. My mind might have caught on to the inconsistencies. Yet I never could have imagined why Zora, at the top of her game, would do so much to risk it all.

Miracle Jones.

I remembered Zora's stories. Her parents. The young filmmaker who'd saved her. The truth, or at least part of it, was piecing itself together. But I needed to know for sure. I needed to catch Zora in the act.

Standing alone in my apartment, I thought about Jessica. About how she had left the project earlier. How she had said Zora had told her that I shouldn't call anymore. She was in on it too. Zora's little helper. As I realized that, a plan slowly took shape in my mind. I called Jessica.

"Hey," I said. "Are you available?"

"Sure," she said. "Did you finally edit that footage?"

"Well," I said, pausing. I had to know. The hunger had to be fed. "No. I actually need you to meet me at the train station. Bring all your camera equipment."

I listened to her breathing for a moment. When she spoke, her confusion seemed louder than her words.

"I thought we had all the film we needed?"

"One more shot."

I pictured it. A grand confrontation where it had all begun. Standing on the dune. The song of the ocean as our score. Miracle's birthplace as the backdrop. Zora, Miracle, and me. The truth revealed below a sprawling sunset. It would never happen. Not like that. But it was visually stunning to consider.

"Where are we going?" she asked.

"Back to where it ended. I'm onto something new. Something *big*!" And, with a smile on my face, I set the hook. "Just don't tell Zora."

* * *

I didn't purchase train tickets. I didn't pack up my equipment. I didn't call an Uber for a ride to the station. No, I sat on my couch and waited until my door handle rattled. The lock popped. And Zora strode into my apartment, uninvited but not unexpected.

"You're a persistent little shit, aren't you?"

"Jessica called you, huh? I figured she was your plant."

Miracle walked in behind her. She moved to the window and low-ered the shade. Zora shut the door behind them, locking it tight.

"I guess it's time for this to end," she said.

"Yeah," I agreed. "I guess it's time for the truth."

Zora shook her head. "I guess it is."

*   *   *

ACT THREE/SCENE 14—**ALTERNATE ENDING**

EXT. MOTEL—NIGHT

The Halo Killer stalks the shadows outside a dark motel. A light in one of the rooms comes on. A silhouette passes in front of the glass, small, almost childlike. It is Miracle Jones. And the trap has been set. A CHYRON appears on the screen: AUGUST 13, 2016.

After finding the key card in that abandoned parking lot by the sea, Jasper haunted the motel for hours. Like a siren of the ancient tales, it sang to him, beckoning him into the light. Urging him to try every lock until one revealed his prize.

Patience, planning, purpose.

That had been his mantra. Even in the darkness of that night, his dry lips moved as he repeated it softly, over and over again. Those three words had kept him free. Yet, with each passing second, they became harder to pronounce. Harder to understand. Slowly his whispers lost meaning, slipping into the animalistic rumble of a predator.

After so long. After so much practice. What could call him this strongly? With such passion? Only the past wielded that weapon with such success. Only the closing of a circle left open for far too long.

"Who are you?" he whispered.

As if in answer, she appeared. Or, at least her silhouette did. A light flickered to life inside one of the ground units. A lithe shadow slipped between the glow and the gossamer curtains. With no detail, without even seeing her face, he knew.

Jasper moved. He stalked through the gloom, inching closer and closer. With each slithering step, he watched her. He had to have her. She was it. She was the one. The only one. He was closer. So close. Almost there.

The light cut off suddenly. The soft glow through the translucent fab-ric turned to blackness, swallowing the shadow of his prey in a single blink of the eye. Jasper froze, confused, panicked. Frantic. All control slipped from his fingers as he clutched the key card even tighter. Breaking into an awkward sprint, he covered the last few feet separating them. Without a pause, he jammed it into the lock. The mechanism clicked. He burst into the room. And fingers that felt like five steel rods wrapped around his thin neck. As he gasped for breath, Jasper was slammed into the wall. The windowpane rattled and the door swung shut. The light turned back on, blinding him for a moment. A dangerous voice hissed in his ear.

"If you move, I'll fucking kill you."

*　　*　　*

The light blazed. Zora's pupils focused to pinpricks of black as she stared into the eyes of the Halo Killer.

"If you move, I'll fucking kill you."

Would she? Certainly. Was she tempted to just do it? Very much so. As her fingers tightened, however—as she relished the idea of ridding the world of this pathetic little man—she saw her in the periphery. Miracle stepped away from the light switch, her eyes wide and as dark as Zora's mood.

Zora's grip loosened as she remembered why they had come this far. Why she had risked everything. She felt him against her palm as he struggled to take a breath. Turning her shoulder, she dragged him toward the single queen-sized bed. When she tossed him down onto the mustard-yellow bedspread, she marveled at how little he weighed.

The Halo Killer sputtered, his frail hand covering his throat. He did not look human. His hairless skin glowed a shining pink. No stubble. No eyebrows. No arm hair. Not even lashes. Nothing. And he was small, almost childlike, with the mannerisms to match. But it was his eyes that troubled her. They stared back at her undaunted, as if looking for an opportunity to strike. Air hissed between his lips, and her hand slipped into her front pocket, finding the revolver hidden beneath her leather jacket.

Miracle inched closer. When the movement caught his eye, his attention snapped toward her. His hands moved, fingers bending into claws. Zora gripped the gun, pulling it free. Before she could level the barrel, she stopped, staring, for something had changed. As he focused on Miracle, his fingers relaxed. The murderer became a man. The Halo Killer became Jasper Ross-Johnson once more. As if, somehow, he already knew.

"Who are you?" he whispered.

Zora took a silent step backward as Miracle sat beside him on the bed. He remained still, transfixed.

"You killed my mother," she said softly.

"My first," he said.

There was no way he could have known that. It was impossible. The gun dangling at her side, Zora had never experienced something as surreal in her life. Joined together in a cheap motel room that smelled of marsh and chlorine bleach, the three could not have been more different. A professional, a victim, and a killer. That's how she saw it, at first.

Miracle met those eyes without flinching. Her right hand slipped across her stomach, cupping the growing child within.

"Do you remember her?" she asked.

"Every day," he said.

Zora flinched. She wanted to lunge across the room and smash the avian bones of his face in with the butt of her gun. Miracle's presence held her in check. All she could do was watch and listen.

"What did she look like?"

His eyes closed. "Broken."

Miracle flinched. And he noticed. His tongue darted out, moistening his lips. At the same time, two fingers pinched at a nonexistent eyebrow.

"Tell me about her."

"Are you certain?" he asked.

"I am."

"I wasn't ready. It wasn't planned. I saw her at night, on the beach. Much like . . . But it wasn't that. She was alone. But there was something else. Something . . . calling me.

"It might have been the way she moved. It was not . . . right. She lurched. Staggered. Like a wounded . . . I couldn't take my eyes off of her. But it was something . . . more, too. Something that slipped through the night and entered me. A . . . sadness."

She shifted closer. "Sadness?"

"Broken," he whispered. "I could tell you more. I could tell you everything. But that's not what you're after, is it. That's not why you brought me here. Because that's what you did, correct? Somehow, you found me and you brought me here. How?"

Miracle glanced at Zora. Zora cleared her throat.

"Tell him," Miracle said.

"I waited for a missing-person report in this area."

"So, what," he said. "I was careful. I was always careful. They could not figure me out. No one could."

"I didn't have to figure you out," Zora said coolly. "I needed to figure them out. All the women you murdered. I stepped into their shoes, not yours. I bought a neon-yellow Walkman, the exact model that her mother had with her. I added the flower to make sure the hook set. But otherwise, I became one of them. One of your victims. You did the rest. You found me."

He nodded slowly. "You should be a detective."

She ignored that comment. A silence spread between them. Jasper returned his attention to Miracle.

"She said something about your birth."

"What?"

"Your mother. I believe it all happened that same night. Your birth. Her death. Beautiful . . . in a way."

"My mother abandoned me in a sink—"

"You are the Miracle Baby," he said, his voice rising. "I remember. I remember well."

A new expression grabbed his face. His lips pursed. His eyes focused, and he nodded his head over and over again. Zora had never wanted to kill anyone as desperately before.

"You're strong," he said. "Not like the others."

"I survived," Miracle said. "I don't know if I had a say about any of it."

"Oh, you did," he said. "Not in what was done to you. What you did with it. But it haunts you still. Anyone could see that. You want to know why she did it."

"No," Miracle said, her head turning. She rose, moving to the window. Peeling back the curtain, she stared at the darkness, cradling her stomach. "I need to know that I won't."

CHAPTER

10

I COULD ONLY STARE at Zora, trying to comprehend the story she'd told me. It had been her on the beach that night in August 2016. The one from the very first story Jasper told me. Not Barbara Yost. Not Miracle Jones. All along, as we searched for the answer to that mystery, she had stood right beside me.

When I didn't say anything for a time, Miracle approached me. I can't say I understood. Maybe I never would. I had questions. A million. Before I could ask, however, she reached out, her phone in her hand.

"That's my son," she said.

I took it and looked at the screen. A chubby, healthy, glowing young boy smiled up at me.

"I know. He's beautiful," I said.

"He is," she agreed, taking the phone back. "Sometimes, when I look at him, I wonder. When they found me, I weighed under three pounds. He weighed over nine when he was born. I saw a picture of me when I was in the hospital. My body had eaten away what little muscle I had been born with. I looked so frail. So unlike him. He means everything to me. And I will do anything to keep him safe."

My eyes shifted. I looked at Zora, how she stood in front of the door. How one hand was in the pocket of her jacket. For the first time, maybe ever, I was scared. Not that I would die. Not really. No, I feared that I would never get to finish this story. As I felt that, everything became clear to me.

"You're protecting her," I said.

Zora smirked. "You are something else, Theo Snyder. I've never met anyone like you. A pit bull with no teeth."

I laughed. "If I didn't have teeth, would you be here?"

She blinked slowly. Miracle moved back to her side. Lightly, she touched the exposed wrist of Zora's left arm.

"Let me tell him the rest," she said.

Zora nodded.

* * *

ACT THREE/SCENE 15—***ALTERNATE ENDING***

INT. MOTEL ROOM—NIGHT

They come together for the first time—Miracle and the Halo Killer. Between them, the detective, ZORA MONROE, stands, pointing a handgun at her prey.

Miracle sat in the motel room, beside her mother's killer, her stomach in knots, her entire body covered in a cold sheen. She wanted more than anything to run away. To get as far away as she could. She couldn't even remember what had brought her to this moment. How she'd ended up face-to-face with the Halo Killer.

After meeting Bunny, she'd made the appointment at the clinic. How could she be a mother? How could she be expected to take care of a child? What choice did she have? The genetic test only made it worse. Meeting Bunny, the same. It proved that at the most basic level, she was simply a copy of who had come before her. Her mother was inside her. Her mother made up at least half of her. And her mother had left her in a filthy sink, alone, to die.

On the morning of the procedure, she drove there. She parked her car. She even walked up to the door. The test hadn't told her anything, really. Nor had Bunny. She knew her mother had disappeared after that day. That was it. What she still didn't know was who her mother was. And without that, she couldn't know who she was. Not really.

Maybe there was a reason. One she could not imagine on her own, but something that could fill the hole that had bored so deeply into her soul. She had thought to talk to Meg. Tell her the fears that had crushed every moment of every day since she'd found out that she was with child. It was one thing to survive alone; it was another to bring someone else into her damaged existence. Her mother could never understand, though. She thought of her daughter as a whole person, not as the remnants left in a bathroom.

Miracle wished she'd had an epiphany before entering the clinic. Some great self-realization, some spout of strength that would turn her away. Instead, as kismet would have it, her phone rang. When she answered, it was Zora Monroe.

"Hi, Miracle, do you remember me?"

"Of course," she said. "How are you?"

"Great. Look, I was . . . just . . . thinking about you." She laughed nervously. "Not in a crazy way, I mean. I just wonder . . . if you might want to meet up for—"

A tear ran down Miracle's cheek as the words tore free without her permission.

"Will you help me find my mother?" she asked.

Zora's voice cracked when she said, "Yes, I would . . . really like that."

* * *

Miracle sent her the genetic test results. Zora said she would not see Miracle in person until she found her birth mother. Not two days later, the call came. Miracle knew when she saw the number on the screen.

"Hello," she answered.

"I'm outside," Zora said.

Normally, that might have troubled her. She'd never given Zora her address. But this was the woman who had found her mother in forty-eight hours.

"I'm coming down."

They drove into town and got a table at the same café at which Miracle and her mother had sat weeks before. Zora looked pained as she pulled a yellow envelope out of her biker bag. She placed it on the table between them.

"She's dead," Miracle said, before touching the file.

Zora nodded. Miracle's head throbbed. The discomfort under her ribs, one that grew with each day, screamed out, threatening to break her will. She had to know. But her questions would be left forever unanswered.

"There's more," Zora said, as if immediately regretting her own words.

She pulled a copy of an old news article out of the envelope, cautiously sliding it across to Miracle. Miracle's eyes lowered. She saw the words:

LONG UNSOLVED MURDER MAY HAVE BEEN HALO KILLER'S FIRST

"What is this?" she asked, tears running down both cheeks.

"Do you know about the Halo Killer?"

"Everyone does. It scares the shit out of all of us. But what does this have to do with . . ."

"A few years ago, a detective made a connection. A body was found near the ocean. Six months before that monster's first victim. She was a young woman . . . only nineteen. She had been strangled. But they didn't find her for over three months. The autopsy. . . . maybe this is too much."

Fighting back the tears, Miracle shook her head adamantly. "No. Tell me."

"The autopsy showed signs that she had recently given birth. There were whispers, I guess. Even then. That this woman might have been the Mir . . . your mother. But there was no way of knowing then. So it got shelved."

"But . . . why didn't they . . ."

"They couldn't prove anything. It was just a theory. The body—there was just no way of knowing for sure."

"What does this have to do with that serial killer? You said this was before he . . ."

"It was. But about three years ago, a detective reopened the file. There was a picture, I guess. Of the body. She had one of those old Sony Walkmans, the neon-yellow ones, over her head. It looked like a halo."

"But he leaves flowers."

"The detective looked at all the evidence they had. And he put out another theory. That your . . . mother was the first. It makes sense. The first time for men like that tends to be raw and unpracticed. They learn. And, as bad as it sounds, they get better. More careful."

"You believe this? You think the Halo Killer murdered my mother?"

"Yes, I do."

"But there's no proof. You said it yourself. They're just guessing that she's my . . ."

"There is proof. Now."

"What?"

"I gave the detective your DNA test results. He ran them against the Jane Doe. It was a match. He was able to positively identify her. Her name wa . . . is Abbie Henshaw."

"Honey," Miracle whispered.

"What?"

"That's what they called her," Miracle said, her lip quivering.

Zora nodded sadly. "If I had known it would be so . . . sensational, I would have never given my contact with the police your results. The information is going to be public. The press will pick up on it quickly. I tried to stop it, but I can't. I can only delay the inevitable. He said he'd do what he can, but at most, it will come out in a month."

Miracle stared off at nothing. "I have to find him."

"The Halo Killer? Why?"

Without realizing it, Miracle touched her stomach for the first time since they'd sat.

"He was the last person to see my mother."

*   *   *

Somehow, Zora used her magic and found him. The man who had murdered her mother. Miracle found herself sitting closer to him on the bed. She could not take her eyes off the man. He was so small. So broken. Yet so confident. It dripped from him, telling both her and Zora that he was better, stronger, smarter. Regardless of the fact he had just been manipulated and that he might not leave that room alive.

The more they spoke, the more he entered her thoughts. He probed her soul. Then he said it, even before she could.

"You need to know why she did it."

Need? Was that it? Or was it something else?

"I need to know I won't," she said.

Miracle let out a slow, agonizing breath. That's when the true pain hit. When the last of her tattered heart broke. For she realized that wasn't enough. That wasn't why she was there. Why she'd done what she had to get there. It was so easy to say it was about her child, but so untrue as well. Though admitting that hurt almost as much.

"Did she love me?"

The question burst from her like a blood clot breaking free and storming through the synapses of her brain, burning them out, erasing everything else. Her childhood. Her unborn baby. His father. Her mother. Everything.

"Did she love me?" she repeated.

And somehow, Miracle felt emptier than she ever had before. Jasper just stared at her, an even stranger look in his piercing eyes.

"Amazing," he whispered.

"Why?" she asked.

"The hunger. It's in us all. We're all trying to find it. To devour it. In the hope that it will help. That it will make a difference."

Miracle nodded. "When I was young, my . . . mother would take me to the ocean. After playing in the water, for hours sometimes, I would leave Meg in her old beach chair, reading some novel she'd bought on discount at Browseabout. And I'd cross the sand. I'd feel the warmth from the day's sun against the soles of my feet. It would grow hotter and hotter the closer I got to the dune. But I would keep going until I couldn't take it. Then I'd sit in that hot sand, utterly alone. And dig.

"Despite the beauty around me. The soft sound of the ocean singing. The gulls crying out above. I only saw my fingers scooping sand out. Faster and faster. And with each swipe, the sides caved in, refilling the space, undoing my best effort. But I kept going, kept fighting, like I could win, like the sand was some challenger. Some enemy that cared as much as I did. But it didn't. It just did what it does. Erases what I did.

"Eventually, I won. At least I thought I did. I dug deep enough, fast enough, that I reached the damper sand below. The hole became a deep, dark eye staring back at me. I leaned back; I looked at what I'd done as sweat dripped down and burned my eyes. And you know what I saw? A hole. Nothing more. And I was left wondering why I'd tried so hard to begin with."

"Because what would you do if you didn't," Jasper Ross-Johnson said.

"What would we do if we didn't," she agreed. "Maybe that's the answer. Maybe the big questions don't matter. Because you can never truly fill the holes inside. Because they're not holes. They're just a part of us. Pieces that make us who we are. Maybe we'll keep trying. Maybe we don't have a choice. But in the end, it doesn't really matter, because they'll always be there. No matter how much you are loved. Or how much you are feared."

They stared at each other for a moment. Zora moved closer. She looked to Miracle, who subtly shook her head. With a nod, Zora left them on the bed, walking into the bathroom.

Jasper watched her leave. Then he turned back to Miracle, the smile on his face strangely human.

"She left you alone with me," he said.

"I'm pregnant," Miracle replied calmly.

"Yes, I know." His head shook. "Is she going to kill me now?"

"I don't think so," Miracle said.

"I think . . . I wish she would."

His eyes never left Miracle's as Zora reentered the room. She held a damp washcloth in her hand. Without pause, she slapped it across the bottom half of his face. In three seconds, the homemade ether dropped him into a sound sleep.

"WE LEFT HIM at the parking lot where it all started," Miracle said. "It felt right."

"And the police found him there just as he was waking up," Zora added.

"Wow," I said, for so many reasons.

They stood beside each other, so close that I could not see the doorway behind them. I sidled to the left until the knob came into view. Maybe, if I made a sudden lunge, I could surprise them. I could make it out into the hallway.

As I tensed the muscles of my feet, ready to spring, Zora turned. She opened the door, and Miracle followed her through. Standing in the threshold, she stopped.

"Theo," Zora said. "It's up to you now. Understand that everything I did, I did to try to protect her. It was stupid. A risk. But once we started, it just snowballed."

"It's amazing," I said, breathless.

"She's been through enough. If her part in this gets out . . . it would be like reliving it all over again." Her head shook. "But there's nothing left. You have the truth now."

"Do I?"

Her eyes clouded. "What does that mean?"

"You're leaving something out. You broke him out of prison. Why?"

"I had nothing to do with that," Zora said, but I didn't buy it.

"Why would you allow that maniac to be free again? It makes no sense. But that's why you've gone so far. Why you've risked so much. Why you are still protecting her."

Like a flash, she attacked. Zora grabbed me by the throat, pushing me across my apartment and up against the far wall. Her nose nearly touched mine as she growled at me.

"You have enough, you asshole. Make the movie and move on. You'll be rich and famous. Everything you could have ever wanted."

A laugh slipped out. "It's not enough."

Strangely, I felt no fear. No concern at all. Instead, something else engulfed me. Fueled me. And I realized that Jasper was right. It wasn't desire. It was a hunger. The truth was a drug, the perfect ending my hit. I would dig, claw out the clues. Tie up the loose ends. I would prove that they'd broken him out of jail. I would learn the motive. My film would shake the world.

Why?

The question was much softer than everything else. A whisper in the storm of endorphins. This time, though, it was not directed outward but at myself. For some reason, I thought of that pop star who had slipped into my DMs. My childhood dream. Birthed to reality by my sudden fame. And when it happened, when I had it all, I'd ended up on my floor, empty and alone.

In that moment, I realized something. Looking into Zora's eyes; seeing Miracle stepping back into my apartment. Picturing Jasper's dark eyes. Seeing myself, maybe for the first time. Were we so different?

The hunger. The need to fill some deep emptiness inside our souls. Zora's family had broken her. Her parents had turned their backs on her, made her the villain. Miracle had been left to die by the one person who should have loved her beyond life.

I never truly learned what had made Jasper a killer. But I'd built a profession convincing people that I could. That my work dissected the unexplainable. Parsed it into predictable slices that the rest of us could easily swallow, making us feel better. Safer. Superior. Letting us believe that we could never. That our children could never. And that tragedy like that would never touch the ones we loved.

I was the true American dream. I'd made it. I was rich and famous. I could get a table at Nobu myself now. I had it all. And the second I did, I realized that it wasn't enough. Not that I needed to be more famous. Make more money. Instead, I learned that I'd spent all my life chasing a dream. I'd run myself ragged. Paranoia and anxiety had racked my psyche, tearing it to bloody shreds. My career had skyrocketed, then plummeted to the literal basement. I'd worn my hands and knees raw climbing my way back up. As I stared into Zora's eyes, I wondered why. Why had it been so dire to me? What was my motive? And I had no answer. I didn't even know what hole I'd been trying to fill. I just knew, for certain, that this wasn't the answer.

Miracle eased beside Zora. A hand snaked out, taking hers. I glanced down as their skin touched. I saw how that simple contact eased the rage that had creased Zora's entire face. And I understood her hunger as well. What Miracle meant to Zora.

"It's okay," I whispered. "It'll all be okay."

THE ENDING

December 17, 2018

TIME HAS PASSED. I stand behind the counter, one hand atop the La Marzocco espresso machine. The morning's been slow, just the regulars. Often, as I do this morning, I find myself watching the guy who comes in and writes between nine and eleven every day. As always, he wears noise-canceling headphones and sits there, alone. Every day. Doing the same thing.

I assume he is or is trying to be a novelist. An air of torture surrounds him, keeping the other patrons at bay. I picture myself approaching him. Sitting down across the table and asking him the question. *Why?* I won't, though. Because his journey is not mine.

As I watch him, my phone rings. It is my mom and dad on speaker.

"Hey," I say. "Did Meechie land yet?"

"We're on our way to pick her and the kids up," my mom says.

"When can we expect you?" Dad adds.

"Cass is coming in to cover for me in an hour. I should get there in time for dinner. I can't wait to see the kids."

They both talk at the same time. Eventually, Mom wins.

"They can't wait either. They keep talking about your famous scavenger hunts."

"Oh," I say, smiling. "I have a great one planned. I'll see you all soon. Love you, Mom. You too, Dad."

"Love you too, buddy," he says.

When I end the call, I glance over at the writer again. As I do, the door swings open. Without really looking, I slip the cleaning rag from my shoulder, rubbing it between my palms.

"Can I help you?"

"Hello, Theodore," a familiar voice says.

My heart stops. My head jerks up. And I find Martino standing across the counter from me. His teeth shine brightly, in contrast to his smooth, bronze cheeks. He holds a thickly stuffed manila envelope in his left hand.

"What . . . how'd you find me?"

"It wasn't hard," Martino says, his tone unnervingly familiar.

"Wow," I say. "Um, how are you?"

"I saw your movie last night," he answers.

"You did?" I shook my head. "*The Basement?*"

He laughs. "No, *Miracle and the Halo Killer.*"

Though my back stiffens, I try to smile.

"That's not my movie, Martino."

He nods. "I forgot. The woman got the credit."

I blink slowly. "Her name is Jessica Ransom. I hear it's amazing."

The truth—after Zora and Miracle left my apartment, I sat down and edited the footage from the night I shot the Halo Killer, careful to avoid any hint of Miracle's involvement. We plugged it in and I called Kent's father. I asked to be removed from the credits and from any press junket. He fought me—until he watched the film. Saw how great it was. In the end, he plugged Jessica into the director role, at my suggestion. I watched her Academy Award acceptance speech from my tiny house on the shore of Rehoboth Bay, smiling the entire time.

Understand something: as altruistic as this all might sound, I kept the money.

"It's funny," Martino says. "He actually predicted that would happen."

I can barely get the next question out.

"Who?"

"Jasper," he says, the smile gone from his face. "He left this for you."

Martino reaches out, handing me the envelope. I take it, my hand so numb that it slips from my fingers, floating to the counter. I snatch it back, pressing it against my chest.

"He asked me to give this to you after the movie was released. He had some . . . parameters as well. Having to do with the ending. So, I had to watch it first. You understand."

"You've had this since . . . ?"

He nods and backs away.

"It was a true pleasure meeting you, Theodore. I hope you're happy."

I have nothing to say. All I can do is watch Martino walk out of the coffee house. I am so transfixed that I don't even notice the novelist craning his neck, staring at me.

"You know him?" the guy asks.

I startle. "Martino? Yeah."

"Martino?" The guy squints. "That's Malcolm Grander. He's kind of a local legend."

"Malcolm. Grander?"

"Yeah. You didn't know that?"

I shook my head.

"Wow," the guy says.

"Who is he?" I ask.

"Did you see *The Face of a Killer*?"

I knew the documentary well. It was Cassandra's finest work. But I had stopped watching competitors' films a long time ago.

"He was in that?"

"Yeah, he played the killer in all the reenactments." The guy pulls out his phone. "He runs a local troop of actors down here, out of the Rehoboth Theatre. I wrote a short for them. Here."

He tilts the phone, and I stare at the photo on the screen. It is a group shot. My eyes immediately find Martino—or Malcolm—standing in the center. When I see who stands next to him, my stomach turns. Though she wears neon sunglasses and a theatrical cape, there is no mistaking Ginny Harris, Miracle's landlord. As I stare at the picture, I think about all the background the woman provided me. And the confusion I first felt begins to melt away. I sense, not for the first time, that I have been masterly played. It's just the author I got wrong.

The writer from my café kneels beside Malcolm in the picture. I glance at him, and he smiles.

"Yup, that's the Rehoboth Beach Players."

I remember my last conversation with Zora. We knew Jasper had help. As my eyes slowly move across the other faces, I recognize some of the others as well—the prison official who took me back to see Jasper that second time. The man who kept me up all night on the red-eye with his inane stories. Tilting my head, I stare at another one. A tall guy in all black. With thick, stylish gray hair. And I swear he is the one I ran into outside my apartment the night I found the flower at my door.

"We all go a little mad sometimes," I say out loud, remembering his words.

"That's from *Psycho*. I love Hitchcock." The writer guy laughs, then continued in his best Norman Bates impersonation, "A boy's best friend is his mother."

And I picture that group of nefarious, geriatric thespians haunting me. Cleaning out my apartment. Leaving that damn flower outside my door. Keeping me on edge, exhausted, so I wouldn't notice. I imagine an elderly would-be actress named Edith following me in New York. And as I fled to New Jersey. Making phone calls and holding a cell up to the receiver, one connected to Jasper in Delaware. That was why he had sounded so distant. How he had appeared to be everywhere at once. Jasper hadn't had a single obsessed follower, but a troupe.

My heart misses a beat. The phone disappears. The man, next. Even the café. Everything but that envelope and its contents ceases to exist. I tear it open. I know, immediately, that it is a script. A letter is attached to the cover page with a shining silver paper clip.

DEAR THEODORE,

I truly hope that this letter finds you well. I have a feeling, as long as Mr. Grander follows my instructions, it will. I am sorry I've kept this from you for so long. As you will surely understand upon reading this correspondence, it was necessary.

First, let me thank you. To my vast surprise, prison was both a blessing and a curse. I knew that the situation was not viable, long-term. I certainly was not going to allow my own ending to be written in that place, by our pathetic government. Horrid concept, really. Yet, it did provide me the focus to understand my final purpose. The time to craft my greatest tale. And the focus to realize my inspiration. "Did she love me?" That was her question, not mine. Oh, how it did inspire me.

At this time, I assume you believe that the other one, that so-called detective, found me. That is a lie, though one originated by me. The truth is that, when I read that article, printed on July 15th, I found her the very next day. The detective had nothing at all to do with it. She was nothing but an annoyance, though her skills came in handy near the end. I needed to see the girl. Maybe I intended her harm. I am not sure. But I found her. And when I met her, everything changed.

I will not enlighten you on our full connection. That is mine, alone. But I will say that, in many ways, where I was empty, Miracle was full. And vice versa. We had no convenient motive. No lust, no love, no greed or passion or hatred. That, my friend, you understand. For those things are not necessary for the truly beautiful stories.

You might wonder why Miracle and the other one fed you that final story. I was not sure it would be necessary. I wrongly assumed that, due to your troubles, you would be more pliable. That you would follow my lead and end our film as I intended. I should not have been surprised. I chose you not solely because of the Bender scandal, but for your miraculous work to date. I was in awe of you from the day we met. How quickly you neared the truth. That Miracle and I were connected. And that we had met prior to my capture.

When, even after my choreographed end, you still questioned, I was prepared. They were to tell you the alternative ending. And, in truth, it was only a test. I would never have let you tell that story. If you had tried, things would have gone poorly for you. Evidence would have materialized linking you to my escape. A trusted assistant has a recording of you talking to me about it. And there is the physical evidence you left behind when you broke into my home. You would have been arrested. And someone else would have stepped in to complete the film.

You might wonder how I did it all. I imagine you have figured much of it out, already. It was very simple, really. I switched hats from writer to director. I had a very loyal cast to work with. They assisted me at every turn, fulfilling their roles perfectly.

And then there were my stars. Miracle required little effort. She understood the danger she was in. And I understood her motivation. She would do anything for her child. Ironic, really, considering her insecurity on the matter led to our connection.

Why did she help me? A month passed after they knew my identity. We met not in August, as our alternate ending suggested, but the very day after the article was printed. They knew my true identity, even my whereabouts, from that day until my arrest almost a month later. During that beautiful time, I cherished my moments with Miracle. But, alas, the hunger struck after our first meeting. I took a woman, and completed the process. The detective figured it out. And when I took the Yost woman, she turned me in without Miracle knowing.

Both knew that if the authorities learned of our . . . fraternization, they would be charged with a crime. Miracle would have been sent to prison, abandoning her small child. And Zora would lose her Miracle. Alas, with such danger hanging over them, they played their roles perfectly as well. I believe the detective wavered. At times, I think she attempted to dissuade you from our collaboration. I warned her, eventually, that if you left, their prior involvement with me would come to light. And she would never have let Miracle suffer such a fate.

In the end, you chose correctly. You learned that a single life, Miracle's in this instance, was worth more than the empty dreams you once chased. That is the true beauty of our connection. All four of us. All servants to some dark past. All broken. A desperate need to fill an emptiness that we never truly understood. And all of us, in the end, reborn. I am at peace, my own ending lovingly written. Miracle received her answer, though she knew all along that her true role model, her own mother, would guide her as a parent more than any genetics could. The detective, well, I assume you understand her desires. I cannot guess how that will end for her. But Miracle is a truly special being. One way or another, she will heal Zora Monroe. As she did me. And they will both be better for it.

And lastly, it comes to you. You passed the test. You saw through your own trap. Happiness cannot be bought. Or earned. It does not come hand in hand with money or fame. For it is nothing but a figment. One lit from within. I am happy for you, young man.

In closing, a warning, though I doubt you will need it. The story is finished. The ending told. If, in learning the truth, you think to change that, to use my words to incriminate Miracle, it will be your mistake. As is my expertise, and as I have mentioned, I have carefully planted physical evidence, enough to convict you of aiding my escape. I am truly sorry to end on a threat, Theodore, but I cannot have you undoing my ending.

Yours forever,
Jasper Ross-Johnson
The Halo Killer

The letter finished, I pull it out from under the clip. Under it, as I expected, is a script. The thick green sheet of the cover page reads:

MIRACLE AND THE HALO KILLER
by
Jasper Ross-Johnson

Holding it in my hands, I tell myself I will not read it. I will throw it away. Set it aflame. But I hesitate. And a strange, almost proud smile creeps onto my face. I flip through the pages, my eyes catching a few of the scenes:

ACT ONE/SCENE 1

EXT. THE BEACH—NIGHT

A full moon shines down on the rolling surf of the Atlantic Ocean. We see the pale rise of a sand dune, and a figure appears out of the darkness.

A CHYRON flashes across the jet-black sky: AUGUST 12, 2016.

Flip . . .

ACT ONE/SCENE 13

EXT. FRONT PORCH OF RESTAURANT—DAY

Martino holds court at a café table just off the sidewalk. Surrounded by smiling faces, his eye wanders. And he catches sight of YOUNG JASPER. His blood chills.

Flip . . .

ACT TWO/SCENE 7

EXT. PARKING LOT—DAY

The sun backs that same dark asphalt, those same faded white lines. The outhouse still juts from the corner of the lot. Miracle Jones steps out from behind it, her dog by her side. The weight of the entire world in her eyes.

Flip . . .

ACT THREE/SCENE 1

EXT. BEACH—NIGHT

Jasper Ross-Johnson stands over the battered, half-naked body of his first victim. In that moment, the HALO KILLER is born.

Holding my breath, I turn to the last page. Read the last scene before *The End.*

ACT THREE/SCENE 20

INT. HOSPITAL—DAY

Our hero awakens. A television shines in the corner of his dimly lit hospital room. Although the volume is down, we see a banner cross the screen. CHYRON: FAMOUS DOCUMENTARIAN SAVES THE MIRACLE BABY AND ENDS THE NIGHTMARE REIGN OF THE HALO KILLER.

I didn't know if I should laugh or cry.

THE END

EPILOGUE

January 13, 2019

T HE RAIN FALLS in icy sheets as I run across the parking lot, avoiding the larger puddles. The cold bites through the dampness spreading across my thighs. I put a hand in front of my face, protecting the exposed skin, but I do not slow. I run until I reach the large canopy over the entrance to the assisted-living facility in Dover, Delaware.

Water drips from everywhere as I walk slowly to the receptionist's desk. A middle-aged man in a flannel shirt and thickly lensed glasses stares at me until I stop a pace away.

"Can I help you?" he asks with a touch of suspicion.

"I'm here to see Carla Ross."

His brow lowers. "Are you that fellow that . . ."

He trails off. But I nod, knowing what he means. He looks like he would say something more but doesn't. Instead, he leads me down the hall to the dining area. It is empty but for a single resident. She sits in a padded chair by a lit fireplace. The logs crackle, and the light from the flames dances across her deeply lined face. She turns, looks at me, and I see her son's eyes, sharp and focused.

"Ms. Ross, the gentleman's here to see you."

"Thank you, Clarence," she says.

She has Jasper's voice, too. Or he had hers. As I stand there, unsure how I will proceed, Clarence does the same. With a smile that disarms me, Carla assures him that everything is okay. He leaves, slowly, and she leans forward and pats the seat across from her. I sit.

"Thank you for seeing me," I say.

She nods. "Don't feel bad about what you did."

Her statement comes so suddenly, I have no response. She smiles again, this time at me, and I may never have seen something as gentle in my life.

"I'm glad he's at peace now," she says. "I've had time to think since he's been gone. I miss him, very much. He used to come see me once a week. And everyone here loved him."

Tears fill her eyes. Without really thinking about it, I reach out and place my hand on her forearm. It feels frail and birdlike under my fingers.

"I didn't believe it at first. I can imagine no one believes that. But here they do. Because they met him. And they saw how he treated me. We talk about it some. It's hard to understand, really. How someone can be two people at once."

"I'm sorry," I say softly.

"But that's not why you're here, is it? You mentioned that you had to ask me something. Go ahead."

I pause. Suddenly, I don't really care about the answer. Instead I feel a very deep urge to just sit by the fire and listen to her voice. Let her fill the time with her stories.

"Go ahead," she repeats. "It's okay."

"You're nothing like how he described you," I say.

She laughs. "Jasper just loved making up stories. Since he was a little boy. He would sit in front of the television all day. He'd watch shows that I knew he'd seen a million times. He'd recite the lines, sometimes even before the actors said them. And how he loved movies."

"Hitchcock?" I ask.

"Oh, yes. That one with Jimmy Stewart and Grace Kelly."

"*Rear Window*?"

"Yes," she says, and she claps her hands together, just as Jasper did that first time we met. "He used to write, too. Screenplays. He sent one off once, and they said he wrote very much like that Hitchcock. Oh, how he loved it all. Even when he was just a little boy. When he was ten, he had me get him a subscription to this little magazine from all the way out in Hollywood. I think it was called *Variety*. He'd read each one a hundred times over." She shakes her head. "I really thought he'd do something with all that. I imagined he'd make movies one day. Guess I was wrong."

"Maybe you weren't," I say softly.

"Excuse me?"

"Oh, nothing. He told me about his father, too. Is he—"

She puts up a hand. "Stop right there. Jasper never knew his father. But he always made up stories. Told everyone. Even his teachers at school. They'd believe him, too."

"He never met his father?" I ask.

"Nope. Not once."

We continue to talk, she and I. At first, she tells me more about Jasper and his love of movies. Eventually we move on to her life. Lower middle class. Rural. Two-bedroom track house. Career at the local library. I listen, but I'm lost in my own thoughts. Maybe an hour passes before she mentions that she has to leave for therapy. We both stand, and I find myself giving her a warm hug.

"Can I come back and visit again?" I ask.

She nods. "I'd like that very much."

ACKNOWLEDGMENTS

I'D LIKE TO thank those that helped turn all these words into a book. Stephanie Rostan has had my back for a long time. Without her, I'd still be working on my first book. Jessica Renheim swooped back in the nick of time like the superhero she is. Great editor who has made every book she's touched better. I owe gratitude to Matt Martz for giving this book a chance. And everyone at Crooked Lane Books, especially Melissa Rechter and Madeline Rathle. And most importantly, I have to thank my wife and kids. They are everything. And they're fairly good at putting up with the daily challenges of living with an author. For there are many.